# Charisma Grey

## Blood of the Gods

Anthony D. Phillips Jr.

ISBN: 0-9910582-8-3
ISBN-13:978-0-9910582-8-0

# Table of Contents

Prologue.............................................................................

1 Stalker.......................................................................... 6

2 Weird and weirder .................................................... 15

3 A little less safe ..........................................................32

4 Just plain ol' creepy ..................................................54

5 Welcome to the team .................................................78

6 The Blue Room ........................................................102

7 All Boys....................................................................124

8 So much for fresh air...............................................149

9 A win for the home team ........................................188

10 Fright Night, or Fight Night?................................208

11 Final Showdown, who are you?..............................233

About the author ........................................................250

"The U.S. Government hasn't maintained secrecy regarding UFOs. It's been leaking out all over the place, but the way it's been handled is by denial, by denying the truth of the documents that have leaked, by attempting to show them as fraudulent, as bogus of some sort. There has been a very large disinformation and misinformation effort around this whole area, and one must wonder, how better to hide something out in the open than just to say, 'It isn't there. You're deceiving yourself if you think this is true, and yet, there it is right in front of you."-DR. EDGAR MITCHELL, lunar module pilot of Apollo 14

# Prologue

I never knew my real parents. Heck, until recently I didn't even know I was adopted! What I am, and what I am capable of, are beyond normal comprehension. The events and changes that I have endured are what science fiction fantasies and nightmares are made of. My new life is something far from the norm. At times it can be a little disheartening because all I've ever wanted to be is a normal teenage girl. Normal in the sense of, keeping up with my social media accounts and going crazy over the latest boy band or pop idol. My life was forever changed on the eve of my fifteenth birthday. There are forces in our universe that are devoted to Mankind's enslavement and Earth's destruction. It's my responsibility to make sure that those things don't happen. I am Charisma Grey and I am one of the last beings on Earth with the blood of the Gods coursing through their veins. It gives me enhanced abilities unlike anything else on Earth. I along with six others, are the planet's last line of defense.

# Chapter 1

# Stalker

**I CAUTIOUSLY TREKKED** through the dark and foreboding forest. I sensed the dragon was near. Its presence was undeniably evil. Fear made me quicken my pace, but my courage made me contemplate confronting it. I could hear the breaking of branches underneath its heavy leathery feet. The silence of the forest made each of its movements louder and more pronounced. From what my ears could detect, it was now only mere meters away. Its snarl was bone chilling. A weird buzzing sensation swept over me, as it got closer. My small petite strides of distance were swallowed up by its huge four-legged gait. I had grown too tired to continue running. I might as well have been in quicksand.

My lungs burned from the over exertion put upon them by my hurried pace. My heartbeat, as well as my panic, increased rapidly. Sweat saturated my tattered clothing. It made my shirt stick to my body like a sticker to a Trapper Keeper. Most of all, I kept feeling an incessant buzzing sensation. It was a nagging attention stealer. It was amazing that on the verge of becoming a dragon's dinner, I paid enough attention to the buzzing to become annoyed by it. It was so annoying that it distracted me from my plan of sticking to the thicker parts of the dense seemingly endless forest. I wondered if the dragon blew fire like in the myths and legends. I know it was a silly thought to think, and maybe if I'd seriously considered the absurdness of such a thought, I wouldn't have thought it. I should've realized that it would be nothing for a creature that could indeed blow fire, to set ablaze the entire forest and alleviate the distance between us and any chance of my escape.

The ground started to rumble beneath me, I knew my time was almost up. It was odd, but comforting that before my violent, gruesome death, I still found myself irritated by the buzzing. It was successful in distracting me from the hopelessness of my predicament. It was so distracting that it caused me not to pay attention as an elevated root caught onto my foot. Like a scene out of a movie, I fell to the ground like a helpless damsel in distress. I turned over just as the creature came upon me. It opened its mouth and it was like staring at death itself. I readied myself and weakly scooted back along the ground. The buzzing was like a faithful stalker that wouldn't take no for an answer. No, I'm not going to the school dance with you, no I don't need you to carry my books, and for the last time, I will not accept your friend request. You may call it persistence; I call it a serial killer in the making. This buzzing was becoming one of those. Even in my last moments of life, it still vied for my full attention, AAAGH!

I woke up with my head between the pillows and my cotton sheet wrapped around my ankle. In spite of my groggy, 'I just need a few more minutes of sleep' state I still felt the buzzing sensation. It was underneath me. Realizing I was in my warm comfortable bed, I knew exactly what it was; I sluggishly withdrew my right hand from its comfortable nest underneath my pillow, slid it under myself, and wrapped my fingers around my beloved buzz happy phone. After retrieving it, I held it up, almost dropping it twice before managing to look at the touchscreen. The word "MOM" and the associated number and picture graced the screen. I awkwardly fumbled with the green phone icon and answered.

"Hello?" I croaked out in a deep raspy voice.

"Hey honey, are you up?" My mom asked in a bubbly tone.

"Now I am," I murmured in a not so enthused tone. It was only days before my birthday and my mom's excitement was building more than my own. I know a birthday is a big deal, but it was only my fifteenth birthday, not the highly revered "Sweet Sixteen". Seeing as how I still had to wait until I was fifteen and a half to get a driver's permit put a damper on the upcoming celebration. I longed to feel myself behind the wheel of a car just as much as I longed to meet Jason Niles from All Boys. My bedroom walls were a shrine to the hunky teen heartthrob. Waking up to his beautiful image every morning instantly, put a smile on my face. I look back now and wish life didn't change so dramatically.

"So, have you decided what you want for your birthday?" My mom asked igniting a war between thoughts of All Boys concert tickets and images of the latest iPhone and a pair of shoes that I had been salivating over since my last trip to the mall.

"Well," I paused and thought one last time about my options, "the All Boys are coming to town next month, and I would really love to see them." Thinking about them instantly woke me up. *"Sorry new iPhone and oh so cute shoes,"* I thought to myself as I pictured being close enough to the stage to have Jason hold my hand while singing one of his solos. It gave me a warm euphoric feeling. Ah, the innocence of ignorant bliss, I so miss those days. The days when my biggest problems were deciding what to wear the next day and who to excommunicate out of my social circle.

"Are you sure about that pumpkin?" My mom inquired, with a hint of disappointment in her voice. She is the type that wears her heart on her sleeve. She really looked forward to buying me things that I could instantly enjoy. Sure, she would be able to see me explode with joy over the chance to see my idols live, but she would have to wait to see her gift put to use. This was something new to her. She struggled to realize that I was actually making the transition from a giddy birthday cake, colorful cartoon, princess party theme loving kid, to a sophisticated, slightly boy crazed young woman.

"Yes, I am absolutely one thousand percent sure mom." I murmured before stumbling out of bed and stretching. My room was slightly on the messy side, but given the abundance of homework assignments, the cleaning of it was a stagnant work in progress. For a brief moment, my thoughts journeyed back to the nightmare dragon. The image of the tyrant reptile snatched my attention from the conversation and focused it on the creepy horrific nightmare that kept forcing itself into my dreams on a now frequent basis.

"Okay, well if you're sure about it… oh yeah, and before I forget, I need you to take the ground beef out of the freezer for me. Thank you, and please tell Karen I appreciate her giving you a ride to school today."

"Alright, gotcha," I replied as I looked at myself in the bedroom mirror. I was starting to notice slight changes in my appearance. Nothing major, but it gave me hope. My golden skin appeared smoother and there was a bright glow in my hazel eyes. My muscles looked toned, which was odd because I hadn't been working out on a consistent basis. I also took into inventory the fact that my figure looked somewhat curvier. It was a small improvement, nowhere near as much as some of the other girls at school, but it still counted as one regardless. I compared myself regularly to some of the most popular ones; which in turn left me with a slight complex. Some of them could easily pass for college students. My small five feet, one hundred pound petite frame, had yet to show substantial signs of it transitioning into womanhood. I tried different subtle things to age my appearance. Well, as much as I could without getting a lecture from my parents. Especially my dad, he really stayed on my case in regards to makeup and clothing. He always told me that I was perfect as is, which I highly doubted and put it in the generic category of 'things all dads say to their daughters'.

"Okay, honey. I love you and I'll see you later," My mom said in a rushed manner.

"Love you too," I blurted before hanging up. I still had a lot of stuff to do before my best friend Liz and her mom Karen arrived. I opened one of my bedroom windows to catch a quick sample of how the weather was behaving. It looked nice out. Just to be sure, I clicked my phone's weather app and viewed the forecast. The expected high was seventy-three with a minimal chance of rain. It was exceptionally warm for the first week of May in the Bipolar, weather-having state known as Ohio. Living close to the city of Cleveland, I had witnessed my fair share of crazy weather. Armed with the knowledge of the day's weather, I started getting ready. Like an organized drill, I went through each drawer methodically grabbing all of the items needed before rushing into the bathroom.

Once in the bathroom, I grabbed my shower cap, turned on the shower, and began brushing my teeth while waiting for the water to heat up. With the pearly whites handled, I jumped in the shower and quickly washed up. I contemplated taking the cap off and washing my hair, but I decided it would be too much of a hassle to blow-dry it. I hate having wet hair! My long flowing curly locks can be a real bother when wet. Since it was already Thursday, I decided to let it go until my birthday on Sunday.

After I finished getting dressed, I doctored up my mess of curls and made my way to the kitchen. Remembering the conversation with my mother, I opened the freezer and removed the pack of ground beef before searching the refrigerator for breakfast. I felt the rumble of my stomach as I tried to decide on something quick and easy to eat. I ended up grabbing an already opened cereal bar that I had sampled the day before, and a bottle of water. As I closed the door, there was more momentum with it than normal. It was odd because I didn't feel myself using any additional force. I lightly pushed it as I had normally done countless times before. I dismissed it to me rushing. While chewing the last bit of the cereal bar, my phone began to vibrate. I already had an idea who it was so I finished the bar, took a quick swig of water, grabbed my things, and headed for the door. Before reaching the door, I checked my phone just to make sure of my assumption. I swiped the screen lock and opened a text message from Liz. *"We're outside ☺,"* The message said. Not paying attention, I nonchalantly grabbed the doorknob. I gave it a light twist/tug, and it broke off!

*"What the…?"* I thought as I examined the knob. It looked as if someone had whacked it off. *"Maybe my father was working on it recently."* I thought dismissively before doing my best on the spot reattachment job and rushing out the door.

Once outside, I saw Liz and Karen pulling up to the house. Liz always contacted me a few minutes before she arrived. Liz is the kind of person that one can't help but like. Sometimes when I think about her, I wonder how she has adjusted without me. We were the absolute closest of friends. There was not one secret, which either of us kept from the other. She is one of the things about my former life that I miss the most. As the car came to a stop, I could see a bright, bubbly, smile plastered on Liz's face. Her brown skin glowed and her dark brown eyes were full of excitement. Her short black hair was cut in a style similar to that of her idol, pop star Jade Phoenix. Karen looked like an older version of Liz with darker skin and long hair. Looking at them made me wonder why my mom and I didn't favor each other as much. I jogged to the car and was just about to carelessly yank on the door handle when I thought about the doorknob. With that in mind, I gently pulled on the handle. Liz must've noticed because she had a weird look on her face.

"Is everything alright?" She questioned as I got into the back of the car.

"Yeah, of course," I responded with a slight giggle.

"Good Morning Charisma, did you let your mom know that you were staying over tomorrow night?" Karen asked as she adjusted her body to turn toward me.

"Good morning and yes, I did," I answered as I softly closed the door.

"There is something different about you," Liz blurted without turning back to address me. I definitely felt different, I mean I noticed a change in my appearance and strength, but I didn't know the cause of it.

"Wish I knew what it was bestie, you would be one of the first to know," I responded as Karen began to drive.

"So Liz tells me that you girls are going to a concert for your birthday, what group was it again, Some Boys?"

"All Boys Mom, All Boys," Liz responded in a slightly annoyed tone. Don't get me wrong, I was a fan, but Liz was a fanatic! She practically based her whole future around meeting them.

"Yes, I confirmed it with my mom earlier." I murmured as I stared out the window. I drifted off into my thoughts and hardly noticed that Karen and Liz had stopped talking.

*"Wow, I remember when I was stir-crazy over my first boy band,"*

"What band was that Mrs. Bemis?" I asked aloud.

"Huh?" Karen responded.

"I was responding to what you were just saying about boy bands."

"Well… I didn't say anything about boy bands," Her response completely threw me for a loop.

"But I thought you just stated that you used to be stir-crazy over your first boy band."

"No, um… actually… I was thinking it. How did you…" Karen was completely confused. She couldn't even finish her statement. She just continued driving with her mouth gaped slightly open. Liz turned around with the strangest look on her face.

"My mom didn't say anything." Liz uttered with eyes wide as saucers. I knew what I had heard her say. I heard it clear as day. *"I knew there was something different about her today."* I heard Liz's voice state, and I was about to respond until I realized that her lips didn't move. I couldn't understand how it was possible. It was as if I'd read her thoughts. Then, like a flash of lightening, I had one of those Ah-ha moments. You know one of those moments when the metaphorical light comes on and illuminates your thoughts. It was a very weird, awkwardly silent moment. I had to think fast.

"You know what, I was thinking about what my mom said earlier and I was so deep in thought, I guess I assumed you said it, Mrs. Bemis," I responded with an on the fly explanation.

"Oh, okay," she replied. Liz continued looking at me.

"What? I'm okay." I stated as I looked at my confused best friend.

"You're scaring me Charisma," She murmured as she forced her best attempt at a smile to melt away the shock on her face. I giggled in response, not sure of what to say. I myself was scared and didn't have the slightest idea what had occurred. Things were definitely getting strange.

# Chapter 2

# Weird and Weirder

"DOES ANYONE WANT TO COME UP TO THE BOARD AND SOLVE THIS PROBLEM?" Mrs. Mallory asked as I sat somewhat paying attention. I was still trying to make sense of the strange incidents from earlier. *"Is everything alright?"* Liz's question lingered as well. I started to question if I were in fact "alright". I was lost in thought when Mrs. Mallory called me up to the board. "Ms. Grey, would you like to come up and give the problem a try?" Her request snapped my attention back into the classroom and off the thoughts inhabiting my brain.

"Huh? Uh… sure, I guess," I uttered with a lack of confidence evident in my voice. I hate when a teacher does that. Out of the thirty-one students in the class, she picked me. I slowly got up from my desk, and awkwardly made my way up front. The room was quiet, and I could feel everyone's attention focused on me. Once I reached the board, I grabbed the marker and glanced at the problem on the board. It was a type of problem that I'm not too particularly fond of you know, the ones that have letters in the place of numbers, like B plus A equals… yeah, one of those problems. I was in the middle of concentration when the voices started up. *"Any day now,"* I heard Justin, a guy that sat next to me say. I turned around, shot him a quick evil look, and then resumed assessing the math problem. Then, I heard another person *"She must be slow,"* so I turned around again.

"Is everything okay Ms. Grey?" Mrs. Mallory asked with a weird puzzled look on her face.

"Yes, it's just a little hard to concentrate." I murmured before turning back to the board. I removed the cap off the marker and was on the verge of making my first mark when more voices started up. At first there was just a couple. Then, numerous voices started to flood in. There were so many that it was hard to decipher them all. It was like being in the school auditorium waiting for a program to start and everyone's chattering away and making the best of the idle time. I tried to tune them out, but they continued to invade my mind. *"What's taking her so long?" "I'm glad it's not me!" "She has a nice butt." "Hmm, I wonder what's for dinner? I hope it's not leftovers." "Maybe I should ask her for her number after class." "I shouldn't have stayed up so late playing that game."* Were some of the thoughts being picked up in a variety of recognizable voices by my psyche, it got so bad that I stopped working on the problem, dropped the marker, closed my eyes, and cupped my ears with both hands.

"Charisma," Through the flood of thoughts I heard Mrs. Mallory. I opened my eyes and turned to face her. "Is everything alright?" She inquired with a concerned look.

"I have a headache," I blurted as I quickly put my hands down. "May I go to the restroom?" I asked.

"Yes. Do you need to see the nurse?"

"I don't know… maybe." I wasn't sure if I should milk the opportunity for more than a pass to the restroom.

"Perhaps it would be best if you did." Mrs. Mallory insisted before writing me out a hall pass. I reluctantly took the pass, grabbed my personal belongings, and went to the door. Without thinking, I grabbed the doorknob. It began to crumble in my hand like aluminum foil. I quickly looked back to see if anyone else noticed. Their eyes were all focused on me, but fortunately, my body covered their view of the doorknob and it went unnoticed. Not wanting to risk having Mrs. Mallory come to the door, I gently wrapped my hand around the knob and lightly gave it a twist. The door swung open with little effort on my part. I knew that there was definitely something going on but I was clueless as to what. I left the room and headed to the restroom. As I was walking, I noticed everything around me was blurry and out of focus.

"Whoa, slow down!" I heard someone yell. I stopped and glanced around the hall. I saw Mr. Russell the security guard down the hall a short distance from where I had just walked.

"Huh?" I responded.

"What are you doing, practicing for the speed walking marathon?" Mr. Russell asked sarcastically.

"I… I was just walking." Which at the time, I honestly thought I was.

"Well, it looked like you were practically running. Do you have a pass?" I handed over the pass. Mr. Russell gave it a quick glance before returning it. "Okay Ms. Grey, slow it down,"

"Yes Mr. Russell," I responded sheepishly before resuming my journey. Not wanting to risk another confrontation with Mr. Russell, I made sure to walk extra slow. As I walked down the hall, I continued hearing random voices. They changed from room to room. After passing a class where there was a test in session, I decided to stop and wait by the door to see if I could tell exactly where the voices were originating.

I sat quietly outside of the classroom observing the students as they took their test. The voices were still present, but not a single person in the room was moving their lips! After seeing that, I thought I was really losing my marbles! I decided to forego the restroom, and head straight to see the nurse. Everything around me was changing. I was scared senseless! It wasn't even after ten o'clock and I was already having a terrible day! I reached the nurse's office and lightly tapped on the door.

"Come in," The nurse yelled from inside. Remembering the classroom doorknob, I cautiously grabbed the knob, took a deep breath, and gave it a soft twist. The door opened and I strolled inside. The nurse, a petite woman in a powder blue outfit had her back turned to me as I entered the room. She appeared to be in the middle of filling out paperwork. Her dark hair was neatly bunched into a ponytail and the smell of a faint flowery perfume hung in the air.

"Have a seat. I'll be right with you." She stated as she continued scribbling on the papers. I took a seat as instructed and patiently waited for her to finish. After waiting for a few moments, I noticed everything was quiet; the voices were gone! This was a good thing because I didn't have the slightest idea as to how I would explain it and sound sane. "So what are you here for?" She asked while still facing the opposite direction.

"Well, uh… let's see…" I stopped and thought about how to explain everything. "Have you ever had one of those days where everything just seemed weird, and unexplainable things occur?" The nurse must've caught on to what I was saying because she stopped writing almost immediately. She turned to face me, and the first thing I noticed was how bright her blue eyes were. They were unlike any I'd ever seen. There was something different about her. She had a strange presence about her.

"Okay… would you care to elaborate?" She asked as she sat down in front of me.

"Yes, but I don't exactly know how to say it. Things are happening that I have no logical explanation for."

"Like what exactly?"

"Well, for starters, when I woke up this morning, I noticed several changes in my appearance."

"Okay, well as a growing teen your body is supposed to change. What else did you notice?"

"Um, well, I seem to have more strength today than I had yesterday, oh and I'm faster."

"It could just be because you're maturing, quite a few teens experience changes that seem drastic, and like they happened overnight."

"No, I don't think you heard me correctly. The changes are <u>drastic</u>."

"How <u>drastic</u>,"

"Well, when I grabbed my doorknob earlier, it broke off."

"Broke off?"

"Yeah, it came right off, like someone used a hammer and whacked it loose."

"Oh, excuse me for a moment." The nurse got up and went into an adjoining room. It was unclear why, but I got this creepy vibe. Then, I began to hear her voice as clear as day speaking in a weird foreign language. The clarity of it made it seem as if she was standing right next to me!

"What did you say?" I asked aloud.

"What are you talking about? I didn't say anything." She stated as she returned to the room. There was a weird, creepy, expression plastered on her face, and her eyes were even brighter than before.

"I thought you were saying something to me from the other room." I murmured while taking notice of the slight changes in her appearance. In addition to the increased brightness of her eyes, her skin had a not so subtle glow. It was almost as if it were radiating with some weird energy.

"I was thinking aloud." She replied as she moved closer to me. "Is there anything else you would like to share?" I was beginning to notice something abnormal in the way she talked. It made me feel uneasy. I wanted to get up and run full speed out of the room, but I decided that it might not be the best thing to do considering the circumstances.

"You know what, you're probably right. Maybe all of the things I'm experiencing are just a result of normal growth and I need time to adjust to them." Based on the strange vibe she was giving off, I decided not to divulge any further details.

"So you're fine now?" She inquired while looking intensely into my eyes.

"Yes, I'm great thanks," I said as I began to get up from my chair.

"You're welcome," She continued staring. It was as if she was staring into my soul.

"Okay, see you around," I replied and hastily made my retreat. I was almost out the door when a strange calming energy swept over me and made me stop dead in my tracks.

"Sooner than later, it will all make sense." The nurse said cryptically. I didn't know what to say in response. I gave her one last look and left.

As soon as I reached the hall, the bell rang. Within seconds, students filled the halls. I had just begun walking to my next class when, "Charisma," I heard someone yell. I looked around and saw Justin coming toward me. "Hey, you got a moment?" He asked as other students whizzed by. His bright green eyes were full of excitement. His wild blonde hair and boyish grin reminded me faintly of Jason from All Boys. If not for his slightly boorish ways, I would've considered making him my first boyfriend.

"Yeah, what's up," I answered, "but make it quick cause' I have to make it up to Mr. Kroger's class before the bell or I'll get sent to in-school. He's a real stickler for punctuality."

"No problem, I can walk you there." Was his reply, I knew that he had a crush on me, but I wasn't ready to start seeing someone, my schoolwork and studies came first.

"Okay, whatever," I replied and continued walking.

"Is everything okay? How did it go with the nurse?"

"Everything is fine. I just have a slight headache." I murmured as we made our way through the sea of hustling bodies all racing to get to their assigned destinations.

"Okay, that's good, well if you're not doing anything this weekend…" I knew he had an ulterior motive. He had been hounding me since the school year started, "how about we catch a movie this weekend?" Justin was so predictable that it was almost cute in a weird quirky way.

"Well, I sort of have plans. I'm spending the night at Liz's tomorrow, and Saturday my parents are taking me out to dinner for my birthday." My parents had taken me out to dinner every year for my birthday since forever.

"Uh, well, maybe we can go on Sunday? I mean, if you don't have anything else planned." He was persistent, to say the least. I took a second to think about it before responding. "Well?" He was like an anxious dog wagging its tail in anticipation of a treat.

"I will let you know tomorrow before class," I responded as we reached Mr. Kroger's room. "Thanks for walking me," I uttered as I flashed a quick smile.

"You're welcome. I guess I'll see you later." Justin said bashfully, almost blushing. I gave him another look before going in. Mr. Kroger was my biology teacher. His class was one of the few classes that Liz and I shared. Most times while in class, we tried our hardest not to chatter and giggle. I remember when Liz showed me this video of a woman falling off a bus. We laughed so much that we both ended up having to do extra homework for according to Mr. Kroger, "disruption of class". Once inside, I saw Liz in the usual part of the class, closest to the windows. She looked troubled. Normally she would be all smiles. I went over and settled in next to her.

"Hey," I said as I took out my supplies.

"Hey," She responded while keeping her attention focused on her phone. That wasn't like her; something was definitely up.

"Is everything okay?" I questioned. I was determined to find out the truth.

"I don't know, you tell me," was her snappy reply. I realized that she was upset with me for not being truthful with her, but what was I supposed to say? Liz, I can read your mother's mind as well as yours, oh and I broke my door with my newly discovered super strength? It sounded crazy just thinking about it.

"Look, I don't know what's going on, but I'll tell you all about it later, I promise okay?"

"Okay," Her attitude instantly went from standoffish, back to the normal Liz I know and love. The bell rang, and everyone took his or her seat. Mr. Kroger rushed in with a cup in one hand and notes in the other.

"Good morning class, let's get right down to business. Everyone take out your books and open them up to page one hundred eighty-three. We're going to read about the Mendelian Inheritance." Mr. Kroger said as he placed his cup down and flipped through his notes. Once he finished sifting through his notes, he opened his teacher's copy of the assigned biology book and began to read. "In the 1800's, an Austrian monk named Gregor Mendel performed breeding experiments with pea plants in his garden…" As Mr. Kroger continued reading, Liz and I began texting back and forth. Most of the stuff was just silly typical teenage nonsense, like boys, celebrities, shows, and All Boys. Everything seemed as if it were back to normal.

*"Why do you think Jason's the hottest?"*

*"Have you seen his smile and green eyes?"*

*"What about Barry?"*

*"He's okay, I guess, Idk…"* were some of the messages sent back and forth between us as we pretended to pay attention to the lesson. We always made sure to read everything ahead of time. We continued back and forth with the messages for the remainder of the class.

Class let out and I was anxious to leave. The next class was gym; which I didn't mind too much. Liz shared that class with me as well. Some of the activities were actually quite fun. A few of the girls with larger bust sizes often complained which made me thankful for not having the same dilemma. I didn't mind playing volleyball and dodgeball. I know it sounds sadistic, but I actually liked hitting people with the ball. The only thing I didn't like about the class was Paige Shuster. She and I had been rivals since the Sixth grade when she purposely spilled juice on my new outfit. She held great disdain for me and I wasn't particularly fond of her either. She hated me even more after she found out that Justin, the guy she really had it bad for, had a crush on me. That was another reason on top of him being boorish, that made me hesitant to give him the green light.

Liz and I rushed to the locker room to change before class started. As we were headed in, Paige and her two flunkies, Tiffany Grace and Gina Delanie were headed out. Paige was a leggy menace with cold blue eyes and dirty blonde hair. Tiffany was a dark brunette with a few extra pounds, and Gina was a green-eyed redhead freckled face lackey that seemed to follow along and laugh at everything Paige said or did.

"Hmm, make sure you two Lesbos don't leave the locker room smelling like dead fish." Paige murmured with a malicious smirk on her face. I felt like punching her teeth out but I knew that it would end up in an altercation and no All Boys concert tickets.

"It takes one to know one, and the dead fish smell is a little closer to home. You might want to hit the showers before class starts." I retorted in a nasty tone.

"Touché," She stated bitterly. I shut her down. She was floored. I smiled as she and her cronies gave me nasty looks before walking away.

"Touché, that was so lame," Liz commented before we went inside. We laughed the whole time while getting dressed. It felt good to shut Paige down. She was the type of person that had the courage to insult or do malicious things to others, only when she had an audience. She seemed so self-conscious.

After getting dressed, Liz and I rushed out to the gym floor. The Gym teacher Ms. Velez had a penchant for making people that were late to lineup run five laps around the gym before being able to participate in class. And those that didn't want to participate ran at least ten laps before having to sit down and do a writing assignment for the remainder of the class. Ms. Velez was a hard-nosed ex-marine that didn't tolerate too many things. Her looks fooled many. She was a petite but curvy woman with long flowing black hair and an attractive face. Almost all of the boys in class had a crush on her. While waiting in line up, I would often overhear them talk about the things they wanted to do to her. It was gross, to say the least and obviously influenced by the stuff they saw while sneaking onto adult only sites.

Ms. Velez stood silently in the center of the Gym staring at her clipboard, looking up periodically as she made checks on the paper. I knew she was in the middle of taking attendance. After about a month of the class being in session, she had memorized everyone's name. "Alright, I need everyone's attention, we're about to have a dodgeball match. After the warm up, everyone will gather with the rest of their designated team!" She said as she briefly looked up from the clipboard. "The Red Team," she pointed to her left, "will go over there, and the Blue Team," she pointed to her right, "will go over there." I got a weird sensation in my gut before she began naming the teams. "Team Red will be Brian, Chris, Paige, Liz, Tiffany, and Rochelle, James, and Stewart as subs; Team Blue, Gina, Charisma, Jonathan, Jasmine, Mya, and Angelo, Sean and Jennifer as subs." Liz let out a sigh. Paige looked less than enthused as she stared in my direction. As we stood staring at each other, I began to hear her voice.

*"Well on the bright side, I'll get a chance to hit old ugly in the face. It might make her look better!"* Was what I heard her say without her lips moving. A smirk quickly formed on her face.

I was without a doubt positive that the voices I'd been hearing were people's thoughts.

*"What the (expletive)?"* I thought as I realized the magnitude of such a revelation. I contemplated whether I was losing my mind, or if I were indeed experiencing things that had no logical explanation.

"Ms. Velez I don't want to be on teams with her!" Gina said in a highly displeased manner while pointing in my direction. It quickly shifted my attention back to reality. She was expressing her displeasure in regards to us being on the same team. Don't get me wrong, I wasn't pleased with the situation either, but it was either play together, or run laps and write, so I wasn't going to say a single word.

"Well, if you don't like the teams, you're more than welcome to run laps and write." Ms. Velez responded. The look on Gina's face made it hard not to laugh. It took every fiber in my being to restrain it.

"Can you switch her out with one of the subs?" Gina asked, fully expressing her disapproval. She had a lot of nerve and I was already irritated with her and her friends.

"How about you switch with one of the subs?" I countered in a brash tone.

"Girls that's enough," Ms. Velez said in a strong commanding voice, "Gina, since you have a problem playing with Charisma, you can switch with Sean."

"But—" Gina tried to protest, but was quickly silenced.

"Either switch or start running."

"Fine," Gina fumed in a bratty tone as she folded her arms. She stood in silent protest for a brief moment before making her exit. Her walk was hard and full of attitude as she left the gym floor. Shortly after Gina left the floor, Ms. Velez blew the whistle and the warm-up session began. We stretched and did minimal exercises that had become a routine at the start of every class. After a few minutes of warming up, Ms. Velez blew her whistle again.

"Okay everyone, choose your positions," Ms. Velez instructed. I quickly went to one of the center positions. I was ready to clobber Paige and Tiffany. Liz looked so pitiful and downtrodden, standing on the opposite side of the floor. I felt sorry for her, but I was motivated to win. Paige was going down, and that meant the entire team. I waited in place anxiously for Ms. Velez to blow the whistle. As soon as the whistle blew, everyone ran for a ball. There were three on each side, so I had to hustle for one. I ended up grabbing the first of the three placed on my side and ran for the attack line. Before I could reach the line, I felt the shock of a ball hit me in the back of my head. It almost made me lose my balance. I heard the blow of the whistle and the squeaky sounds of tennis shoes, stopping abruptly on the waxed floor.

"How many times have I said no hits above the shoulder?" Ms. Velez yelled out angrily. "Paige what was that?"

"I was on the attack line, and I didn't mean to hit her in the head," Paige responded innocently. Which I knew was an outright lie. Even though I didn't see her throw it, I knew she had every intention to hit me in the head. I stood angrily rubbing my head waiting for my chance of vengeance. I made the meanest face that I could muster at Paige. She flashed a mischievous grin before directing her attention back to Ms. Velez.

"If that happens again, you'll be running laps and writing for the rest of this class and the next!" Ms. Velez warned. She blew the whistle and we went back to playing. I dodged an awkward throw from Brian and watched as Liz was hit by Jonathan. The hit distracted Paige and I saw my window of opportunity. In a pitch of fury, I released the ball. In my moment of anger, I completely forgot about the weird incidents from earlier. The ball flew abnormally fast. As I watched it, the memories hit like a flash of lightening.

"Oh—" Before I could finish my thought, the ball hit its target. It hit Paige square in the right shoulder. She let out a quick moan as the force of the hit sent her to the floor. Ms. Velez's whistle blared out as Paige's body crashed onto the hard waxed surface. The voices followed shortly after. Everyone's thoughts flooded my consciousness along with their audible reactions. It was pure chaos. I barely heard Ms. Velez's shouts.

"Charisma," Ms. Velez rushed onto the floor with a flustered expression. She shot me a displeased look before going to Paige's aid. I stood motionless as I watched Paige cry and writhe in agony. As she clutched her shoulder, it reminded me of this nature show I watched when I was younger. In the show, a young bird with a broken wing is slowly nursed back to health by a little boy that found her in his backyard. My feelings were mixed, I wanted to celebrate and kick myself at the same time.

*"There goes my chance to see Jason Niles in the flesh,"* I thought as I looked over toward Liz. She had the same look as she had earlier in the car. She was thinking about missing the opportunity to see her favorite All Boys' member as well. I really didn't mean it. In spite of how much I despised Paige and how much hell she'd caused up to that point, I never seriously thought I would physically hurt someone.

I watched as paramedics came into the gymnasium. It was serious. The force of the hit dislocated her shoulder. The bell rung and all of the other students rushed to go to lunch. I was about to go as well, but Ms. Velez stopped me before I had the chance.

"We're going to the principal's office!" She said in a stern voice before directing me to the exit. I felt a lump form in my throat as we made the trek to see the principal. It was the first occurrence for me. For my entire school career, I'd managed to avoid having to make such a trip. I didn't know what to expect. The butterflies in my stomach were definitely a flutter. I felt like dying. I pictured my mom and dad's faces of disapproval. While stuck in the shock of the moment, I begin hearing Ms. Velez's thoughts.

*"Oh my God, please don't let me lose my job over this. How the hell did she do that? How can you dislocate someone's shoulder with a (expletive) dodge ball? Is that even humanly possible?"* Based on her thoughts, she seemed more worried than I did. Her level of worry only increased mine. Once we finally reached the principal's office, we ended up waiting a few minutes for the principal to finish up with these kids caught smoking in the bathroom. It was weird because I could hear the entire thing as if I were in the room with them. Listening to the kids, the principal, Ms. Velez's silent prayers, and the receptionist reminisce about her date the night before, the wait was over before I knew it.

The kids exited the principal's office with dismal expressions and thoughts to match. The principal, Mr. Rose emerged seconds later. He was a real character in the sense that he looked like a principal. I mean, he looked like that was exactly what he was destined to do, run a school for a paycheck. His hair was nearly nonexistent on the top of his head, and he reeked of some type of bland cologne.

"Ms. Velez and Ms. Grey," he said while making a gesture for us to come into the office. To say I was nervous would be an understatement. As Ms. Velez got up from her seat, she continued to pray silently all the way into the principal's office. She prayed fervently in both English and Spanish. Her prayers made me wonder if I should've been doing the same thing. Being inside of the principal's office was like being in a foreign land. It was unfamiliar territory. "Ladies, have a seat," The principal instructed in a very neutral tone. His thoughts started flooding my mind immediately. He was concerned with how Paige's parents would react to the news. He didn't know what to make of the entire situation.

"According to you Ms. Velez, Charisma hit Paige with a rubber dodgeball correct?"

"Yes Mr. Rose, that's correct," Ms. Velez responded timidly.

"So how can a rubber ball filled with air that weighs a few pounds at best, cause that kind of injury?" Mr. Rose Inquired as his mind worked to come up with an answer to his question.

"I, I don't know… maybe it happened when she fell." Ms. Velez responded. *(Expletive),"* was the profane thought that accompanied her answer.

"Well, regardless of how, we need to make sure it doesn't happen again. That's a liability that the school can't afford. I pray to God that her parents don't decide to take legal action. And you young lady," Mr. Rose shifted his attention to me, "Why would you do such a thing?"

"I didn't do it on purpose. I guess I got caught up in the competitive spirit." I really didn't want to reveal the truth. That probably would've led to more questions and psychiatric help. That's the last thing I needed was for school officials to think I'd gone off the deep end.

"I understand Charisma but unfortunately, I have to implement a punishment. There has to be consequences for your actions. This is my first time seeing you in here, so I know you're not a troublemaker, which makes choosing a proper punishment that much more difficult. I had to think fast, I didn't mind being punished, as long as my parents didn't find out.

"Mr. Rose, I know that I have to receive some type of punishment for my actions and I'm fine with that. The thing that I'm concerned about is my parents finding out. I didn't do it on purpose, can you please figure out a punishment that I can serve out at school?" I hoped my pleas were convincing.

"Well, what do you think Ms. Velez? Is she a pretty good student?"

"I've never had a problem with her and she is always on time to class."

"Okay, well let's do this; let's give you a few days of in-school suspension. That might just rectify the situation. Starting tomorrow, you will report to room 228 and every day until next Wednesday. You will pack your lunch and I will make sure all of your teachers give you your assignments that need to be completed. And under no circumstances, other than restroom breaks, must you leave that room. Is that understood Ms. Grey?"

"Y—yes sir," I replied humbly. I wasn't psyched about the punishment, but I felt relieved knowing that my parents weren't going to find out. After signing my signature and apologizing profusely to Ms. Velez, I received a pass and went to lunch late.

The cafeteria was almost vacant when I finally arrived. My stomach growled as my nose invited in the succulent aroma of pepperoni pizza. Pepperoni pizza was always served on Thursdays. I was abnormally hungry, I felt as if I could eat an entire pizza by myself. I ended up buying the last half of the pizza pie that was left, an order of loaded fries, and a pop. As I was leaving the line, I noticed Liz was almost finished with her food. I gave her a brief rundown of my punishment before she had to leave. After she left, I devoured my whole meal in a matter of minutes. It was the fastest I'd ever eaten. I disposed of my trash and rushed to my next class. The rest of the day was filled with the whispers and gossip of the dodgeball incident. In a matter of hours, it had become the most infamous event of the entire school year.

# Chapter 3

# A little less safe...

**WE PULLED UP IN FRONT OF MY HOUSE,** and I could hardly wait to get out of the car. The entire ride home had been very uncomfortable. Liz didn't say much because she didn't want to risk her mother finding out about the incident from earlier. She always had a way of spilling the beans, so her remaining silent was a good thing. I remained silent for an all together different reason, I couldn't stop hearing Liz and Karen's thoughts. I received every single thought and was highly irritated by some of the things Liz thought. It really made me not want to sleep over the following night. As soon as the car made a full stop, I quickly thanked Karen for the ride and said bye to Liz in an impersonal manner. I was out of the car and halfway up the walkway in a matter of seconds. I heard the car pull off as I opened my door. My mother greeted me on the other side of it.

"What happened to the door?" She questioned with her hands on her hips. I wanted to tell her I didn't know, but that would've only made matters worse. My mom has always been big on security. If she sensed the slightest threat to our safety, she didn't hesitate to call the police. I guessed part of that stemmed from her house being broken into when she was a child.

"Uh, well… I'm not quite sure." I replied as I tried to come up with a humanly feasible explanation as to why the doorknob looked so mangled.

"What do you mean you're not sure?" My mother's eyes had a strange disconcerting look within them.

"Well, I was rushing to get ready, and while rushing," I had to make it sound as convincing as possible, "I fell into the door, and the knob broke. After it broke, I tried to use dad's tools to fix it."

"Are you alright? Do you have any pain?"

"I'm okay, and no, I don't have any pain." I quickly changed the subject, "So how was work?"

"Work was work, dealing with sick people that have attitudes, typical stuff. How was school?" was her response.

"Um, it was okay." I responded. I didn't want to risk saying too much. "So what do you think dad will bring us?" I questioned as my mom examined the knob.

"Probably some of the usual suspects, shirts, trinkets, or both," She replied. She looked at the door and then looked at me. "Are you sure you're not hurt?" She asked. Her nurse instincts were in full gear.

"<u>Yes,</u> mom. I'm fine." I replied in a slightly irritated tone. I wanted to tell her the truth, but I didn't know how to explain it. I didn't know how to tell her that her daughter had freakishly, weird super strength.

"Okay, honey," She uttered, though her thoughts reflected something different.

"So what's for dinner, burgers, tacos, hamburger helper?"

"You'll have to wait and see," She said with a sly grin as she fumbled with the knob.

"Okay," I murmured before heading upstairs. I felt extremely tired. I had homework to do, but figured I'd have plenty of time to do it in in-school suspension. I took off my clothes, put on something comfortable, plopped down on the bed, and turned on the TV. I began flicking through the channels. A weird story on the news caught my attention.

*"I'm here in front of the home of the Linux family. Earlier today, police found the bodies of five brutally beaten victims. The victims were beaten beyond recognition and are missing their eyes. Police, are desperately looking for leads to bring the guilty parties to justice. Anyone with information should contact the Oak Hills Homicide Division at 440-555-5455."*

Hearing the news report sent a strange chill through my body. Oak Hills was only thirty minutes from where I lived. *"Why would someone take their eyes?"* I pondered as I turned the channel. I felt an unsettling sensation in my stomach the more I thought about it. I resumed flipping through the channels and luckily found something more upbeat, but I still couldn't get the story out of my head. I was mortified. I wondered if it was the work of a serial killer, a satanic cult, or just an isolated incident. The more I thought about it, the more it made me think about the broken front door. I decided to go back downstairs and check on my mother's progress.

Halfway down the stairs, I could see my mother still hard at work on the door. My father's toolbox rested on the floor next to her.

"How's it going?" I inquired as I reached the landing.

"I've almost got it," she replied as she turned the Phillips screwdriver. "There," She said in a breathy tone. "It's not the best as far as the cosmetics go, but it's functional. Your father will probably have to get a new one or fix this one when he gets home."

"Okay, sorry for breaking it," I said as she put the tools back in the box.

"It's okay, accidents happen, how about you wash your hands and help me with dinner." She said as she wiped off beads of sweat from her forehead.

"Alright," I replied before rushing upstairs to wash my hands. I made sure to tread lightly out of fear of another "accident". I did everything cautiously, from turning the knobs on the water faucet, to removing a towel from the rack. I felt like I was living in a glass house! I wanted to tell my mother so bad, I was even willing to show her, but I knew that it would only complicate things even further. I was tremendously conflicted. I needed someone to talk to. I needed someone to understand and to help me make sense of it all.

Once I reached the kitchen, I began receiving my mother's thoughts. Most of them were basic things such as work related matters and concerns in regards to my father's trip home.

"Okay chef I'm ready, what's on the menu." I said in an enthusiastic tone as I grabbed an apron.

"Well, since it's just the two of us, I figured we'd have your favorite."

"Tacos," I blurted excitedly as I tied the strings of the apron.

"Yep," She replied with the smile that I love seeing. My mother has the brightest smile. I've often tried to emulate it, but to no avail. Looking at her made me think back to what I noticed about Liz and Karen.

"Hey mom,"

"Yes," she responded.

"Can I ask you something?"

"Sure," She replied as she set some ingredients on the island counter.

"Have you ever noticed how Liz and her mom look alike?" I questioned.

"Um, well to be honest, I've never really paid that much attention to them."

"Seriously," I questioned. I knew she was downplaying it. Their resemblance was too obvious.

"*I hope she doesn't say what I think she's going to say,*" was the thought that preceded her response. "I guess they do a little, why?"

"Well," I paused and thought about how to delicately get my point across, "I've noticed that we're the opposite of them, we don't favor one another as much." I got it out as best as I could.

"That's because you take more after your father." She responded in a weird unconvincing tone. Her thoughts said otherwise, *"Please don't let this be what I think it is. I don't think it's time to tell her."*

"Tell me what?" I blurted out without thinking about it. It was more of a reflex than on purpose.

"What are you talking about?" She looked puzzled. I didn't know what to say. I contemplated telling her what was going on, but I was lost as to how I would explain it.

"Nothing, just forget about it." I responded and began prepping the food.

"No, how… did you do that?"

"Do what?" I played dumb, hoping that it would work.

"It was as if… it was like… like you read my mind." She uttered in a dumbfounded manner.

"Mom, how can I read minds?" I asked sarcastically.

"I didn't say that, I—"

"I know what you mean, what if it was something like that. I mean, what if there was something so strange going on, that I didn't know how to explain it?" I expelled it all in a great storm of wordy confusion.

"What are you talking about?"

"What if I could actually read minds and do other things?"

"Huh, come again?"

"What if I'm not normal? What if I can do things that regular people can't?"

"Um, you're starting to scare me. Are you sure you're okay?"

"Here, let me show you," I went to the refrigerator and attempted to pick it up. At first I gave it a light tug, it didn't budge. I attempted a second time with a little more strength added. It still wouldn't move.

"Honey, what are you doing?" She questioned as she stood with a bewildered expression on her face.

"I'm trying to show you." I responded, frustrated with my lack of a demonstration.

"Show me what?" I could tell that I really wasn't making sense. I was only making things even more confusing.

"Uh, think of something." I instructed.

"What?" She looked at me as if I were a crazed mental patient.

"Think of something, anything." I instructed. Confused as to why my strength wasn't working.

"Okay," she responded. There was a long pause. I knew she was thinking something, but I wasn't receiving it. I was about to get angry, but then a voice began to speak.

*"Relax,"* is what it said in a firm authoritative tone. Even though the voice sounded familiar, I knew it wasn't my mother's. Something inside, urged me to follow its instruction. I let my frustration dissipate and became calm. Almost instantly, I began to hear my mother's thoughts.

*"Why are we sitting in the kitchen not doing or saying anything?"* She questioned mentally.

"So I can read your thoughts," I divulged, a shocked look appeared on her face almost instantly. "Now watch this," I said before walking back over to the refrigerator. I took a deep breath, wrapped my arms around it, and lifted. It rose with the greatest of ease. It felt as light as a paperweight. I put it back down just as effortlessly as I had lifted it. I turned to face my mother. She stood frozen with her mouth slightly gaped open.

"H-how…" She was at a loss for words, and I didn't have a good explanation to give her.

"I'm not sure, it just started today," I responded as I tried to figure out the origin of my powers.

"Hold on, I need to take a seat." My mom said, before going into the dining room. She returned seconds later with chair in hand. "Oh, and I definitely need a drink," she expelled before walking past me and going into the refrigerator. She grabbed her bottle of wine, picked up a glass from one of the cabinets, and sat down on the chair. She filled the glass almost to the brim, and took a healthy gulp of it before speaking. "So, is that what really happened to the doorknob?" She questioned before taking a small sip.

"Yeah," I responded. "I was rushing to catch my ride and it broke as I was pulling and twisting it. The mind reading ability started when I got in the car with Liz and her mom."

"Okay, so what else can you do? Can you shoot laser beams out of your eyes, fly, or freeze things?" She inquired as she continued drinking her wine.

"I don't think so," I responded as my mind ran wild imagining the possibility of having other powers. "Besides, I wouldn't really know how to find out. I don't even know how I got these powers. Do you or dad have any powers?"

"No, well… see the thing about it is… remember when you were questioning the lack of a resemblance between us? Well, there's a reason for that." My mother finished the rest of her drink before continuing. "We're not your real parents." Her revelation, made it seem as if time itself had slowed down. My whole world shattered. I was left speechless. My heart sank and it felt as if every dark cloud in the world came over me. It felt as if someone had just ripped me apart like a piece of paper. I wanted to cry, I wanted to run out of the room. I wanted to leave the house and never come back. I wanted to do everything but stay and confront the newly revealed truth. I felt my eyes start to water up as I looked at my mother. Her eyes were watering up as well. I felt a deep urge to go and embrace her. The knowledge of having my freakish uncontrollable strength made me rethink my initial instinctive impulse.

"So when did you plan on telling me, never? I mean, how could you and dad keep a secret like that?"

"It's not what you think—"

"Well, what is it?" I interjected in a nasty tone. I felt like dying. "Who else knows? Does Liz or her mom know?" Paranoia had set in. I didn't know who to trust or what to believe. I couldn't wrap my mind around the fact that the people I loved the most, were capable of keeping such an incredible secret.

"No, Liz and Karen don't know. I'm quite sure that no one outside of our family knows. We were planning to tell you on your eighteenth birthday." She replied with shame evident in her voice.

"Why would you wait so long?" I asked as tears burned my eyes. I tried my best to hold them in, I fought them back, but they kept pushing to escape. One began to fall, and then another. More followed after that. They began to flow like a stream of dreary emotions. I broke down and gave in to them. I accepted the pain like a long delayed visitor that had finally arrived. I felt my lips quiver as a low muted sob escaped from them.

"I'm sorry honey, I really am, but we decided that it would've been best to wait until then. Once you were mature enough to handle it." I wanted to hate her. I wanted to use my power to pick her up and throw her as far as my new gift would allow. I wanted to hurt her so bad. I wanted her to feel as awful as I felt.

"I'm not hungry," I said before fuming out of the kitchen. I quickly retreated up the stairs, and into my room. Once inside, I locked the door and collapsed onto my bed. I sobbed into my pillow until I slowly drifted off to sleep.

I was almost out of the forest. I could see the clearing in the distance. My feet were heavy and my legs were burning with pain, but I refused to give in. I refused to die. I pushed myself harder as the dragon steadily gained ground. Its beastly snarls and footfalls echoed in the near distance. It wanted me as bad as I wanted to escape. "You're so close to the clearing, come on Charisma make it!" I mumbled as my body began to give in. I was less than twelve feet away, when suddenly a small figure emerged almost out of thin air. It appeared to be somewhat human. The sight of the figure, gave me hope. It renewed my strength. As I got closer, more details about the figure became apparent. He or she was floating a few feet above the ground. It was also surrounded by a weird blue glowing aura. Those details, made me question if I should continue running toward it. I felt the ground beneath me shake, and decided that the strange being was my only way out. Time seemed to slow down as I reached the strange entity. As our eyes connected, a thought slowly manifested in my mind, *"SOON,"*

I woke up drenched in sweat. My eyes quickly scanned around the room. Everything looked familiar, no dragons, little floating beings, or wooded areas. I was in my room and relieved to be in it. I remembered the tiff with my mother the night before. The argument and revelation were far worse than the recurring nightmare with the dragon. I was so upset that I didn't even eat one of my favorite meals in the entire world. I grabbed my phone from the nightstand and checked the time. I had slept for close to twelve hours. It was Friday, and in spite of the damper, from the night before, I was looking forward to getting away from home and hanging out at Liz's house. One thing that I wasn't looking forward to, and was absolutely dreading, was the first day of in-school suspension.

I pondered whether it really even mattered. All Boys meant everything to me, but knowing that I was adopted took precedence over it. School didn't matter, and any punishment handed down from my parents didn't matter. The only thing that kept me from going off the deep end, the only reason I decided to stay the course was Liz. My best friend in the entire universe mattered. Making sure that she had the chance to smile and sing along to her favorite All Boys' songs mattered. With that in mind, I reluctantly got up and did my usual routine. As I got myself dressed, my mind kept hanging on to the little floating creature from my dream. It seemed so familiar, like something from my past. Once I was dressed, I went into overdrive. I only had ten minutes or so left to spare, so I had to rush in order to eat before Karen arrived. As I was gathering my things, I accidentally knocked a jar of Anti frizz hair cream off my dresser.

On the way down the hall, I peeked into my parent's room. My mother was fast asleep. It was her first day off in almost eight days and she was taking full advantage of it by catching up on her rest. Her hours as a registered nurse often fluctuated from time to time. I felt bad about what happened the night before. There were things that were left unresolved. I wondered if she tried to wake me and talk things over. I wanted to say something to her before I left, but I figured it best to let her sleep. Finding out I was adopted was life changing. Most of the initial anger had subsided and although I was slightly depressed, I began to appreciate the way my parents treated me.

My dad was scheduled back into town that night from a business trip to Connecticut and I couldn't wait to see him. My dad was a Sales Consultant for some type of company that worked with other companies it referred to as its clients. I wondered what trinkets he would bring back from the trip. He always brought us back things. Shirts, key chains, and figurines, were just a few of the items added to my collection over the years. When he went to different countries, he would often return with amazing stories of the people and the cultures, oh and the strange delicacies too. When it came to experiencing new things, he was adventurous to say the least. I remember when he came back from Asia and he told me that he ate centipede soup and crickets. The thought of it made me so sick, that I didn't eat for the rest of the day.

I made it downstairs and grabbed a quick bite to eat. I was halfway through the meal, when my phone began to vibrate. *"It's Liz,"* I thought as I gobbled up the last morsels of food. I grabbed my book bag and carefully opened the front door. After school, I planned to return home before going to Liz's for the night. I had so many questions that I wanted to ask both of my parents, I couldn't wait to get out of school. The warm sun greeted me as I stepped outside. The breeze softly caressed my face as I walked to the car. I saw Liz bright and bubbly as usual, which helped to make me feel better.

"Good morning Liz, Good morning Mrs. Bemis," I said as I entered the car.

"Good morning Charisma," They both responded almost in unison.

"So are you ready for your birthday weekend?" Mrs. Bemis asked as she pulled away from the curb.

"Yes, I guess." I responded with a forced smile. My mind was full of concern and I was still slightly depressed. *"Some birthday,"* I thought sarcastically as new questions began forming in my head.

"I planned on getting pizza later and in honor of your birthday, Liz wanted you to pick the toppings. So which toppings would you like? Three's the limit unless you get the works or a specialty." Mrs. Bemis said as she looked at me in the rearview mirror.

"Okay, how about grilled chicken, steak, and bacon?" I responded remembering how great the combination tasted the last time I had it. It temporarily helped to take my mind off everything. Liz and Karen were in a talkative mood and I just wanted to be left alone. Not wanting to rain on anyone else's parade, I kept my true feelings to myself, and engaged in conversation. I couldn't let them know how I was really feeling. I maintained an upbeat façade for the duration of the ride. I felt like crap, and that was putting it nicely.

We arrived at the school, and said our goodbyes before heading in. The halls were bustling with life. It was Friday and everyone, well everyone except me, was looking forward to the weekend. I didn't know what to expect. I didn't feel like the normal carefree teen. I wasn't the normal carefree teen. It seemed as if I was fourteen going on thirty. My life was changing fast, and I was playing catch up trying to adjust. The incident with my mother, gave me a vague idea of how to control my powers. Relaxing and focusing my mind, made them work, and cluttering my psyche shut them off. I didn't know exactly how it worked, but I was glad it did. The last thing I needed was a bunch of other people's thoughts picking up in my head like radio stations. I didn't want to know about their plans for the weekend. I was actually contemplating canceling mine. It was shaping up to be the worst birthday weekend ever! I dreaded the actual day. I dreaded the day that I would officially become fifteen.

"So are you excited about hanging out tonight?" Liz asked as we hastily made our way to our lockers. "We can stay up all night if you like," Liz was really anticipating the sleepover. I envied her. She was normal and not adopted!

"Great," I responded sarcastically.

"What's wrong?" She inquired in a concerned manner, briefly stopping in front of me.

"What isn't wrong?" I responded dryly.

"Why are you acting like this? You were fine a few minutes ago in the car."

"Maybe it's because I have to spend the entire day in one class, or maybe it's because of the weird stuff happening in my life, or maybe, just maybe it's because I'm adopted!" I found that getting out my frustrations were easier than keeping them bottled-in. As soon as the last words escaped, I quickly walked around Liz and continued down the hall.

"You're what?" I really didn't feel like responding. Part of me just wanted to keep walking. "Why are you acting like this to me? I didn't do anything to you!" I could hear the anger building in Liz's voice. She couldn't understand why I was taking it out on her. I wasn't taking it out on her intentionally. She was just the hapless victim.

"Liz I'm sorry, but my world is falling apart, everything is going wrong!" I stated as I turned to face her.

"How did you find out you were adopted?"

"It's a long story. I'll tell you everything tonight after school when I come over okay?"

"Okay,"

We went our separate ways. I went to room 228 and got ready for the long, boring day that lay ahead. Once inside of the room, I sat at one of the desks closest to the door. The teacher was an old lady with a mean withered face. She looked like she could pass for one-hundred years old easy.

"Make sure you sign in on the clipboard by the door," She said in a stern but shaky voice. I settled my belongings, at the desk, and went to sign in.

*"I wish I could just fast forward to the end of the day."* I thought as I put my signature on the sign-in sheet. I wondered if I could indeed do such a thing or if someone else could. I started to see a bright side to having powers. I felt better walking back to my desk. Thinking of the limitless possibilities gave me a glimmer of hope. I sat down seconds before the sound of the first bell erupted throughout the building. *"Do my real parents have powers? Are they real life superheroes, or maybe they're super villains?"* I had questions that urgently needed answers. Pandora's Box was open and its contents were running wild. *"I wonder what my limits are. Can I pick up cars, trucks, buses, trains? Are there other people like me?"*

Focusing on my work was going to be a difficult task. I couldn't block out my unanswered questions. There were only a handful of students in the class, which only made the isolation factor worse. I felt like one of the misfit toys on the Christmas special that my grandmother would watch every year around Christmas. I always managed to get bored or fall asleep when it was on. I can't remember ever watching it in its entirety. It didn't interest me in the slightest. It seemed so ancient and outdated. My grandmother enjoyed every moment of it. She sung every song, and knew all of the scenes in the movie like the back of her hand. Thinking back on it made me look forward to the day when I would no longer be forced to endure it every year.

I finally managed to calm my excited thoughts, and start my work. I zipped through my English, Biology, and Social Studies work without a hitch. Algebra was a bit of a hurdle, but I managed to finish it ten minutes before lunch. After finishing it, I remembered that I forgot to pack a lunch. I was so busy being depressed that it completely slipped my mind. *"Great, now I'm going to starve!"* I thought as I stared at the clock. I had to think of something fast. *"Liz,"* popped in my head and I discreetly removed my phone from my purse and somehow managed to text a legible message to Liz. *"Hey Liz, I need lunch! ☺,"* I texted swiftly, while keeping an eye on the fossil of a teacher. She looked tired as if it was past her nap time.

*"Ok, just let me kno what u want 2 eat ☺,"* She responded promptly.

*"Just a sandwich, chips, & juice, I'll pay u Bk,"*

*"No need 2 its 4 Ur bday,"* She replied exactly how I knew she would. I knew she would refuse the money.

*"Thx,"* I texted a second before the teacher looked in my direction.

"What are you doing?" She questioned with a suspicious look.

"Nothing, just checking my makeup," I responded as I tucked my phone back into my purse.

"Aren't you a little too young to be wearing makeup?" She asked dryly.

"I don't think so," I replied, which resulted in a few small chuckles from the other students.

"Well, I beg to differ," She murmured in a bossy manner.

"May I go to the restroom?" I asked as I glanced up at the clock.

"Hmph, I suppose." She replied. "Make sure you take the hall pass and don't be longer than ten minutes is that understood?"

"Yes," I uttered as I got up from my desk. I quickly walked up to the table by the door where the sign-in sheet was and grabbed the absurdly large wooden hall pass that rested on it.

"I'll be watching the clock," She blurted out.

"Gotcha," I replied with a quick look before I opened the door and stepped out into the hallway. I knew the old bird would probably be timing me down to the last second so I had to make sure that I was back before the time was up. As I started to walk, I realized another power that I possessed. I realized that I had slightly enhanced speed. That was probably why Mr. Russell stopped me and told me to slow down. I figured it would be the perfect time to use it to my advantage. I could meet Liz, go to the restroom, and return to class in no time. I would have to keep an eye out for Mr. Russell and other school faculty, but it would be my only chance. The lunchroom was on the other side of the building, so I didn't have a choice.

I zoomed through the halls with mere minutes before the lunch bell was scheduled to ring. I made it to the cafeteria in record time. The bell rang as I reached the doors. I contemplated sneaking in and getting my own lunch. In-school students weren't allowed in the cafeteria and based on the notoriety I was receiving from the dodgeball incident I didn't want to risk it. Liz came a minute later and gave me a quick hello before heading in to get my lunch. I waited nervously outside as crowds of hungry teens followed suit. My stomach growled as I checked the time on my phone. I scanned through the crowd of lunch goers and noticed Paige and her cronies coming down the hall. *"If they see me out here, I'm toast!"* I thought before ducking into the closest place to hide, a janitor's storage closet. As I opened the door, the strong smell of musty, damp mop heads filled my nostrils. "Ewww," I mumbled as I covered my nose and closed the door behind me. I waited until the bell rang before ducking my head out. The hallway only had a few stragglers left in it and thankfully, Paige wasn't among them. Liz emerged from the cafeteria just as I was exiting the closet.

"Hey, I got you the turkey club, some plain chips, and an apple juice." She stated before handing me the items.

"Thanks Liz, you're a lifesaver," I replied before taking the items.

"I'll see you later, okay?"

"Yup, right after I see my dad. He's due back into town from his trip," I left Liz and practically ran back to class. I managed to avoid Mr. Russell and use the restroom. I was beginning to like having powers. I felt like a superhero. I made it back to class without even breaking a sweat. I couldn't wait to get my lunch out of my purse. Being famished was an understatement, I felt like I was about to die from starvation. With my stomach growling like a ravenous mountain lion, I calmly opened the door and stepped inside of the class. Once inside, I noticed the teacher's eyes glued to the clock. She really was serious about making sure I came back in time. The other students in the class were already eating their packed lunches. After carefully closing the door, I sat the wooden hall pass back on the table, and returned to my desk. I tried to avoid looking at the teacher, but I felt her watching me. I tried to ignore it as I carefully pulled out all of my lunch items. I devoured everything like I'd been without food for a week. After I finished, I noticed that all eyes were on me.

"Pretty hungry huh?" The teacher muttered as I finished my meal. She had a slight smirk on her face. I guess she found it amusing that a small female such as myself could eat at such a frenzied pace. I must admit, I felt somewhat piggish having eaten in such a manner.

"Yeah," I responded in a garbled tone as I chewed up the last bit of food. "Absolutely starved," I uttered while wiping my mouth. Most of the other students were still engaged in eating as I was discarding my trash. The meal didn't quite quench my appetite. It felt as if I could eat an entire buffet and still have room for dessert. Within minutes, it was as if I had never eaten.

After lunch, the last few hours of school went by without a hitch. I finished most of the work packets that were suppose to last until I went back to my normal classes, and I managed to get some reading done. I decided to call it quits at ten minutes to two-thirty. Questions about my past and my parents filled my thoughts. I wondered what other secrets they were keeping from me. I wanted to be angry at them, but at the same time, I was trying to understand the real logic behind it. *"Maybe my real parents are high profile criminals and I wasn't informed of their existence as a means of protection. What if my birth parents are dead?"* While in deep thought, a mysterious voice emerged in my consciousness.

*"Soon,"* it said in a faint, whisper like tone. It startled me. I quickly looked around the room to find the source of it. It sounded familiar. It sounded as if I had heard it before somewhere in my past, but at the time, I couldn't figure out when or where. They had to be nearby. It sounded as close as when someone whispers in your ear. What was really startling was that it didn't sound human. As I looked around the room, I noticed everyone was preoccupied with his or her own stuff, everyone except for the teacher. She was staring at me with a weird look in her eyes. The eyes themselves were glowing with a bright radiating blue energy. They were similar to the school nurse's eyes. I sensed that whatever was going on wasn't threatening. It was quite the opposite. I was captivated by those eyes. They held me in a trance like state.

The ringing of the last bell, snapped me out of it. *"Whoa, that was weird,"* I thought as I looked back at the teacher. The captivating presence that was in her was no longer there. She was back to her normal fossilized, bitter faced self. I got my things together and headed out. I was glad the day was over. I was eager to talk to my parents. As I battled my way through the crowded hallways, I accidently bumped into Paige.

"Hey, watch where you're going," she said before turning to face me. She turned around with a scowl on her face. She was about to say something else, but stopped when she realized it was me. Her scowl instantly turned into a look of fear. She quickly turned back around and frantically pushed her way through the crowd. It was a pleasant surprise considering that she'd normally insult me or become confrontational on sight. I giggled to myself as I watched her frantically escape. I made it to my locker and collected the rest of my things.

Once outside, I saw my mother and father parked and awaiting my arrival. I excitedly jogged to the car. I was so happy to see my father.

"Hey dad, hey mom," I blurted as I got inside the car.

"Hello Charisma," My mom murmured.

"Hey Honey, did you miss me?" My dad questioned as he turned around with a bright smile. "Your mother told me about what happened." He said in a more serious tone.

"Yeah," I murmured as thoughts from the day before popped, into my head.

"I just picked up your father from the airport, and we decided to surprise you." My mother said as she began to drive. "How are you feeling? Do you feel like talking?"

"I'm okay, and yes, I would like to talk now." I responded as I adjusted myself in the seat. "When was I adopted?" I asked as I looked out of the window.

"You were less than a year old when we found you, or rather when someone left you." my father responded in a weird solemn tone. "We were returning home from celebrating my recent job promotion when we noticed the front door of our house was ajar. I feared the worse, so I told your mother to wait outside while I checked it out. I nervously stepped inside and went to grab a knife out of the kitchen before cautiously beginning my search. I checked the entire first floor and didn't find any signs of a typical break in, which made the situation even more ominous. *If the intruders didn't break in to steal stuff, what other reason could they have to be here?* I wondered as I started making my way upstairs.

When I reached the second floor, I could hear faint voices coming from one of the rooms. It was definitely not a good sign. My logic wanted me to leave the house and call the police, but this overwhelming urge from within made me continue my search. I lightly crept down the hall and noticed all of the doors open except one, our master bedroom. It was odd because I specifically remembered running back in at the last minute to get my wallet before we left. That door was definitely open when we left earlier that evening. Anyway, there was a bluish glow reflecting on the wooden floor under the door and the voices were coming from inside of it. Panic started to set in as I slowly moved closer to the room. I knew someone was inside, but I didn't know why. I tightened my grip around the knife and prepared myself for the worse as I reached the outside of the room.

I took a moment to mentally get myself together before grabbing the doorknob and turning it. I gave it a gentle nudge, and the door slowly creaked open. I was sweating bullets as I peeked inside. The room appeared to be empty. I let out a sigh of relief. I assumed that whoever was responsible for the noises had long since left. I was just about to leave the room when a strange sound stopped me dead in my tracks. It was a weird wet chewing sound coming from the area by the foot of the bed. The way we had the bed positioned, prevented me from having a clear view. A Picture of a flying saucer flashed on the TV screen and briefly diverted my attention from the sound. Someone had left it on a special about aliens. Then suddenly, I heard a small giggle.

It almost scared the life out of me! Battling against my fear, I forced myself to walk over to the foot of the bed.

I reached the foot of the bed, looked down, and there you were. You were so small I was perplexed as to how you ended up in our upstairs bedroom. You looked up at me and gave me one of the brightest smiles that I'd ever seen. I dropped the knife, picked you up, and fell in love. Giddy from my discovery, I gave your mother the green light to come in. She came in and instantly fell in love with you as well. We had been trying to have a baby for years, but doctors told us that our chances were slim to none because of medical reasons. Finding you in our house that night was... it was as if our prayers had finally been answered." My father lifted his glasses and wiped his eyes before continuing, "We contemplated calling the police, but what could we tell them, someone broke in and left a baby watching TV in our bedroom. We were compelled to keep you and didn't want to risk losing you to the system. That night, something came over us. It was as if some strange force had taken hold of our hearts. It was as if you were meant to be ours all along..." My father trailed off as he searched for the next words to say.

"So did you ever find out anything or did anyone come looking for me?" I questioned with a burning curiosity.

"No, that was the strangest part of it all, we never found out where you came from, or why you were left in our house." My mother answered while stopping at a red light. My father continued the story.

"After returning to the bedroom to show your mother where I found you, we discovered a small metallic box resting near where you were. The box contained all of your birth records and personal data. While sifting through the papers, something on one of the pages got your mother's attention. She scanned over the rest of the papers and saw the same anomaly. She noticed that we were listed as your parents on every single document pertaining to your birth. To make matters even more confusing, there were even photos of all of us together in events that we knew never happened. Such as pictures of your mother holding you in the hospital the day you were born. It was like something out of the Twilight Zone."

"Twilight what," I questioned, completely unfamiliar with the reference my father gave.

"Never mind, it's a show that was way before your time," He responded, "but anyway, it was as if someone defied the laws of nature and altered time itself." I didn't know what to believe. I wanted it to be some kind of bad birthday gag. I wanted my father and mother to laugh and tell me it was a joke. I wanted things to go back to normal. The truth was scary, and it made me feel vulnerable.

"So what happened with the door and the refrigerator? Is it true what your mother said? Did you read her mind and pick up the fridge?" My father asked. I knew he was astonished by the possibility of me having powers.

"How about I demonstrate them for you?"

"Okay, well… can you do anything else?" He was genuinely amazed. When he was younger, my father had been a big comic book buff. He still had his childhood collection of comics stored away in his home office. Every now and then, I'd catch him reading one of them or bringing home a newly acquired one to add to his collection.

"Not that I know of, it just started yesterday." I responded. It felt weird talking about my powers to my father. The tone of his voice did little to mask his excitement. It was the closest that he would ever come, to knowing a real life superhero. "Can we stop and get a bite to eat?" I asked. My stomach growled like a ravenous tiger. Hungry was an understatement! It felt as if I hadn't eaten all day.

# Chapter 4

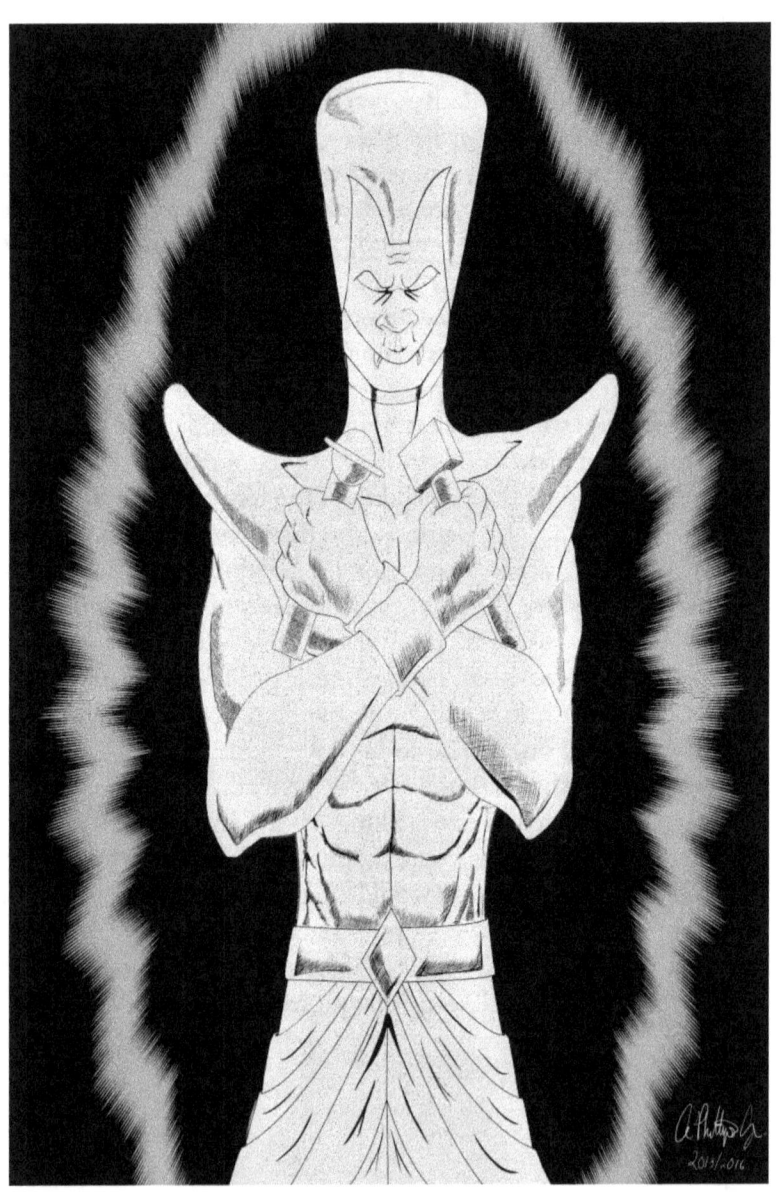

# Just plain ol' creepy

**WE ARRIVED HOME** after grabbing a bite to eat. The sad part was that my food didn't make it home with me. I managed to eat every morsel of it within minutes of leaving the drive thru. My father was in awe of how I dispatched the meal so quickly. My parents went into the dining room to finish the rest of their food, and I went upstairs to get my stuff ready for the sleepover. I was excited to spend the night at Liz's house. The sleepover was one of the only normal things that I had to look forward to. I still hadn't told her about my powers. I decided to show her like how I had done with my mother. It had proven to be effective.

In the midst of getting ready, my stomach was yet again hosting hunger pangs. My insatiable appetite was really bothering me. I had to figure out a way to curb it before the sleepover. I had just finished off a large Wendy's Baconator combo meal and my stomach still growled like a hungry badger. I didn't understand why my appetite had increased so drastically in such a small amount of time. I went from eating, like a normal teenage girl, to eating like a college linebacker. I feared that I would surely end up becoming overweight if I kept consuming so much food! I didn't have anything against heavier people. I just didn't want to risk getting the diseases associated with that type of lifestyle. My mother always scared me with her hospital horror stories involving clogged arteries, Diabetes, and heart attacks. She always made sure that I ate well-balanced meals and got some type of exercise weekly. *"Preventive steps are always the best steps,"* Is what she'd say when I would groan and complain. I've heard it so much that it's permanently stuck in my brain!

When I entered my room, I felt this weird sensation like someone other than me had been in it. I would have thought I was going crazy, if not for the small footprints that I found in the mess of anti-frizz cream that I spilled while rushing to get ready for school earlier. They were the size of a small child's foot and the shape was foreign. There were four toe imprints on each of them. They started by my dresser, where I had spilled the cream, and ended abruptly just steps away. I spilled quite a bit so the tracks should have ended closer to the middle of the room. It was as if whatever it was, simply vanished into thin air. I briefly entertained the thought of ghosts, but if that was the case, why hadn't I experienced anything prior to it? More importantly, why did its feet only have four toes?

*"Maybe I should tell my parents,"* I thought as I examined the prints. I grabbed my phone and snapped a few photos before calling out for them. "Mom, Dad," I yelled while keeping my eyes glued on the prints. Then, like a trick out of some magic show, they started to disappear right before my very eyes! "What the," I uttered as I tried to process what had just occurred. I wiped my eyes and looked again. They were definitely gone.

"Yes, you called me?" My mother asked as she entered the room. I remembered the pictures that I took.

"Uh, yeah, hold on." I replied as I flipped through my photos. I looked frantically through the photos but could not find the ones I had just taken mere seconds ago. "Where did they go?" I mumbled as I closed the app and reopened it.

"What did you say?" My mother asked. She was really puzzled by my seemingly erratic behavior.

"Wait, I just had them," I responded, not taking my eyes off the screen for a second. They had to be there. They had to be on my phone. I was positive that I was not imagining it. It was frustrating scrolling through the same photos countless times with no change in their lineup. I felt like throwing my phone out of the window. Not having anything to show, I had to think of a substitute reason as to why I summoned her. "I was wondering, do you think my biological parents will ever try to find me?" I blurted the first thing that came to mind, a question that had been nagging me since the talk with my father in the car.

"Well, I really don't know." My mom responded, "If they wanted to find you, they would've already done so." She stated coarsely. I noticed a change in her demeanor. "Sorry, it's just that, well, maybe I don't want them to. I don't want them to take you away from us." My mom then walked over to me and gave me a hug. I hugged her back lightly. I made sure to restrict my own strength. I had already had enough accidents. The last thing I needed was to break my mother's back, by hugging her too hard. "I don't care if you're not a normal girl, you're my girl, my daughter, and I love you all the same." She said in a congested tone as she sniffled.

"I love you too mom," I replied in a muffled tone with my mouth partially covered by her shirt. My mother released me from her embrace, cleared her throat and nose, and wiped her face.

"Now hurry up and finish getting your stuff together so you can spend some time with your father before we leave." My mother said in a partially choked voice.

"Alright," I replied. My mother left the room and I began to clean up the cream from off the floor. I still couldn't quite register what was going on. I began contemplating whether it was all a hallucination. I unlocked my phone and scrolled through the photos one last time. *"Did I really see what I thought I saw?"* I questioned to myself as I slowly looked over each individual picture starting from the most recent. There was nothing! I didn't know what had transpired, but a part of me didn't want to think about it any further. I already had enough on my mind and it just added to the list of unfortunate revelations that were slowly destroying my life. I wanted some sense of control back. I needed to have some sense of normalcy. While in my moment of reflection, a strange blue glowing orb slowly began floating across my room. The presence of the glow had an effect on me. It temporarily paralyzed me with some unknown force. I tried to focus my strength and break free from the invisible hold that it had over me, but it did little to bring about the desired result that I so desperately needed. An immense fear swept over me. I didn't know what was going on, and I didn't like it one bit.

*"Be still and listen,"* a voice said to me. It was the same deep voice from earlier. I wanted to continue struggling, but my logic prevailed. *"The time is almost near. Unfamiliar enemies seek your destruction."* The voice warned in a cryptic manner. I wondered if it had anything to do with the disappearing footprints.

"Huh?" I murmured as I tried to understand the message. "What are you talking about? Who are my unfamiliar enemies?" I asked while looking around the room.

"Who are you talking to?" My father asked as he entered the room. I had to think fast.

"Um, I was singing this new song." I responded. My lie was quick and poorly thought out, but effective.

"Oh, well it doesn't sound very good. Who made it?"

"Uh, this group called Mysterious Voices." I said the first name I could think of, which I thought sounded like a cool name for a band after the fact.

"Okay, you kids and your music," He replied in typical parent fashion. "Are you ready to show me?" He asked while looking at the cream on the floor.

"Yes," I answered while stuffing the last of my things in an overnight bag. He looked around the room and then responded.

"How about you pick up the dresser?" He said as he smiled like a child at a magic show.

"Okay, help me clear it off," I responded. We cleared it off, and I got ready for my demonstration. I prepared in the same manner as before, except this time I closed my eyes because I was nervous. For some reason my father always had that effect on me. Like this one time, my dad came to one of my school plays and I had to turn my back to the audience in order to recite my lines. I think it strongly had to do with me being a daddy's girl. I never wanted to disappoint him. Don't get me wrong, I felt the same way about my mother, but I guess the fact that we were both female, helped me to relax around her as opposed to my Dad. With my eyes closed, I got into a squatting position, took a deep breath, and found sturdy areas on the dresser to grip. I rose up with the greatest of ease. I didn't feel any of the stress or tension that is often associated with lifting such an item. The dresser was so light that I had to open my eyes to see if I had actually lifted it. When I opened them, I saw that my little arms had hoisted up the entire dresser as if it were a cardboard replica. I didn't feel the slightest strain on my muscles what so ever. I looked over at my father. He was in complete shock. I placed the dresser back down on the floor as easily as I had lifted it.

"Holy crap, how… how did you do that?" He asked in an astonished tone.

"I don't know. I just took a deep breath, focused, and lifted." I responded gingerly.

"So does the mind reading thing work the same way?"

"Yeah, I believe so,"

"Does Liz know?"

"No, not yet, I was planning on telling her later."

"Honey, I don't think that's a good idea. I mean I'm not saying she would tell the wrong person, but what if she tells her mom and her mom tells someone else, and then it gets out to the wrong person. All I'm saying is that this is something that can cause a great deal of trouble."

"I understand, but she's my best friend and we never keep secrets from each other." I protested. I already felt bad for keeping it from her for a whole day.

"Look, sometimes certain secrets are meant to stay secrets." My father stated in a serious tone.

"Well, if that's the case, I guess I should never tell you or mom about me getting in-school suspension for dislocating someone's shoulder." I responded as my anger began to build. When I look back on it, my dad was right, but at the time, it was hard to realize it.

"Wait, what?" My dad questioned, completely thrown off by my response.

"I, I dislocated another girl's shoulder accidentally in gym class yesterday." I looked away from my father in shame. I didn't know what to expect from him. I dropped two bombs in one chaotic package, I kept a secret, and my actions resulted in a severe injury.

"Why didn't you tell your mother?" He asked sternly. "Furthermore, why didn't the school inform us?"

"Because it was a legitimate accident and I handled things on my own with the principal. He decided to not inform you guys and gave me a few days of in-school."

"And why weren't you planning on telling us?"

"Um, because I didn't want to get grounded and not be able to see All Boys,"

"Why would we punish you if it was a legitimate accident?"

"I don't know. I was afraid. It was my first time getting in trouble at school, so I didn't know how you or mom would take it."

"If it was an accident, we would address it as an accident. Honey, I know you're a good kid and an excellent student. I'm going to have a talk with your principal on Monday. In the meantime, I don't think it's a good idea to sleep over at Liz's tonight. At least not until we figure out what's going on with you and your powers."

"That's not fair!" I protested in a slightly elevated voice.

"Now don't you take that tone with me young lady, you don't realize how dangerous you could be to your friend or her family! Think about it, what if you have another accident?"

"The accident happened before I figured out how to control my strength."

"Okay, well what about reading thoughts, what if someone thinks something bad about you. Will you be able to control your temper and not let on to the fact that you know what they're thinking?"

"I know how to control that too."

"Okay, but you have to take everything into consideration. What if you have more abilities that you're not aware of? What if you can ignite things and accidentally end up setting their house on fire, or what if some other physical ability manifests while you're at the dinner table or watching a movie with them! Honey, you're not normal, and you can't pretend to be!"

"You don't understand I'm not trying to be normal, I'm just trying to be me! I'm trying to enjoy my birthday weekend with the people I love, and that includes Liz! I wish I had never told you anything!" Hurt and confused, I stormed out of my bedroom and went into the bathroom, locking the door behind me. It seemed as if things were indeed getting worse as my birthday drew near. Lost in frustration and despair, I turned on the water and splashed my face several times to mask the tears that had started to flow. *"How dare my father try to keep me from spending time with my best friend, it's my life! I have control over myself, I—"* My thoughts were interrupted by a series of knocks on the door. "Go away!" I yelled in a shaky evidently angry voice. "I wish I could fly, I would fly away right now and never come back." I mumbled as I glanced out of the window.

"Charisma, open this door. I just had a talk with your father and now I want to have a talk with you." My mother said in a loud but calm voice. It always amazes me how good she is at neutralizing and resolving disputes.

"Hold on a second," I responded while grabbing my towel off the rack. After wiping my face and making myself presentable, I unlocked the door and let her in.

"Your father told me what happened. I'm not taking sides, but you really should hear him out, and why didn't you tell me that you dislocated someone's shoulder?"

"I didn't tell you, because it was an accident and I was afraid that you wouldn't buy me the concert tickets." I muttered sheepishly.

"You mean an accident because of your powers?"

"Yes, I was in gym class and we were playing dodge ball. I honestly didn't mean for it to happen, it just sort of did and I couldn't do anything to stop it. I wasn't thinking about my powers. I was so into the zone that they had completely slipped my mind."

"Honey, if it was an accident, you should've told me right away, especially if it involved your powers. Not getting concert tickets should have been the least of your worries. I know it may have all seemed a bit overwhelming, but you should always be able to come to us about anything."

"Okay, well sorry for not telling you and thanks for understanding."

"You're welcome now let's get back to this sleepover business. The reason your dad is so adamant about you not going to Liz's is that he's not sure if you have full control over your powers. And I have to say that I agree to a certain extent. We love you and Liz and would hate for anything to happen to either one of you. With that being said, I convinced your father to let you go to the sleepover on one condition..."

"*Oh boy, here it goes.*" I thought as I tried to tune into what was on her mind. I focused, but was unable to pick it up. Frustrated with my ability, I decided to hear her out. "What's the condition?" I asked dryly, making no attempt in the least to cover up my disdain about the whole situation.

"If you sleep over at Liz's house, you have to promise us that you won't tell or show her anything, at least not until we have a chance to ensure your safety and learn more about your abilities. I mean, sure you have super powers, but there is no telling what people will do when they find out. I'm sure you can still get hurt or even worse die and I don't want that to happen, at least not before you're old and gray with grandkids. You have a bright future and I don't want anything to get in the way of it. Okay," not satisfied with the comprise I looked away and hesitated before responding. I felt so conflicted. I didn't want to keep lying to my friend until God knows when, but I had to honor my parents' wishes. "Also, whatever it is that you do to keep your powers under wraps, I need you to stay doing it." She added.

"Okay," I murmured unenthusiastically.

"Great, finish getting your things together, and I'll give you a ride over." My mom said, before hugging me and placing a kiss on my forehead. I followed her out of the bathroom and went back into my room to finish packing. Not that I had much left to pack, I was only staying for one night. Once I was done packing, I decided to have another talk with my father to smooth things out between us. I found him in his study engrossed in reading an issue of Superman. He was so preoccupied with the comic book that he failed to notice me in the doorway.

"Hey," I uttered as a means of getting his attention. "Got a moment?" I asked after making up my mind to be the first to apologize. I felt bad for yelling at him. Looking back on it now, I definitely wish it never happened. It unquestionably made the list of top regrettable moments.

"Yup, come in." He replied, as he placed his comic book down and continued looking away from the door entrance. I knew he was still upset. The telltale sign was how he avoided eye contact with me. I remembered him doing the same thing countless times before when he and my mother would get into arguments. He would stay upset for a short while, but he always managed to return to his lovable, warm self.

"Um, I just wanted to say sorry," like my father, I was avoiding eye contact as well. My guilt fought against my pride as I struggled to come to terms with the fact that I was indeed wrong and was now trying to apologize.

"Mmm, hmm," His response was less than encouraging. It didn't motivate me to continue, but I had to get it out.

"Is that all you have to say?" I had the notion to walk away. He was being difficult, but I guess he was taking a page out of my book. He turned around to face me and I managed to look him in the eyes.

"What more do you want me to say honey?" He asked sarcastically with a smart-aleck expression plastered on his face. I felt my frustration mounting, but I held it in and stayed the course. I was there to make things right, and that's exactly what I was going to do.

"Dad, I shouldn't have snapped at you. I understand that you're concerned for my safety. I still need time to adjust to these changes and—"

"That's enough, actually, that's too much." He joked. At once, his expression changed from sourpuss to sweetheart. "I understand honey. I just wanted to see how much you've matured and I must say that I'm pleased. That was a quick turnaround, especially considering the circumstances. As you probably already know, your mom and I had a talk. We want you to enjoy yourself tonight, but keep in mind that, you must not tell or show Liz anything until your situation is sorted out, fair enough?"

"Yes and thank you!" I ran over and was about to give him the biggest hug possible but he stopped me.

"Whoa, slow down Risma, I enjoy having the use of my full body," my father joked as he playfully, put his hands up to block me.

"Dad really," I said before making my best pretend angry face.

"Just kidding honey, now give your Papa Bear a hug." I focused and gave my father a normal strength hug.

"No matter what, I'm still your little bear." I murmured with my face partially buried in his shirt.

"I know, honey, I know. Now hurry up and get out of here, you have a sleepover to get to." My dad's smile was so bubbly and cheesy that it was contagious. I felt my face muscles form a dorky smile in response. We had a goofy chemistry like that I suppose.

"Okay," I responded before rushing out of the room. I went back into my bedroom, grabbed my things, and texted Liz. *"OMW ☺,"* Was the quick text that I sent her before I headed downstairs to meet my mother. "Hey mom, I'm ready," rushed out of my mouth before my body came to a complete stop.

"Whoa, slow down. Did you contact Liz?" My mother asked as she finished folding one of her dark blue uniform tops. I don't know how medical staff can wear scrubs. They look so uncomfortable and not cool.

"Of course," Was my response. I couldn't wait to be around my best friend. I was looking forward to engaging in mindless girl talk, watching a cheesy B movie slasher flick, and stuffing my face with steak, grilled chicken, and bacon topped pizza. Unbeknownst to me, that night would be one of the last normal nights of my life.

We left the house and I noticed that even though it was still quite early, there was a dark cast over the horizon like a storm was brewing. It seemed as if something of epic proportions was approaching. I was glad that we were going to be inside. I hate storms.

"It might get kind of nasty tonight. I hope it doesn't get too bad." My mom stated as she looked at the sky and unlocked the car.

"You and me both," I replied while opening the passenger door. I felt my phone vibrate as I stepped inside the car.

"*K,*" was the response I read while buckling my seatbelt.

"*That's odd,*" I thought as the car slowly backed out of the driveway. I looked back up at the sky and then proceeded to type a new message. "*Is everything okay, or are you busy?*" I sent the message and turned up the radio. One of my favorite All Boys songs was on and it completely distracted me from everything else going on around me.

"Oh lord here we go," My mother said as she shook her head. She was probably sick of hearing All Boys. When their second album came out, I played it every day nonstop for two weeks straight. My mother was on the verge of pulling her hair out by the end of the first week. She was seriously considering getting me professional help. I guess you might say that I have an addictive personality. When I get into something, I really get into it.

"Mom, please let me have this moment. I love this song!" I stated with an absolute seriousness.

"Okay honey, but only because it's almost your birthday,"

"Alright Mom," I murmured before getting back into my All Boys moment. I sang along while the song blared through the car's speakers. Once the song was over, I remembered the text message that I sent to Liz. I unlocked my phone and saw a message notification. I must've been so busy bouncing and singing along that I didn't even feel it vibrate.

"*Of course I'm okay, silly. I was in the middle of finishing my chores.*" Is what the message read. I was relieved that things were still the same between us. She was the closest friend that

I had. The secret was definitely getting to me. I mean, why wouldn't she be okay? She didn't have a reason not to. We arrived at Liz's house a short while later.

*"God, please let everything be okay,"* my mother thought as we pulled into their driveway.

"Everything will be fine mom, you worry too much." Was my aloud reply to her thought. My mind was so preoccupied with the night that lay ahead that I forgot to tune out her thoughts.

"I hope so, please don't have any slip-ups," She replied as she put the car in park.

"I won't, I promise," I uttered while unbuckling my seat belt. I got out of the car and my mother got out as well. She walked over to me and gave me a big hug. I carefully reciprocated.

"Okay Honey, enjoy yourself, oh and tell Liz and Karen I said hi." She replied in a somewhat shaky voice. I could tell that she was about to start with the water works, which explained why she didn't want to go in herself and say hi. I began to feel a weird dreadful feeling as I walked up to the front door. Liz opened the door before I had a chance to ring the doorbell.

"Hey bestie," She gave me a warm bubbly welcome.

"Hey Liz,"

"Hi, Mrs. Grey!" Liz yelled past me to my mother.

"Hello Liz, tell your mom I said hi." She replied. I looked back just as she was getting back in the car. She slowly backed out of the driveway, and headed back home. I went inside with Liz and followed her into the living room.

"Do you want to have that rematch?" She inquired as she turned on the TV. I knew exactly what she was talking about. She wanted to play against me in Dance Central 3. The last time we played, I danced circles around her and the rest of the girls that attended her birthday party the year before.

"Only if you don't mind losing," was my bold response. Which I suppose was rightfully spoken seeing as how I had beaten her almost every single time that I played against her. Liz was persistent and I really liked that about her.

"We'll see about that. I've been practicing." She responded with a confident look in her eyes.

"Fire it up and let's go," I replied. Liz powered up the Xbox, and within minutes, we were engaged in a heated dance competition. She had gotten better, but I was determined to win and keep my title as champion. Her moves were less cumbersome than previously, but they were still nowhere near as graceful as mine. I was so caught up in the competition, that I almost felt normal. When we finished the first round, Liz had already broken a sweat. Whereas, I was the complete opposite. I felt as if I had been sitting down and watching the entire time. We played a few more rounds, all of which I ended up winning. Liz didn't even come close. She was good, but I was unnaturally great. It was as if I had transformed into a professional dancer. Karen even sat in and watched for the last round.

"Okay, that's it. I think it's time to hang up my dancing shoes," Liz blurted, heavily panting and out of breath.

"Well, if it's any consolation, you are much better now. I barely beat you." I said as a means of making her feel better about her loss.

"You both looked great." Karen interjected with a lively look on her face.

"Thanks Mrs. Bemis" I replied and smiled at her.

"I bet you girls worked up an appetite with all of that dancing. Are you ready for the pizzas?"

"Yes," Liz and I said in unison. I felt my belly rumble as thoughts of eating delicious steak, grilled chicken, and bacon pizza appeared in my head. I felt ravenous enough to eat two pizzas by myself.

"Great, I've already placed the order for two large pizzas. Both of them have the same toppings. I'm stepping out on faith by not getting my regular toppings. I hope I won't be disappointed." Karen stated with a slight smile.

"Oh, don't worry, you'll love it! I guarantee!" I responded with absolute confidence. The combination of those toppings made others pale in comparison. The sound of keys rattling outside of the front door ended our conversation.

"I have a surprise for you honey," Karen said to Liz. The door opened, and in walked Liz's father, decked out in his military uniform and lugging a large duffle bag on his shoulder.

"Dad," Liz could hardly contain her excitement. She ran past me, then Karen, and affectionately pounced on her father. He dropped his bag and they spent a silent moment embraced in one another's arms. It had been months since her father had deployed on a top secret assignment. Her parents made the sacrifice of being apart for sometimes months at a time to keep Liz in a stable environment. Liz's father was an army brat, and as such, was frequently shuffled around from state to state and sometimes country to country. According to Liz, he seldom kept friends, and was never able to adapt to civilian life. It conditioned him for a career of travel. His experience growing up was probably a major motivating factor for them to sacrifice their quality time for Liz. I watched as Liz and her Dad had their moment. Taking their situation into account made me grateful that I only had to deal with my dad being gone for days at a time. I smiled as he wiped her tears with his handkerchief.

*"Thank God I'm home! I don't know how much more I can take!"* was what I picked up from Liz's dad as he briefly looked away. Something was bothering him deeply. He held a heavy burden that was unbeknownst to Liz and possibly Karen as well. It was unsettling. His thoughts and burdened aura put a damper on the mood in the room. I wondered what demons he was silently wrestling. True enough, he did for all intents and purposes seem genuinely happy to be

home, but there was without a doubt, something eating at him. "Hey Charisma, I haven't seen you in ages!" he exasperated as he took notice of me in the doorway of the living room. Sounds from the idle video game persisted in the background as I walked over to Liz and her father.

"Hey Mr. B, It's good to see you back." I faked full excitement as best I could but something about him just didn't seem right. It made me uncomfortable. I gave him a quick hug and resumed my stance. Liz and Karen were probably too caught up in the moment to realize anything but for me, it was sticking out like a sore thumb. My curiosity was fully vested in the mystery that he held. I had to know what was going on in his head. Karen walked over to him and gave him a hug and kiss while I moved further away from him.

"Are you hungry?" She asked after their brief moment of affection.

"A little," was his response. *"I don't know if I can handle going back."* was another one of his thoughts that projected into my consciousness, like a forceful intruder. It further fanned the flames of curiosity. I had to find out the secrets that he kept.

"Okay babes, go upstairs and get washed up. The food should be here shortly." Karen stated. Like a good soldier, her husband followed her orders. He slowly ascended the stairs and seconds later, disappeared into the recesses of the upstairs. Liz turned off the game system and changed the TV back to the regular setting to see what was on cable.

"Do you want to watch anything?" She asked while skimming through the guide.

"Not that I can think of," I murmured before having a seat on the couch.

"So how did you dislocate Paige's shoulder?" Liz's question caught me completely off guard. The promise I made to my parents came to mind. I was conflicted but I knew what had to be done. I had to lie to her.

"I don't know. I was angry after she hit me in the head so I threw it as hard as I could. That and the fall caused it, I think." I weaved the lie like a spider weaving its web.

"Really," The look on her face was full of disbelief. She was digging hard for something to explain it, but I wasn't going to give her anything. I made a promise to my parents so I had to keep the truth hidden.

"Oh yeah, that's right, I forgot about my super powers." I said truthfully but in a sarcastic tone.

"Very funny, I'm serious!" Liz became slightly agitated.

"I don't know what else to tell you. I'm not even sure how it happened, it just did. I honestly didn't mean to do it." I proclaimed as Karen entered the room.

"Is everything okay?" She asked with her left brow slightly raised.

"Everything is fine Mrs. Bemis." I stated and smiled to conceal what I was really thinking. Everything wasn't fine and I was getting irritated holding in such a big secret, but what else could I do? I agreed to the conditions.

"Yeah, everything's cool mom." Liz added. "We were just having a friendly debate over something that happened at school the other day."

"Okay, well make sure you listen out for the door. I'm going upstairs to help your father. The pizzas should be here soon. I left the money for them on the table in the kitchen." Karen said before heading up the stairs. I made sure Karen was completely upstairs before resuming the conversation.

"Alright Liz, since you obviously don't believe my story, why don't you tell me what happened."

"Well, I don't know. Are you some kind of witch?" Her question made me burst into laughter. "Why is that so funny?" She asked in a slightly defensive tone. I took a moment to settle my giggles before speaking.

"I'm sorry, but that's ridiculous." I responded as I struggled to keep a straight face.

"How else can you explain it? And, what about that weird thing you did in the car the other day? It was like you read my mother's mind." Liz was really prying, for some answers.

"Oh that, that was nothing. Like I told your mother, I remembered my mother saying something similar so I pretty much just assumed what she was going to say." It seemed like a sufficient explanation. "It was just a coincidence trust me, I don't know any spells or incantations. I'm just me, regular old Charisma." I replied bluntly.

"Yeah, o—" The ringing of the doorbell interrupted Liz.

"Pizza's here," I blurted out with a smile. I was grateful for the distraction. It quickly helped to put an end to the conversation. Liz rushed into the kitchen to get the money, and I went to get the door. I opened the door, and there stood one of the hottest seniors at our high school, Drave Duncan. Looking at Drave, a girl couldn't help but form an instant crush. He has deep brown eyes, a slim but muscular physique, flawless medium brown skin, and a smile that could melt a block of ice. Drave is a bad boy/rebel, but not in the typical sense. Now I know what you're probably thinking, you're probably thinking, *"He must not be that cool or that much of a rebel if he's a pizza delivery boy,"* but like I said, he isn't the typical bad boy/rebel. He's the type of person that can make anything go from taboo to the latest trend of the minute. He's the type that could get caught picking his nose while driving and suddenly, everyone else would be openly doing it because of him. He is a rebel with a cause, several actually and he's a wiz when it comes to anything related to math or science. An example of him not fitting into the typical bad boy/rebel archetype is the time he organized a rally for equal treatment of gay and lesbian students at our school. He got the crowd worked up and almost ended up getting arrested.

Another example would have to be the legend of how in his freshman year, he managed to steal the then senior football captain's girlfriend, Sienna Craft. Sienna was the "it" girl. Every girl wanted to be her and every guy dreamed of being with her. She was a junior with the popularity of a senior. By the time I started attending the school, the story had already reached mythical proportions. The story was so distorted that the only way I found out the truth was that I got it straight from the horse's mouth. During a visit to the mall with Liz, we ran into Drave and Sienna. I wanted to know the truth for myself so I decided to ask them. I told Liz what I planned on doing beforehand and she freaked out.

*"Are you serious? You can't just go up to them and ask them that!"* I remember her saying in a dire tone. I did it anyway and got the straight facts, and ended up somewhat befriending the both of them.

"Hey Charisma, how's it going?" Drave said in his regular abnormally cool voice.

"It's going," I replied, wishing I had another leg so I could kick myself for releasing such a dorky response.

"Hey, I heard about what you did to Paige the other day. People are saying that you have some type of super strength or something." Liz walked up just as he was finishing his statement. I knew she probably heard a good portion of it, so I had to downplay it.

"Wow, really? Super powers, that sounds like something out of a comic book. You know how people like to stretch the truth and—"

"I was there and that's what it looked like," Liz interjected.

"Liz, c'mon now stop being silly," I said through my teeth as I smiled falsely. "You know how people at school can be, something happens out of the norm, word travels, and people add their own twist to it until it becomes a legend like the Greek Gods and Titans." I stated in an attempt to suppress any further interjections from Liz.

"Yeah, you have a point," He replied. He must have recalled his own experience with the rumor mill. "Well anyway, I got two steak, chicken, bacon pizzas for you. By the way, that sounds like a good combo. How does it taste?"

"Like slices of heaven," I replied as my mouth watered from the hot pizza aroma entering my nostrils.

"I'll have to try it sometime. Well anyway, your total is fifteen fifty." Liz handed him the money with a three-dollar tip included and Drave slid the pizzas out of the delivery carrier. The smell was on the verge of intoxicating. As he handed Liz the pizzas, my stomach began to growl. "Alright, well I guess I'll see you guys at school," He said as he closed up the carrier.

"Okay, see ya'," we replied in unison like a pair of twins. Drave smiled showing off his gorgeous pearly whites and walked back to his car. His car looked cool in spite of the dorky *Captain's Pizza* magnetic sign on the roof of it. As we watched him walk away, I began receiving these strange messages in another language similar to the one that I heard in the nurse's office.

*"That's weird,"* I thought as I closed the door.

"Mom, Dad, pizza's here!" Liz yelled as we walked toward the kitchen. "I'm surprised that he's still with Sienna." Liz said as she placed the pizzas on the counter.

"What do you mean?" I inquired while grabbing a paper towel.

"Think about it, he can have any girl in the entire school if he wanted to and he's wasting his time with that old lady." Liz said in a disappointed tone.

"Liz, that's not a very nice thing to say." I responded as I shot her a less than pleased look. "That's downright mean, if you ask me."

"No, it's not Riz think about it, she's almost old enough to be my aunt and—"

"Anyone of any age can be an aunt Liz, I remember this show I watched where this guy was like seventy with all adult children and he ended up having a baby with a woman younger than his youngest child! And that baby was an aunt to his ten year old grandson, so age is irrelevant when it comes to that."

"Well, she's still too old for him, and it's about time they broke up. He's practically wasted his whole high school career on that one girl and—"

"Liz, do I detect a slight bit of jealousy?"

"No, not at all, I'm just saying." She tried to deny it, but the jealously she harbored was so obvious, it was practically screaming, *"Hey I'm right here!"*

"Okay bestie, get ready to feast on the best pizza combo ever." I said with glee.

"Great it's here," Karen said as she entered the kitchen with her husband not far behind. The smell of the pizza permeated the entire kitchen. "Okay girls grab your plates and have at it," I quickly grabbed a plate and piled on a few slices of steamy cheesy goodness. I was starving, but I didn't want to seem like a pig, so I only grabbed half of what I really wanted, which did a great disservice to my appetite. I finished my food before I reached the dining room table. When everyone filed into the room, they all had shocked looks on their faces as they gazed at my empty plate.

"You must've been real hungry huh?" Mr. Bemis asked as he pointed at my plate. "You finished that meal faster than that little Asian guy that wins all of those food eating contests." I was familiar with the person. I had watched a few of his competitions with my dad. In one of them the Asian guy, I think his name is Takeru Kobayashi, ate like over fifty hot dogs.

"Yeah a little," I replied bashfully, I was slightly embarrassed by him noticing.

"You can have some more if you want?" He offered which only increased my embarrassment.

"No thank you, I'm full." I murmured, letting my embarrassment win out over my hunger. "On second thought, I could use a little bit of water." I said, remembering that water was said to curb hunger.

"Okay, well help yourself to a bottle out of the fridge." He said. I quickly exited the room, grabbed a bottle of water from out of the kitchen, and then went into the living room. I downed the water in a matter of seconds before plopping down on the Bemis's plush cushy couch. The water seemed to do the trick. I actually felt full, though the feeling was short lived. After about a minute, I felt hungrier than I had felt before I ate.

*"What's wrong with me?"* I wondered as I tried to suppress the hunger that raged inside of me. I needed to figure out a way to appease it. If I were at home, I would've easily grabbed more slices of pizza or a snack or two out of the cabinet. *"Maybe some TV will do the trick."* I thought as I sat down and began flicking through the channels. Something on one of the channels caught my eye, the image of a reptilian humanoid like creature. It sent a weird chill through my being. It was part of a special on Aliens. Something about it intrigued me. I couldn't quite figure it out, but there was a weird familiarity about it. I wanted to turn the channel but my fingers refused to move.

*"The Draakunaki are believed to be an alien race that came to Earth millions of years ago from their home planet Draakonus. According to legend, they came to this planet and created the dinosaurs based on DNA derived from their home planet. The dinosaurs in essence, were their pets. Ancient tablets tell stories of giant reptilian men like creatures riding dragons like horses and controlling them like dogs on leashes. Then suddenly, a global catastrophe reduced their earthly population, and gave rise to another species, Man.*

*The Enocians, another race of aliens, are believed to have come to Earth after the fall of the dinosaurs and their reptilian masters. According to one ancient civilization, the Enocians came to Earth and created mankind in their own image and likeness. This enraged the Draakunaki, and led to what was considered the first major intergalactic war—"*

"What in the world are you watching?" Liz asked, diverting my attention from the program.

"Uh, I don't know. I was just flipping through the channels and—"

*"Why is she watching that?" Does she know? Nah, not Charisma,"* Mr. Bemis's thoughts caught my notice like a ball in a catcher's mitt. I shifted my gaze in his direction. Our eyes met briefly and I sensed a great distress permeating from them. Something was troubling him, and I wanted to know what it was.

# Chapter 5

# Welcome to the team

**THE NIGHT HAD BEEN UNEVENTFUL.** We did the typical things that girls do while having a sleepover. We played a few more rounds of Dance Central 3, and then we watched a movie with Liz's parents. The whole time, her father had been distracted by his thoughts. He kept thinking about some deep secret. It had something to do with a device called a Zykotron. It was tearing him apart at the seams. I made every attempt to downplay it, but it was impossible. The only time I felt relief was when he left the room. I tried to block him out, but I couldn't seem to control my powers around him.

After some time, his thoughts became jumbled, almost on the verge of being incoherent. By the end of the night, I had a burning desire to know what he was hiding. His secrets had heavily aroused my curiosity. I had to know what a Zykotron was, and why he couldn't stop thinking about it. After Liz was asleep, I decided to do some investigating. I slowly slipped out of bed and tiptoed across the room to the door. I focused myself and cautiously grabbed the doorknob. The door was already ajar so I gave it a slight push and quietly exited the room. Once inside the hall, I could hear the sound of keyboard buttons being pressed rapidly. It was coming from Mr. Bemis's study. I silently crept down the hall toward it. As I cautiously trekked toward the study, I began picking up his thoughts

*"They've already started. It's almost too late, the end is near!"* were his disturbing thoughts. Whatever he was thinking about, was of epic proportions. The speed, at which he was typing, made me wonder if he was communicating with someone. I was determined to find out. The door was cracked slightly, which was perfect for sneaking a quick peek. I managed to get within inches of the opening before the unexpected happened. I was literally a couple of steps away, when the floorboard beneath me creaked. Terror shot up through my body as I heard the urgent clicking of a power button, followed by the swivel of an office chair.

*"Oh great way to go Risma,"* I thought as I frantically tiptoed toward the bathroom. I had almost reached the other side of the hall when he called me.

"Charisma," the voice echoed down the hall in a whispered tone. I wanted to pretend that I didn't hear him and quickly slip off into the bathroom, but I knew that he would probably be waiting by the door when I got out. Against my better judgment, I stopped and turned around. He approached me quickly. "Why are you up?" he asked with a crazed look in his eyes. He was paranoid and on edge.

"Uh… I was going to the bathroom." I murmured as I made a quick pointing gesture down the hall.

"Really, then why were you creeping down the other end of the hall when the bathroom is practically right next to Liz's room?" He questioned with military authority. I felt like an AWOLED soldier being court-martialed.

"I got confused. I got the location mixed up with the bathroom at my house. I had just woken up and was slightly disoriented." I'm surprised that I thought of such a sound coherent lie in a matter of seconds. I prayed that it was good enough for him to buy it.

"How much do you know?" was his straightforward response, he saw through my false statement and questioned to know the truth.

"W-what are you talking about Mr. Bemis?" I was confused. I wasn't expecting the question.

"I, I saw you watching that program about aliens earlier." I had no idea why he mentioned the weird show from earlier. It only made his secret even more intriguing and scary.

"I really don't know what you're talking about Mr. Bemis. You're really starting to scare me." I was sincerely frightened. He sounded like a deranged lunatic and I didn't know what was coming next. We stood in silence for a brief moment. He must have realized that he had said too much, and I was scared out of my wits.

"Charisma, I'm sorry… it's just… um…," I could tell that he was struggling for the right explanation that wouldn't reveal too much. "I'm just going through a lot with my work and… I shouldn't have addressed you like that." After hearing his best attempt at an explanation and somewhat apology, I decided to reveal a little on my end as well.

"Well Mr. Bemis, maybe I wasn't telling the complete truth. I wasn't going to the bathroom, but I really don't know what you're talking about. I was actually coming to check on you and see if you were okay. You've looked troubled ever since you came home and—"

"I am," he interjected and paused before continuing, "Charisma, what if the entire world was in danger and you knew about it but were powerless to stop it?" He sounded gravely serious as if the burden was solely on his shoulders.

"Does it have something to do with the military or is it something else?" Now I had to know. I focused my power and tried to see if my question would get me the answers. His thoughts were inconclusive. It was frustrating because it was as if he'd had previous experience with mind readers. I was starting to believe there was some truth to the rumors my father had been telling me about secret experiments and the military. He was a big conspiracy theorist. When he was off from work, I would often hear him listening to a late-night conspiracy radio program called Coast-to-Coast AM. He was big into UFOs and other paranormal phenomena. Sometimes he would share his knowledge of it with me.

When I was younger, he would tell me about secret military bases like Dulce and Area 51, and about alien abduction cases. All of it frightened me to no end. I would often have nightmares of being abducted and carried away to a strange planet surrounded by reptilians. In the dreams, I'm always older. I think my age in those dreams was more frightening than the reptilians. He and my mother would often argue because of it. She felt that he was corrupting my mind with what she perceived to be far-fetched tall tales, while he felt that he was simply equipping me with important knowledge.

"No, well… yes, it does, but I'm not at liberty to share that knowledge with you." Mr. Bemis uttered as he looked away. It seemed as if something prevented him from looking me in the eyes. He was in a real dark place, and there seemed to be no way out for him. He looked like a nervous wreck. He looked like he was falling to pieces trying his best to hold the secret inside. "If I told you, both of our lives and families would be in jeopardy!" The look in his eyes was as dire as his words.

"Uh, okay. Well, I think I'll go to bed now." I mumbled before quickly walking away. That encounter really made me understand the point that my parents had tried to get across to me earlier. Telling the wrong person the right secret could absolutely prove to be a deadly decision. Seeing the way Mr. Bemis was behaving, I was glad that I had listened to them.

Sleep didn't come easy. I sat up for most of the night thinking about what Mr. Bemis had told me, or rather, what he didn't tell me. The possibility of aliens being real left an unsettling feeling in my gut. It was terrifying, so much so that I was close to ecstatic when the first rays of sunlight found their way into Liz's bedroom. I had only managed to get a couple hours of sleep and I was ready to get back to the safety of my own home. Liz's father bugged me out. I had practically slept the rest of the night with one eye open. I checked the clock on my phone and saw that it was a little after six, which wasn't good because my parents wouldn't be up until, eight at the earliest. I didn't want to wait that long. I decided to walk home. I needed sleep and my stomach was practically doing flips due to an almost insatiable hunger. Liz slept undisturbed while I packed my things. Once all of my things were packed, I slowly crept into the hallway. Everything was quiet as sunlight struggled to invade the dark hallway. I made my trek to the stairs. I could hear birds chirping and the barking of a dog not too far away.

"I'm done with sleepovers, goodbye normal life," I mumbled to myself as I headed down the stairs. I reached the first floor and began hearing a deep voice chanting, in the same weird language that I first heard in the nurse's office. It made me stop dead in my tracks. I was frozen momentarily with fear and dismay. I didn't know the source of the sound, which only made me want to make my exit even sooner. I shook off the debilitating sensation and rushed out of the door. A gush of warm air hit me as I began my twenty plus minute walk home. The chanting seemed to follow me. At some points of my journey, it was stronger and louder. Other times, it was almost as faint as a whisper. Regardless of its volume, it was a constant companion throughout the course of my walk. As I reached my street, screams began to accompany the chanting. As I approached my home, something felt dreadfully wrong. When I was mere yards away from my house, a strong indistinguishable odor invaded my nose. It was like the best and worst smells all at once. I wanted to gag and at the same time savor the exotic overpowering scent.

As I began going up the walkway leading to my house, the screams and chanting stopped. I reached the door. When I touched the doorknob, I felt an overpowering sensation of dread. Random images began flashing in my head. The hairs on the back of my neck stood up. Something was definitely wrong. The images were appearing and replacing each other so fast that it was difficult to distinguish any of them. When they ceased, I twisted the doorknob. The door was unlocked! My parents always made sure that all doors and windows were locked before they went to bed! *"What the hell?"* I thought as the door swung open.

Upon entering the house, the weird smell became stronger. I took off my jacket and used it to cover my mouth and nose. The smell was so pungent that the jacket did little to block it. Then I felt it. It started off as a small sensation in my gut, and immediately grew into a raging riot of queasiness. It traveled upward with urgency before finally exiting my mouth in an eruption of stomach contents. I vomited right at the foot of the stairs. Seconds later, the smell disappeared. I couldn't fathom how a smell so overpowering could vanish almost instantly. It was as if the smell was purposely released into the atmosphere for that reason.

*"Oh man, mom is going to kill me."* I thought as I looked at the small puddle in front of me. I figured that once I made sure they were both okay and peacefully, sound asleep; I'd come back down and clean it before they woke up. After wiping my mouth, I placed my overnight bag on the floor and quickly ascended the stairs. The sight of small glowing footprints stopped me dead in my tracks. They looked similar to the footprints that I found in my bedroom. The chanting abruptly resumed. The first room I passed was the guest room. It looked as if one of my parents had been looking for something. The closet was open and its contents were strewn across the floor and the guest bed. The sight was a little

unnerving, but nothing to be alarmed about. Both of my parents had full-time jobs so it was possible that one of them got tired and put off cleaning it up until later. I continued heading toward their room.

As I walked past my room, I noticed that the door was closed. This struck me as odd because I remembered it being open before going to Liz's house. What was even odder was the strange shuffling sound coming from inside. Thinking one of my parents might be responsible for it; I stopped and opened the door. What I saw next, came as a complete shock. It was definitely not my mother or my father!

"What the…" Time seemed to slow down as my eyes locked onto a small being standing in the middle of my room. He glowed with a blue brilliance and his eyes looked like large bright sapphire stones. His skin was a bluish pale color and he appeared to be a foot or so shorter than me.

"You have to come with me," his voice boomed while his mouth remained motionless.

"W-who are you?" I nervously asked as my brain tried to process what I was seeing in front of me.

"We have to go now before they return to eliminate you!" He said in a stern deathly manner.

"What have you done with my parents?" I questioned as I slowly started to back out of the doorway. "Mom, Dad!" I yelled before I began racing down the hall toward their bedroom. I reached their room and the sight of a huge bloody hand print on the door came into view. "Oh no…" I murmured as my brain tried to register what I was seeing. I cautiously entered their room. I wasn't prepared for what I saw. It was a complete wreck. Clothing littered the floor, furniture was overturned, and blood was splattered everywhere!

"They will return to extinguish you, they have the humans." I turned around and saw the creature standing behind me.

"What did they do to my parents?" I questioned madly as tears started to fall from my eyes.

"They took them. Now come with me if you wish to live." The creature's voice was ominous and somewhat frightening.

"I have powers you know. If you touch me, I'll use them." I threatened unsure of what he was capable of, but I didn't care. I was willing to fight if need be. My body shook like a wet kitten as I focused my energy and prepared to defend myself.

"Charisma, I know all about your abilities. I am not your adversary. I am here to assist you. We need to depart at once!" His blue eyes illuminated intensely.

"I'm not going anywhere without my parents!" I protested adamantly. "I'm not afraid of whoever they are! I have powers! I can take care of myself!" I was dead set on fighting whatever was looking for me. I was distraught and angry. My parents were everything to me. I was ready to fight the entire world to get them back.

"You are not yet strong enough to handle such a task. We will assist you in retrieving them but you must come with me. Our enemies will be back soon." I faced a major dilemma. Either I could stand my ground against whatever was after me or go with the strange glowing being. I looked back at the large handprint on the door. It was at least five times the size of my own.

"Okay, maybe your idea is better." I murmured, relinquishing myself over to the little being. A small shiny metallic device appeared in one of his hands and he extended the other toward me. His hands had four digits on each of them just like his feet. I reluctantly took his hand. It was cooler and smoother than that of a human's. As I held the alien's hand, an intense bright blue light engulfed us. When the light dissipated, we appeared to be in someone's living room.

"I tried to make the surroundings reflect a familiar setting." He said while his device disappeared back into his hand. "Forgive me for the lack of proper introduction; I am Anaku, from Pirushan. I have kept watch over you since your powers first surfaced. You will be safe here for now. We must begin your acclimation immediately." His mouth still remained motionless as he spoke in a cryptic sort of manner, but I sensed a good vibe from him. "Follow me and I will introduce you to the others." He said as he started to walk. I followed him out of the room, and he led me into another room significantly larger than the first one. The larger room was completely unlike anything I had ever seen. It was vast and expansive. Just from eyeballing it, I gauged it to be bigger than two high school gymnasiums at least. Its walls had a holographic appearance, with a bluish hue, and there was a strange humming sound emanating from somewhere within it. Standing in the middle of the room were five other people. They appeared to be getting ready for something. "Salutations, I need your attention. This is Charisma." Anaku said while coming to a complete stop. I looked at the others as they came toward us. I instantly recognized two of them.

"Drave, Sienna," I blurted out, taking notice of their weird outfits. They appeared to be dressed in some type of futuristic spandex space suits "What's with the weird clothes?" I whispered to the Anaku.

"You will find out soon enough." He replied as the others gathered around us.

"Hey Charisma," Drave said with his signature smile formed on his face.

"When did you guys get here?" I questioned, as I remembered the fact that he delivered pizzas to Liz's the night before.

"I got here a little after I dropped off the pizzas to you at Liz's house." He stated. "I was driving back to the restaurant and out of nowhere, a group of reptilians appeared in the middle of the road. It happened so fast that I couldn't maneuver in time to avoid them. I almost crashed head on into one of them. It was like something out of a movie. The car was seconds away from impact when the creature sprung into action. It grabbed my car and tossed it in the air like a beach ball. I was already familiar with my powers so I managed to use them to escape. After I escaped from the first group, more reptilians appeared. There were at least ten or so. They surrounded me. I teleported to the first place I could think of, home. I arrived and there were even more of them there! Before I could teleport again, one of them zapped me. The zap paralyzed me. I was rendered completely helpless. I had no way out. Then, a bright light appeared out of nowhere and I ended up here, courtesy of the blue guy." Drave said and pointed to Anaku. Based on his story, I quickly deduced that the handprint on my parents' door was left by the same creatures he encountered.

"I got here around the same time he did." Sienna blurted. She looked slightly different from the last time I had seen her, which was at the mall with Drave. Her normally tan even skin had a glow about it and her once brown hair was pink with streaks of jet black. I glanced at the others. Most of them looked familiar, though I wasn't sure why. One of the other people walked up to me and extended his hand.

"Hey Charisma, I'm Aiden." He said with a boyish grin. His vibrant green eyes glowed energetically. His light brown hair was untamed. His muscular, athletic, frame towered over me. I must admit, I was captivated by his boyish good looks, but a cute boy was the last thing that I needed to concern myself with. I needed to find my parents. "That's a pretty—" Before he could continue, a girl with features vaguely similar to his interrupted the introduction.

"And I'm Alex," She blurted rudely. As I stated, she looked somewhat like the female version of Aiden. Her green eyes weren't as vibrant and full of life and the gorgeous smile was absent. She had fiery red hair as opposed to Aiden's light brown locks and her skin wasn't smooth like his, it was littered with red blotches. Her demeanor was way off too. Her crappy attitude and sour expression gave off the impression of someone that felt threatened. It made me wonder about the two.

"So, are you two a couple?" was the first question I could think to ask; which probably wasn't the brightest choice considering the resemblance between them. Regardless of the slight resemblance, I mainly asked because of her behavior. It was questionable, to say the least. She acted like a jealous girlfriend.

"Are you serious? GROSS!" Is how she responded to the question.

"Actually, we're brother and sister and don't mind her, she woke up on the wrong side of the bed today," Aiden said with a giggle. Alex didn't find his joke amusing, her eyes lit up literally like flames before she walked away. Another one of the people, a boy with wild hair morphed into a fox right before my eyes and his weird space suit morphed along with him. It gave me quite a startle.

"The name's Jackson, Jackson Burges," the fox boy said in a miniature voice obviously ripping off James Bond.

"How did you do that?" I questioned as if I had just been an audience member witnessing a magic trick.

"To tell you the truth, I don't know. I just focus on what I want to become, and my body does the rest." Jackson then morphed back into his human form, which wasn't bad on the eyes at all. He had an almost rugged appearance. One thing that really caught my attention was his golden colored eyes. I had never seen another living creature with such a unique set. They were brilliantly bright and full of life.

"How did your outfit morph with you?" was the next question I uttered, still quite in awe of his ability.

"I don't know. It's some type of advanced organic mimic suit." He said as he poked a piece of it.

"You mean it's alive?" I was freaked out by the possibility of living clothing. It was gross and intriguing at the same time.

"It is alive, but not how you know it to be," Anaku answered. "The garments are specifically designed to fit each wearer uniquely. It is cloned with each individual's DNA."

"Oh, so basically, it's like he's wearing his own skin huh?"

"Yes, that is essentially correct. Enki is the one responsible for creating them. You will receive yours shortly."

"Uh, okay…" I murmured. I could feel my skin crawl at the notion of wearing a clone of myself. It was a disgusting thought. "Who is—" Before I could finish my question, another being emerged. It was taller than Anaku. It looked like one of those gray bug-eyed aliens that you find fake videos of on the internet. The classic slit for a mouth, underdeveloped ears, and nose, the hairless smooth skin, black eyes devoid of pupils. He had five fingers on each hand, but they were abnormally elongated and matched the rest of his rail thin body. He wasn't that tall. At the time, I stood five feet even and he appeared to be a mere few inches taller.

"I am Enki." He said, sounding robotic. "We need to get started right away." He looked stiff. If he were a movie character, I would fire whoever did the CGI effects.

"Is he alright?" I whispered as I tapped Anaku. He felt ice cold.

"What do you mean?" He inquired, clearly clueless as to what I was asking.

"Never mind, so do I have to get one of those suits or is there an alternative?" I still was not sold on the freaky skin suit.

"It's not as bad as it sounds. Actually, it feels like you're not wearing anything at all. Um, I mean," Jackson said leading into an awkward moment.

"I get what you're saying." I started to laugh, but stopped at a smirk. It was one of those moments, one of those juvenile humor moments that briefly brought back a sense of normality. I turned my attention to Enki. "Let's get started," I said.

"Give me your arm," he instructed flatly, not showing any sign of emotion. The guy was like a blank slate. He scored a zero on the personality scale. I stretched out my arm as a weird tool appeared in his hand. It looked like a permanent marker. The tip of it illuminated bright orange. I felt the tool touch my skin. It felt like a thousand needle pricks.

"Ouch!" I blurted and quickly retracted my arm.

"It's done," he responded before making a door appear out of thin air. "Your suit will be done shortly." He said before proceeding through the mysterious door. Once he was completely through, it faded away like a mirage.

"So why do you have all of us here Anaku?" I asked while still coming to terms with the fact that I was talking to real life extraterrestrials.

"All of you are here because Earth needs you. You are its last hope. The creatures that tried to capture you are called the Draakunaki. They are a brutal race of ancient reptilians seeking to enslave Mankind and take Earth's resources to help sustain their dying planet. This group is the only thing that stands in the way of them fulfilling their mission. They will stop at nothing to make sure that you are all eliminated, and the earth is reduced to rubble."

"How can you expect the six of us to take on an entire race of Godzillas?" Alex expressed her concern. The odds were greatly stacked against us.

"You can win by mastering each of your powers and working as a team. You all have the blood of one of the most powerful races in the entire universe coursing through your veins. You are the last sons and daughters of Enocia. This area is where you will hone your abilities. The others are already acclimated to this training facility. I have incorporated every known possible variation of the Draakunaki and their abilities. It will help you to prepare. Let us begin."

"I'll go first." Drave volunteered and stepped forward, everyone else stepped back.

"Proceed," Anaku, said before the entire area transformed into a typical downtown landscape. Before I could grasp everything that was happening around us, two big reptilian brutes burst out of one of the buildings. They looked like something out of a horrific nightmare. I watched nervously as Drave walked to confront the towering twin menaces; both were equally horrendous. I dreaded my turn up to bat. Simulation or not, they terrified me. They each had ridiculously huge energy blades almost the size of my body. I imagined the dread my parents felt coming face to face with the real thing. Based on the condition of my mother and father's bedroom, I kept very little hope of finding them alive if I found them at all. *There was so much blood, how could they have survived?"* I thought as I watched the terrible creatures walk toward Drave.

"C'mon ugly, and uglier, show me what you got!" Drave taunted in typical rebel fashion as the towering behemoths rushed toward him. They didn't move as one would assume nine feet plus tall, creatures would move. Their smooth, graceful strides were comparable to that of professional athletes. The first one closed in on Drave and wound back his weapon to swing. What happened next renewed my hope. The creature swung, and Drave dissolved a split second before the blade sliced through where he should have still been standing. Seconds later, Drave reappeared on one of the buildings. The other one saw him and darted in his direction. Next, Drave did something totally unexpected. He jumped off the building and dived toward the approaching enemy. The enemy swung his weapon, barely missing Drave. He teleported again and ended up directly over his foe. He stomped down on the creature's head and vanished once more. The stomp disoriented the foe. It staggered backward and slammed into a building. The impact caused a small piece of the building's outer structure to crumble. The simulation looked so life like it was scary. While the creature struggled to regain its composure, Drave teleported directly in front of it and began pummeling its face with a barrage of rapid punches. His fists moved so fast that I could hardly keep track of what was transpiring. The other creature tried to seize its opportunity to strike while Drave was preoccupied. It snuck up behind him and wound back its arm. The blade glowed brilliantly.

"Wat—" Drave teleported before I could warn him of the impending danger. I watched in amazement as the creature's blade plunged into the other creature. It sliced clean through its victim's body. The creature stood in a distraught state as its comrade screamed in agony while dying a slow horrible death. With the remaining creature preoccupied, Drave appeared behind it in mid air with a large metal pole. He swung the pole with brute force, sending it crashing into the remaining creature's skull. The creature dropped its energy blade, fell to its knees, and then collapsed sideways onto the hard concrete. Seconds later, everything began phasing out and the room converted back to how it was when I first arrived.

"Well done," Anaku said as a smile formed on Drave's face. "Next," He announced.

"We got this," Aiden and Alex said simultaneously as they stepped forward. Within seconds, another simulation was forming. This one was far different from the last. The room transformed into a middle-class neighborhood. Three more Reptilians appeared and Alex and Aiden went into battle. I watched as Alex hovered off the ground and began to fly. She encountered the first creature. It began firing its laser gun at her. Alex dodged the shots with amazing aerial moves. She moved through the air like a fighter jet at an air show. While the one reptilian was preoccupied shooting at Alex, the other two went after Aiden. As the creatures were approaching, Aiden raised his hands. Seconds later, a fierce and powerful wind started to blow. He motioned his hands and the raging wind slammed into the oncoming Draakunaki, sending each one flying in opposite directions. I turned my attention back to Alex and saw her hurling balls of fire at the creature firing the laser gun. One of the balls hit it directly in the face, causing it to let out a horrendous shrill. I almost laughed as I watched it frantically slap its face in an attempt to put out the fire.

"Are you done playing with them Alex?" Aiden questioned in an annoyed tone.

"Let's put the babies to bed," She replied. I watched in awe as her entire body began to light up like embers in a fireplace. She landed and walked toward her injured foe. Flames formed in her hands and her hair appeared to be on fire. Her powers astonished me. She stood directly in front of the injured reptilian with a sinister smile on her face. "Good Night," She murmured before unleashing her fiery fury. She burned it with extreme prejudice. It shrieked and writhed in agony as the manipulated flames danced over its body melting and blistering its leathery flesh.

After her foe's movements ceased, Alex returned to normal. Her flaming hair reverted to red spiky locks and the lava-like skin changed to its previously blotchy red speckled tone. Alex rejoined the rest of us and let Aiden put an end to the battle. I watched as he squared off with the two remaining reptilians. It was a tense moment. We all stood in silence, waiting for the outcome. I wanted to say something to Alex for leaving her brother alone to finish the battle.

What happened next made me understand why she did. The remaining reptilians raised their weapons. The odds seemed to be stacked against Aiden coming out on top. Then something unexpected happened. I watched in shock and awe as Aiden literally sucked all of the water out of the remaining foes. It happened so fast that the reptilians didn't get a chance to let off one single shot. One minute, they were aiming their weapons. The next, they were dropping them to the ground. Their forms changed rapidly. Their scales became dry and began to flake off as the rest of their leathery appearance lost its sheen. Their skin became dull and brittle as the life escaped from it. Their eyes disintegrated. They let out their last breaths before crumbling to the ground.

When Aiden finished, all that remained of the once formidable foes were two ghastly piles of dried skin and bones. Aiden, Alex, and Drave were frighteningly powerful. I was beginning to understand why Anaku said we were Earth's last hope. Jackson ran into action after Alex and Aiden, I saw Sienna standing eagerly awaiting her turn. I decided to walk over to her and strike up a conversation.

"Hey," I mumbled bashfully. Even with my powers, she was still pretty intimidating.

"What's up?" She questioned not taking her eyes of the session for a second. Jackson was facing what appeared to be a hybrid between big foot and a dinosaur. It was big and ugly, perhaps the ugliest thing ever given the gift of life. I watched as Jackson toyed with it. First, he changed into a cat and began scurrying in and out of every small crevice he could find. This appeared to frustrate the creature to no end. It smashed through buildings like a bulldozer.

"What are your powers?" I asked Sienna as we watched Jackson put on a show.

"You'll see as soon as Mr. Showoff is done." She replied with a giggle. It was pretty entertaining watching a cat outrun the giant monster.

"Okay, I think you've had enough!" Jackson yelled in a weird voice before turning from a typical alley cat into a large tiger. After the transformation, he turned to face off with the creature. They charged at one another and then collided in an uninhibited display of physical rage. Jackson bit and scratched the creature as it grappled his body. While locked in the heated scrimmage, Jackson transformed again into a great grizzly bear. He mauled the creature with raw strength. I was impressed by Jackson but I was super anxious to see Sienna in action. I tried to read her thoughts and she turned to face me and snapped.

"Don't do that." She said in a tone similar to a mother scolding a child.

"H-how did you know?" I was dumbfounded as to how she was able to detect my thought probing activities.

"That's part of what I do." She replied with a smile. I turned my attention back to the battle just as Jackson was downing the beast. He had turned into a silver back gorilla to finish the job. I watched, as he used primate strength, to snap the god-awful ugly creature's neck. The creature's lifeless corpse collapsed to the ground. Jackson stood with a devilish smile. His golden eyes glowed triumphantly.

"Now you'll see what I'm capable of," Sienna said as a cunning expression formed on her face. "Don't go easy Anaku," She instructed as she made her way to the battleground. At that moment, Enki appeared next to me.

"Your custom suit is ready." He said. I noticed a glowing object clutched in his bony hand. I was hoping that I didn't have to leave right away to try it on. I wanted to stay and watch Sienna in action first. The scene around us had changed once again, this time to an abandoned beach littered with wrecked ships and other debris. It looked very post-apocalyptic. Sienna stood by the water's edge among the ghost ships. I saw numerous figures coming into view from further up the beach.

"But—" Before I could finish my protest, Enki touched a section on the glowing device. Like something out of a special effects catalog, my clothes disappeared and my very own suit was left in their wake. "How did you do that?" I asked, completely astonished by what had just occurred.

"It is science, not magic. Anything and everything can be done and explained through science." He said firmly. His statement was puzzling. He somehow assumed that I thought that what had just occurred was some type of unexplainable miracle, a supernatural occurrence that had no physical explanation for it. I was taught the magic of science concept by Mr. Grant, my eighth-grade history teacher. He believed that the Gods of most ancient civilizations were really aliens. His theory was that the advanced technology they possessed appeared deity-like to primitive people accustomed to using stone tablets and cave walls as notebooks. Enki reiterated this fact with the statement. "No offense, but most earth inhabitants are naïve when it comes to advanced technology." He uttered as if he knew how I would react to his previous statement.

"Well, it's obvious that I'm not most inhabitants," I replied in an attempt to be witty.

"That is now noted." He responded blandly. "Do you have any questions about the suit?" He asked. I had so many questions that I didn't know where to start. I wanted to know everything there was to know about the cloned creature that clung to my frame. I looked at the others and noticed their suits were different colors and designs. Drave had a cool dark blue and black suit, Alex's was fiery red and orange, Aiden's was ocean blue and gray, Jackson's was black and hunter green, and Sienna's was pink and black with a pattern that matched Drave's. Mine, on the other hand, was dark gray and looked generic.

"How can I change the look of my suit?" I asked.

"That's a real unique question." He responded sarcastically. "Anyway, once the suit bonds to its owner, the owner will have the power to customize the suit as he or she sees fit."

"So all I have to do is bond with it?"

"Correct,"

"Okay, so how do I do that?" I didn't know the first thing about bonding outside of its normal parameters. I mean other than bonding with other people or pets.

"The suit detects the wearer's vibrations and thoughts. I think the first thing that you should do is name it."

"Uh, okay. I will call my suit—" Enki interrupted before I could finish.

"Don't say it, think it." He said as one of his sticks for a finger pointed to his head.

"Okay," I replied. I closed my eyes and set about thinking of a name. *"Alice"* Was the name that popped in my head. I decided to name my suit after Alice from the childhood classic, Alice in Wonderland. I loved that story when I was a kid. I remember begging my mother to take me to see the live-action film that starred Johnny Depp. When it came out on DVD, I watched it like five times the first day I got it. With my eyes opened, I focused on Sienna and saw that her adversaries were now on the beach and roughly thirty feet away from where she was standing. There were far more than the others had dealt with and they varied in appearance. I counted at least five different kinds.

"It will all become second nature to you. You will have your suit customized in no time." Enki assured. The Reptilians were now in view and were armed to the teeth. I felt a panicky sensation in the pit of my stomach as I watched Sienna ready herself for battle. The way in which she prepared was quite strange. Unlike the others before her, she didn't get into a fierce, ready for war type of stance. She did just the opposite. She sat down in a manner commonly associated with meditation. As the creatures approached, Sienna still in a meditative position, lifted into the air and a pink semi-transparent plasma shield formed around her like a bubble. Some of the Reptilians began firing their weapons. The shots were all deflected by the bubble. They continued firing, but Sienna stayed as still and calm as a leaf on a windless day. She was completely unaffected by their attacks.

"What is she doing?" I mumbled fearing the worse.

"She knows what she's doing, just watch," Drave responded confidently. Then, like a bolt of lightning, she struck. I watched in complete awe as all of the creatures simultaneously disintegrated.

"Wow," I murmured. Watching her display of power was a humbling experience.

"See I told you," Drave commented with his smile shining brightly. "So, what are your powers?" he asked as the room reverted to its original state. My powers felt insignificant as compared to the others. Sienna's powers alone made me feel like a sidekick.

"Uh, well… I, I have super strength, I can move fast, and I can read minds." I replied timidly.

"Oh really, that sounds cool!" Drave seemed genuinely impressed, which made me feel better about my budding abilities. It was at that moment that I understood what Sienna saw in Drave. In addition to his good looks, smarts, and bad boy persona, he was sincere.

"What else can you do?" I asked, assuming that he had more to offer than what he had already displayed.

"Well, aside from speed and teleportation, I also have enhanced agility. I just recently discovered them so I'm not sure if I have more or if those are it."

"So how many powers does Sienna have?"

*"I can float, make atoms disintegrate, produce energy force fields, telepathically communicate, control the will of others, and manipulate matter. I think that's about it."* I looked at Sienna as she gave me a wink.

*"Wow, that's a lot,"* I telepathically responded.

"Oh, I get it. You guys must be having a conversation." Drave said with a smile.

"Just a little girl talk," Sienna murmured playfully.

"It better not be about me." He said in the same playful manner.

"It's always about you," Sienna gave Drave a quick peck before directing her attention back toward me. So, are you gonna show us what you got or what?" She caught me completely off guard.

"I don't know. I don't think I'm ready." I replied as I thought about how dangerous it looked when the others had their turns.

"C'mon, I know you'll do fine," Drave interjected, giving me a needed boost of confidence, though not quite enough to consider seriously giving it a go. I was a newbie or rather a noob, and it appeared as if everyone else already had experience points. Jackson walked over with a big goofy grin. He and Drave were opposites, in the sense that Drave had qualities that screamed sex symbol, and Jackson was more like the goofy boy next door, cute but better off as a friend.

"But—" Jackson interrupted before I could think of more reasons why I shouldn't.

"It will help you learn faster." He blurted enthusiastically, his golden eyes looking like mint gold collectible coins. His goofy smile and positive vibe made it hard to stand my ground.

"Does it hurt when you get hit? I mean can it kill you?" I was intimidated by how real the virtual battles appeared. The realistic appearance made me leery of participating. The last thing I needed was death at the hands of a simulation.

"Don't worry, the simulations are nonlethal. I got clobbered the first time I tried it. One of the reptilians shot me in the head with a laser. I thought I was a goner for sure." Jackson said with a humorous laugh.

"Yeah, it knocked him out cold for a few minutes," Aiden added as he grinned at me.

"I came to and everyone had these shocked looks on their faces." The shot felt like someone whacked me in the head with a rubber ball. The pain subsided shortly after I woke up. Trust me; it's pretty safe… and fun!"

"Are you sure about that?" I still wasn't fully convinced.

"Yes, I'm positive." He replied assertively.

"Oh… alright," I said, feeling somewhat reassured. "Okay Anaku, I want to give it a try," I said before walking up nervously. *"Oh Geez, here goes nothing,"* I thought before the room began to change.

# Chapter 6

# The Blue Room

**EVERYTHING CHANGED.** The blue vast space transformed into a county fair scenario. The recreation was spot-on. There were games with blinking lights and cheesy sounds, food stands displaying everything from Elephant ears to pizza on their posted menus. I could see a Ferris wheel in the distance still operating. Hokey music faintly played in the background. Everything was there except people. The place seemed to be abandoned. It was like a ghost town. It was very unsettling. I felt a chill as I continued walking toward what would be my proving grounds. I didn't want to seem like the weakest link, in the chain of Mankind's last hope. My parents depended on me, the world depended on me. I had to conquer my fears.

I paused when I saw a reptilian coming straight toward me. Based on its features, I assumed it was of the male gender. He destroyed every obstacle in his way. He tossed tables as if they were pieces of paper, and demolished a photo booth by running directly through it. He crushed the booth's metal as if it were a mere pop can. Our eyes connected and in that instant, I felt an inner strength emerge. The creature had to be defeated. And I had to be the one to do it. I didn't have time for fear or doubt. Fear and doubt were luxuries and the impending war made sure I wasn't allotted them. The creature began speaking in some foreign dialect. I assumed it was making a threat or rather antagonizing me, egging me on. It finished speaking and an evil grin formed on its face.

"You really are ugly," was my response. I balled my fists and prepared to eliminate it. I let my rage consume me. I charged full force at the creature. The creature got into its fighting stance. I felt like David facing Goliath. The creature's size dwarfed me. It made me understand why birds and squirrels scatter when in the presence of humans. If not for my powers I would have done the same instead of what I did next. I came upon the creature, and let my fury out in one focused, powerful punch. My fist sunk into the creature's abdomen. It groaned as air escaped from its body. I watched as it was lifted into the air from the impact of the blow. My punch sent it crashing into a 'Shoot the Ducks', water gun game stand. Its body decimated a large portion of the stand.

As I walked over to finish off the reptilian, a gigantic floating ship appeared above us. I watched as a huge beam of light shot down to earth from the center of it. When the light dissipated, three more reptilians stood in its place. The one that I attacked was now attempting to get up. I had a small window of opportunity to take him out before having to deal with the others. I struck fast. I jumped on top of my foe and landed a series of punches to its horribly grotesque face. I beat it until all signs of consciousness were absent. I looked down and briefly took note of the damage. I was in disbelief as to the amount of damage done by my small average teenage girl sized fists. Its face was a complete bloody, mangled mess. My hands were covered in its glowing red blood. It was an exhilarating feeling. Power surged throughout my body as I got up to go confront the new arrivals.

As I got closer, I saw that all of them were armed. A direct approach of attack was not a viable option. I had to figure out a strategy on the fly. Two of the three had lasers and the third had something that I hadn't seen before, it had some type of box attached to its hand. I saw an opening and took it. Judging from the distance that was between us, there was a good chance that they didn't see me beating the crap out of their buddy. I decided to sneak around the booths and stands and take them out one at a time. I crept quietly from one point to next as the creatures stayed in the middle of the fairgrounds. They gradually expanded out to cover more ground.

The creatures were spread out in a triangular formation. They were spaced roughly eight to ten feet apart. It wasn't much to work with, but if I moved fast enough, it would suffice. Since I was on the right side, I went with the obvious choice. The first one was preoccupied with his weapon when I struck. I gave it a swift but deadly jab to the small of its back and quickly retreated back into hiding. The punch sent it flying forward in a manner similar to a stunt double attached to a wire safety harness. It crashed into a food stand that I'd passed earlier. The attack distracted the others. They looked around frantically and talked to one another in a weird foreign language.

While they were distracted, I darted to the opposite end. Once the opportunity arose, I took down the second one in the same manner. After attacking the second one, the last remaining reptilian saw me and immediately began firing from the box mounted on his hand. Each shot that the box released produced a miniature tornado. They ripped apart everything that they came in contact with, in furious swirls of wind and debris. I dived and nearly missed being swept up in one of them. He continued firing, I continued dodging, and after the seventh tornado, I had grown weary of dodging and decided to take a different course of action. I started throwing any and everything I could get my hands on, from tables to food carts, I hurled them all with as much force as I could muster. The creature managed to shoot everything I threw before its weapon jammed. As it struggled to fix it, I seized the opportunity and rushed at it full speed. I was on the verge of taking it down when it switched hands and fired from another box on its opposite hand. A large energy burst fired from out of it. The shot hit me square in the chest and sent me flying into the air.

The impact knocked the wind out of me. I gasped for breath as I flew helplessly through the air. I went higher and higher. The blast had some type of anti-gravity property to it. I looked down at Anaku and the others as I rose like a balloon filled with helium. Other than Anaku, everyone had shocked expressions on their faces. Things looked really bad. I was just about to give up hope when something amazing happened. Another superpower manifested. As I fought and struggled for my freedom, my body began to hover on its own. I was floating! Oxygen returned to my lungs and I felt my strength being renewed. After regaining my composure, a crazy idea came to mind. I chose to implement the idea, which resulted in me dive-bombing directly at the creature. It fired more shots, but I continued to dive unhindered by them. I saw the panic in its face before I felt my fist burst through it. The creature exploded in a splash of glowing crimson. I hit the ground with a heavy thud. The ground shook from my impromptu landing.

"Holy *(expletive)*" Jackson said in an excited voice. "THAT WAS HELLA AWESOME!" His words summed up how I felt perfectly. I felt unstoppable! My petite small body had just destroyed a nine-foot giant. I walked away from the battlefield as it began to change. My confidence was renewed. It was at that moment, that I knew exactly how I wanted my outfit to look. I thought of the design in my mind and suddenly, it came to be. My suit transformed from plain dark gray to royal blue and crimson.

"I see that you are becoming acclimated," Anaku said with his sapphire eyes glowing brightly. There appeared to be a slight smile on his face as well. I knew that I was still a little rough around the edges, but confidence wise, I felt as if I was ready to take on a whole planet of reptilians.

"Yeah, I'm getting the hang of it," I replied with a smile.

"That was okay, I guess," Alex mumbled arrogantly with a less than impressed expression.

"I think you did great!" Aiden said in an enthusiastic tone. His eyes captivated me. They looked like emeralds. I was starting to develop a crush, and I had a feeling Alex was aware of it.

"I think you need more practice. You almost got your (expletive) handed to you by that last one," Alex said in a cold insolent tone. I could tell that she was going to give me hell every chance she could.

"Okay, well, how about we practice together? You can show me a few techniques, and help me tighten up my attacks."

"Uh, well…" My response had her tongue-tied. She didn't expect me to fight the proverbial fire with water.

"That sounds like a great idea!" Aiden chimed in. He seemed truly enthused by the idea.

"Yes, I agree," Anaku said, agreeing with Aiden.

"Nobody asked you for your opinion Aiden," Alex said in a nasty tone before cutting her eyes. "Honestly Charisma, I don't think that would be a good idea. I don't play well with others." She said before strutting off arrogantly. Judging by how she worked with her brother, I knew it was a lie.

"Forgive her disposition," Anaku murmured before following behind her.

"What's the deal with her? I mean, why is she so nasty?" I questioned Aiden as I continued watching them. Alex and Anaku had stopped and begun having a conversation, well if you can call it that considering the fact that Anaku's mouth wasn't moving.

"She's just been having a rough time as of late. Our parents, were recently killed. Don't get me wrong, I'm still in mourning, but she's taking it way harder," Aiden paused briefly as he searched for the next words to say.

"It's okay, I understand. I feel the same way. I'm lost without my parents. Those things took them. Not knowing if they're still alive is killing me." I confessed as my eyes began to water.

"We'll get them back," Aiden said before wrapping his arms around me. I buried my face in his chest. His embrace gave me the comfort that I needed at that moment. I fought my tears, but to no avail. They worked their way out and onto Aiden's suit. I lifted my head and slightly backed it away. The wetness of my tears against his suit felt weird and reminded me of the fact that he was wearing his clone. It didn't feel like fabric, it felt like skin, like tough skin. "What?" Aiden asked with a confused look.

"It's nothing, I just have to get used to the way these suits feel," I said with a small giggle as I remained in his embrace. I wanted to back away from him, but I was so preoccupied by his warmth, it won out over my thoughts of being grossed out. There was no denying my crush. He was dreamy and was someone that I needed in the new world in which I now lived.

"Hey," I heard Alex's voice and released Aiden. Her tone was lighter and she had a friendlier expression on her face. "Sorry for being so hard on you. I didn't know that they took your parents." She said as I wiped the wetness from my face.

"It's okay. I'm sorry to hear about what happened to you and Aiden's parents," I responded sympathetically. Having lost our parents to the Draakunaki was something we all shared, and even though I didn't have the privilege of knowing their fate, I still suffered from their absence all the same.

"Do you still want to practice with me?" Alex was beginning to come around. It made me feel better. "Cause you need all the help you can get!" She joked before extending her hand.

"Ha ha real funny, I don't think I was that bad." I replied as we shook hands.

"All of you should practice as a group. Charisma, I will show you to your sleeping quarters afterward." Anaku said as he walked away and the room changed into a dark wooden scenario. Big redwoods sprouted up, the floor turned into a carpet of grass, soil, and moss. A dark sky formed over the trees and stars and a moon appeared in it. The sounds of crickets and other nocturnal forest life suddenly filled the air. The forest reminded me of something that I had been trying to forget. Everything looked exactly as how it had looked in my recurring nightmare. The uncanny similarity of the scenery triggered something within me. An intense panic emerged. My heart began beating rapidly, and I felt my palms become moist with sweat.

"Are you alright?" Aiden questioned, obviously noticing.

"Yeah I'm fine. Dark wooded areas just give me the creeps." I uttered, downplaying the truth. I was terrified! I remembered the dream as if it was an actual event. I could practically see the big vicious dragon lurking in the recesses of the dark, foreboding forest, waiting for its moment to strike. My mind was really playing tricks on me. "Let's do this," I said in a tone that exuded confidence. I was trying to cover up my fear. I didn't want to give off the weak damsel, 'I'll stay here while you guys save the day' vibe.

As we started walking through the forest, a spaceship the size of a baseball field appeared above the trees. It practically eclipsed the moon. The light that radiated from the object was blinding. I shielded my eyes and continued my trek semi-blindly through the forest. The simulated environment seemed so tangible. I could hear the sound of our footsteps as we stepped on small flora and forest debris. I looked up at the sky just as an even brighter light was discharged from the center of the ship. The force of the energized light cleared a spot in the middle of the forest. As the light dissipated, I could see the silhouettes of several large figures.

"It's time for action," Jackson said with a look of glee. I could tell that he was looking forward to doing battle as a team.

"We should think of a strategy before we reach them," Drave said assuming the leadership role.

"Okay, so what do you propose we do?" Aiden asked as we huddled around Drave like a sports team preparing for a game.

"I think Sienna should take the first attack and while she is doing that, Jackson, and I will go around them and perform a sneak attack. Then, you, Alex, and Charisma finish them off with a final assault." His plan sounded solid and gave me hope that we could, in fact, work as a team.

"Showtime," Sienna said as her energy bubble formed around her. She floated up ahead, Jackson transformed into a black cat and swiftly ran off into the darkness, and Drave teleported in a quick subtle manner. The creatures were fast approaching. There appeared to be a small nation of them trudging toward us. My muscles tensed as I braced myself for battle. Knowing that it wasn't real, gave me some sense of comfort, but it still wasn't something to take lightly. I felt a dull ache in my chest from my previous battle. The simulations though not lethal, still packed quite a punch. I watched as Sienna disintegrated the first few. Then, I saw activity from the rear, which I assumed was Drave and Jackson.

Our turn came and we sprung into action. Aiden made a huge windstorm knocking at least half of the reptilians off balance, and Alex flew into the air and began showering them with fireballs. I charged toward the group and began swinging wildly. One of my punches hit a reptilian and left an impression of my fist in its armor. Not yet knowing my strength limit, I decided to do something different. I grabbed the first one that had fallen and hoisted it over my head. Then, with every fiber of my being, I hurled it into the air. It flew across the sky and disappeared. We finished off the remaining reptilians, and the simulation reverted to what we now refer to as the Blue Room.

Once we were done with the simulation, the others hurriedly scattered like students being dismissed from class. I lagged behind and followed Anaku. He led me down a long curved corridor that looked like something out of a Star Wars movie. From the shape of it, I assumed that we were inside of some type of circular shaped structure. The walls were a metallic gray color and faintly illuminated by some type of light source that was unfamiliar to me. I was confused as to the actual source because evidence of bulbs or fixtures weren't detectable. The ceiling and walls themselves seemed to be emitting it. I wanted to ask Anaku about them, but I had other pressing matters to give my attention to, like where the bathroom was located. I felt horrible after the stressful day that I had endured and was in desperate need of a long hot shower.

"Where is the bathroom?" I asked as we journeyed down the odd hallway.

"Are you referring to the cleansing facility?" was his reply. It was an odd name for something so common.

"Yes, I think." I murmured unsure if we were on the same page.

"You are inquiring about the place in which humans cleanse their bodies and alleviate their waste correct?" The way Anaku communicated was so weird. The odd terms and lack of mouth movement were definitely going to take some getting used to.

"Uh, yeah, that's it."

"I will take you to it after you see your sleeping quarters." Anaku's eyes lit up every time he spoke. I hadn't really paid attention to it before. I assumed that it was the

Anthony D. Phillips Jr.

trade off for not using his mouth. It was so underdeveloped, that I had a hard time imagining him eating.

"Fair enough," I uttered as images of him trying to eat various foods popped in my head. One instance, I pictured him trying to eat spaghetti, another, I visualized him trying to conquer a double cheeseburger. I held back my laughter and tried to keep my face as straight as possible.

"What did you say?" It was quite obvious that he was uninitiated to informal human dialogue.

"Oh, nothing, I was just agreeing with you" I responded.

After walking past several doors, we stopped in front of one of the rooms in the middle of the hallway. The door to the room looked very familiar. It looked like my bedroom door. I'd know it from anywhere. I extended my hand toward the knob, but hesitated and looked at Anaku.

"Open it," He urged. I twisted the knob and opened the door to reveal an exact replica of my room. I was amazed by how much it mirrored my old room. The All Boys posters that covered the walls of my old room were faithfully recreated and the bedroom set was an exact match as well. I also noticed that the clothing I was wearing before Enki zapped on my suit, was neatly laid on my bed.

"How did you do this, I mean… why does this look exactly like my old room?" was the question that I posed as I stood in awe.

"This is an exact replica of it." He stated as I walked inside. "I wanted you to be as comfortable as possible, which is why we reproduced your entire bedroom with one hundred percent accuracy," Anaku answered. Seeing the faithful replication of my room only made me think about Liz and my parents even more. I wished that I had told her my secret.

"So what about my life, will I ever see my friends again?" I questioned. The sight of my old room triggered something that at the time, I was still trying to process. A factor I was still coming to terms with. I didn't know how to let go and say farewell to my old life. I wasn't sure if I was ready to fully adapt to a way of life stranger than fiction.

"Until the threat is eliminated, I cannot permit you to do that." Anaku's words weren't final, but while the threat prevailed, everyone and everything in my life would remain memories, reminders of what was and what might be again if the circumstances changed. The only bright side to the change was that I would no longer have to deal with Paige and her cronies.

"Good riddance Paige," I mumbled as I thought about never seeing her face again.

"You are done for the day. Follow me so I can show you where to cleanse and then we can join the others for sustenance." Anaku said before leaving the room.

"Wait, shouldn't I get changed?" I questioned as I looked at my drawers stuffed with things that I remembered sifting through mere days ago. He duplicated every exact detail. He even accurately captured the mess that I neglected to finish cleaning up, which was especially embarrassing considering the fact that he was an advanced life form.

"No, your suit is a living extension of yourself and requires cleansing and sustenance as well." His statement confused me.

"So am I supposed to take a shower with the suit and how does it eat?" I almost didn't want the answer, but I blurted the question out before I could fully consider the possible response.

"The suit and the wearer form a bond, which is symbiotic. The suit is now a part of you and as such, it will protect you. You must nourish it and keep it hygienically pleasing."

"Okay, well, it's good to know that I have another responsibility to add to my list!" I joked. It apparently didn't amuse Anaku because he still had the same stone expression. His humor level was probably the lowest I'd ever encountered. It was a good thing that he didn't moonlight as a stand-up comedy judge.

"Yes, I suppose." is all that he said, which made the moment even more awkward.

"Never mind, what's for dinner?" I felt hunger pangs in my stomach.

"It will soon be revealed." He replied, not giving me as much as a hint. I was starving and looking forward to a warm meal. I wondered if the meal would be a recreation of an earth meal, or if it would be an authentic man-made dish. I had a craving for a nice juicy cheeseburger and a fresh batch of fries. As I held the thought of food in my mind, the craving changed to a full slab of ribs, a mountain of mash potatoes, and a pile of buttered broccoli with cheese. Before we reached the cleansing chamber, it had changed again to a meal consisting of shrimp, a baked potato, and grilled fish.

"It's not still alive is it?" I asked, thinking of the worst possible scenario. The abundance of alien and horror films that I had watched with my dad contributed greatly to my wild imagination.

"No, it is just sustenance." He replied flatly. Anaku led me to another room a few doors down from my bedroom. "Go inside and be cleansed, I will await your return." He said before waving his hand in front of the door. The door faded and I stepped inside. The room was dimly lit. As I walked further inside, the room illuminated and revealed an actual bathroom. The sight of it made me think about how bad I needed to wash my hair. I turned to ask Anaku a question.

"How—" The door returned to its original solid form before I got the chance to ask my question. I recognized what appeared to be some kind of futuristic sink and an exotic toilet was next to it. On the opposite side from where I stood was a stall. As I headed toward the stall, my suit melted off my body like hot candle wax. The door to the stall automatically opened and the suit slid inside. I cautiously followed. Once inside, the door closed, and almost instantly, a weird mist surrounded us. The mist felt warm and wet on my skin and a weird tingling sensation invaded my scalp. Seconds later, the mist dissipated. I felt clean. Cleaner than I'd ever felt in my entire life. Slits appeared in the walls of the stall and strong gushes of air blew out of them. After the weird blow-drying session ceased, a small robotic arm emerged from one of the walls.

"*Open your mouth,*" a mysterious voice instructed telepathically. I did as instructed, and the robotic arm placed a small tablet on my tongue. Before I had the chance to taste the item, it rapidly expanded and filled my mouth with foam. The foam began to heat up and made a fizzing sound similar to when an Alka-Seltzer tablet is placed in water. The foam tasted like cough syrup mixed with Styrofoam and coffee. I was on the verge of gagging when the foam began to liquefy. "*You may now empty your mouth.*" The mystery voice stated. I quickly spit out the weird liquid. The robotic arm retreated back into the wall and a round dome device lowered down from out of the ceiling and landed on my head.

"*Do not move,*" Is what it communicated to my brain. I complied. A small humming noise began emanating from it. The tingling sensation on my head increased as the device worked its magic, or rather science. The humming stopped and the dome device retracted into the ceiling. My suit worked itself back on to my body and I stepped out of the stall. The door faded again and I saw Anaku waiting patiently on the other side. "Okay, what about my hair? How am I supposed to do it?" In response to my question, Anaku lifted his hand and a mirror appeared and revealed the condition of my hair. I was shocked at the sight of it. My hair was clean and styled neatly, in a basic suitable manner. My long flowing curly locks were tamed.

"Okay, never mind," I uttered, completely floored by the technology responsible for expediently addressing such time-consuming tasks. Showering, washing my hair, doing my hair and getting dressed would've normally taken me close to an hour to finish. The advanced technology did it all in less than ten minutes.

We finally arrived in the dining quarters and it was far from what I expected to see. The dining area looked more like a laboratory than a place where people ate. Drave, Sienna, and the others, were all asleep in clear tubes attached to machines the size of smart cars.

"What is this?" I inquired disappointingly. "Where is the food?" I asked, further expressing my disappointment.

"This is the sustenance chamber. It will provide you with all of the essential nutrients needed to sustain you and your powers." I looked at Aiden and noticed a weird blue glowing substance being absorbed by his suit. "Do not be alarmed, the suits aid with the absorption of the sustenance. That is why they are to be left on when feeding."

"…" I paused and refined my thought before speaking, "How long do they have to stay in those tubes?" I asked pointing at Aiden.

"It all depends on the level of depletion. It can range from thirty earth minutes to five earth hours. It only has to be done once a day and unless the energy is depleted heavily from battle, it will last a full twenty-four hours."

"Let me get this right, I can only eat once a day?" The idea of only having to eat once seemed cool, but un-cool at the same time. I enjoyed the pleasurable task of eating and had grown accustomed to it. Not having to do something that I had been doing my entire life didn't seem right. It made me feel like a fish on dry land. "I like eating! I've been doing it my entire life!" I passionately stated, like a lawyer trying to win the sympathy of the jury.

"It is not as unpleasant as it seems." He assured, though I still wasn't convinced. It seemed like the worst thing in the world and made in-school suspension seem like a trip to the amusement park. Actually, it made me miss the in-school suspension and everything else in my normal life, including Paige. It made me miss anything and everything remotely related to life before my powers. Sure, I had abilities that most people hoped for and fantasized about, but the price for those powers seemed to be a bit much.

"I don't know… it looks weird," I protested. "I don't think they're real. I mean, I don't think they're like me. I don't even think they're human. Maybe they're just clones like my room and new suit!" I stated in a moment of confusion.

"They are indeed real, and some of them are more human than you." I didn't understand what Anaku meant.

"So I'm a clone? Wait, no I can't be. Am I?"

"No, but you are something else. Your birth parents were not from Earth. Your father and mother were Enocian. You and Sienna are not human; the others are all partially human."

"How do you know all of this?"

"I know because I knew your maternal grandparents. We were all part of the Concord of Galaxies."

"What is that?"

"It was a treaty that was formed to protect all known galaxies from the Draakunaki," Anaku paused briefly and then continued, "well," He paused again and his eyes grew slightly dim, "most Draakunaki and other threats. Many years ago, before the evolution of man, the Draakunaki's home planet Draakonus was in turmoil. Centuries of war had depleted it. It was dying. The atmosphere had been heavily damaged and was unable to sustain life. Some Draakunaki left in search of the resources needed to repair it, while the rest left to start life elsewhere. Wherever they went, death and destruction soon followed. Every planet they invaded succumbed to their tyranny. Those that resisted were terminated with extreme brutality. They terminated your biological parents."

"Wait, hold on," Anaku was telling me more than I expected to hear. It went from super non-food nutrients to galactic wars and the deaths of my real parents. "So, that must be the reason I was brought to Earth." It was all starting to make sense. The reason my parents left me with nothing to be traced back to is because they didn't want me to suffer the same fate.

"Your government also had involvement in the treaty. The Draakunaki knew this as well and for a brief period, there was peace. Everyone coexisted.

"So what happened? What led to the Draakunaki starting another war?" I asked.

"I am not completely clear on the details that led to the demise of the treaty. Perhaps we will both discover the cause at a later time. Now please prepare yourself to receive your sustenance." Anaku gestured to an empty tube. I reluctantly walked over to it and put one foot inside. The inside of the machine smelled like a new car, which wasn't a bad thing, but it wasn't a smell I wanted to smell before a meal.

"Okay." I uttered. *"C'mon Charisma you can do this."* I thought as I slowly put the rest of my body inside. Once I was completely inside, a mild panic emerged from within me. I could feel my body tense up as the suit made contact with the tube's cold interior. *"Oh boy,"* I thought as I looked up at Anaku and took an extra deep breath.

"Remain still, relax your mind, and close your eyes. Don't let the sensation that you are experiencing overtake you. The sustenance session will begin momentarily." Anaku said before the door to the tube closed. I did as he instructed, and within seconds felt a warm, comforting sensation surrounding me. I opened one of my eyes just a bit and I could see that the same blue substance that surrounded the others, was beginning to surround me as well. It was squishy, almost like Jell-O, but had a liquid consistency to it as well. I tried to relax as more of the substance invaded the small space. If I were claustrophobic, I would've been panicking like crazy. I reluctantly closed my one eye. As soon as I relaxed, an overbearing urge to sleep came over me. The last thing I remembered before drifting off was how much the color of the substance reminded me of Anaku's eyes.

When I woke up, the blue substance was gone and the tube was open. I emerged from the tube energized and full. My appetite was quenched. The rumbling in my stomach was nowhere to be found, which was a feat in itself considering how much it had increased over the past few days. The others were all gone. I stood alone in the chamber still trying to figure out how it all worked. As I began to walk to the doorway, Jackson appeared. Well, actually, he transformed from a small creature back to his normal cute wild-haired self.

"I see you're up sleeping beauty." He uttered jokingly with a playful look in his eye and a boyish grin.

"Yeah, it wasn't as bad as I thought it would be," I replied after letting out a quick yawn. It felt like I had just had a full night's rest, though remembering what Anaku told me, I knew otherwise. "So what do we do now? I mean what do you guys do for entertainment around here?"

"Follow me and I'll show you." He said before leading me out of the room and back into the self-illuminated corridor.

"Where are we going?" I asked impatiently as we walked past the entrance to my bedroom.

"You'll see," was his reply as he kept walking. We walked past the Blue Room entrance and several other rooms before finally reaching another door at the end of the corridor opposite from the sustenance chamber. "Watch this," Jackson said before taking a step forward. The door dematerialized right before my eyes in a manner similar to the cleansing room door.

"Whoa, I don't know if I'll ever get used to that," I murmured before proceeding through the now open doorway. On the other side was a round circular room. Once we were both inside, Jackson went to the center of the room and motioned for me to follow.

"Brace yourself," He said before the floor lifted and we were taken to another level. When the floor stopped, we were in the center of what appeared to be a ship's control room.

"Where are we?" I asked as I looked around at all of the sophisticated machinery. It looked exactly as one would imagine, futuristic and foreign. There were five sitting areas stationed in different sections with consoles positioned around them. The room was enclosed in a clear glass-like dome that ended at around waist level. I peered out at the vast grassy land that surrounded us.

"We're in a spaceship I think, I haven't been outside to know for sure." Jackson responded "I don't know how far we are from Earth, maybe we're still on Earth, just in a different country." He added. The grassy land was reminiscent of something I'd seen on a Discovery channel program.

"How long have you been here?" I asked after turning to face him.

"One month, five days, seven hours, and twenty-five minutes." He responded, sounding more like a prisoner as opposed to a teen with superpowers. "Now twenty-six minutes." He added.

"You sound like you're serving a prison sentence." I joked. He smiled and released a small chuckle in response.

"This is the longest I've been away from home. It's how I keep it from getting to me I guess. Keeping track of the time gives me a sense of control and keeps me from totally losing my marbles. We haven't been here the whole time, though. We were in space for a while and then underwater before we landed here. I think we're in some sort of spaceship submarine."

"How do you keep track of time?" I asked as I studied his face.

"Anaku gave me this," He responded and pulled a small device from behind his ear.

"What is that?" I asked as I stared at the miniature metallic device in the palm of his hand.

"Uh, it's some kind of futuristic time keeping device." He answered.

"Okay James Bond how does it work?" I inquired sarcastically."

"It locks onto the wearer's brain waves. So no matter what, I'll always know what time it is in my hometown." He answered my question, but I had another deeper one to follow up with, it was a personal question that I wasn't quite sure if I should ask. I proceeded against my better judgment. "Did your parents get kidnapped too?" I asked as I moved closer to him.

"No, I came home from school one day…" He stopped briefly. "When I got home, I… I saw them… they were dead." He finished in a somber, low voice.

"How did they… you know…" I struggled to delicately phrase the question.

"I'm not sure. They looked like they were frozen, and their eyes were missing, and they had wounds… blood was everywhere…" He looked away. "It looked like a horror movie!" He stated as he stared off into the distance. There was a tremble in his voice. It was difficult for him. Heck, it was difficult for me just listening to him. It reminded me of the news report I had watched about the murdered family. It also reminded me of my own misfortune.

"What did you do when you found them? Did you run? Did you call the police? Or did Anaku appear before you were able to?" I wanted to know as much as possible. I couldn't understand why the reptilians killed his parents and abducted mine.

"I panicked, and ran back out of the house. When I stepped outside, I saw a bright blue light and then, I was here.

"So you didn't meet Anaku before coming here?"

"No and yes, I had a dream the night before and in the dream, he warned me that they were coming for me. I tried to tell my Mom about it that morning before I left, but she was busy getting my sister ready for daycare."

"So when you found your parents, was your sister with them? Was she, you know,"

"No, she wasn't there. I don't know where she is, or even if she's alive." Jackson tried to smile as a lone tear rolled down his face. I walked over to him and gave him a hug. He quietly sobbed on my shoulder and I tried to comfort him by lightly rubbing his back. The emotional pain that he was enduring was far deeper than my own. I wondered how he'd managed to keep it together. How he still had it in him to smile and stay so upbeat and jovial.

"How about we change the subject?" I suggested. I felt like a real jerk. I had probed for answers with little regard for Jackson's feelings.

"Sounds good," He mumbled as he wiped his eyes.

"When did you first get your powers?" I asked as he regained his composure.

"Eleven," He replied. "I was up reading a book on magic when an owl came up to my bedroom window. It was the first time I had ever seen one up close in person. I love animals. Anyway," Jackson sometimes manages to get sidetracked when conversing. "I imagined myself being one and before I knew it, I actually became one! Once I realized the change, I panicked and fluttered around the room in a crazy fit."

"So did anyone come in?"

"Yeah, my mother came in and started talking to me. It was weird because she wasn't the least bit bothered by it. She told me that what I was experiencing was normal for our kind."

"Was she a Shapeshifter too?"

"Yeah, she was the one that taught me how to control my powers."

"Wow, well I didn't have that luxury, I'm adopted. Well, I guess I should say I was adopted. When mine started, it was one of the scariest things I had ever experienced."

"I suppose I was fortunate," he replied. A smile formed on his face.

"The rest of your family was normal, I mean regular humans right?" I looked into Jackson's golden warm eyes and felt a connection, a kindred spirit of sorts.

"Yeah. My dad, brother, and sister were as normal as they come." I noticed something that I hadn't picked up on earlier.

"Where's your brother? I don't recall you mentioning that you found him with the rest of your family."

"He wasn't there. He…"

"So they took him too?"

"No… I would rather not talk about him okay?" I could tell that I had touched on another sensitive subject.

"Okay," I murmured as my curiosity loomed.

"Thanks for understanding." He said and flashed a quick smile.

"No problem," was my response. "So anyway, what kind of music are you into?"

# Chapter 7

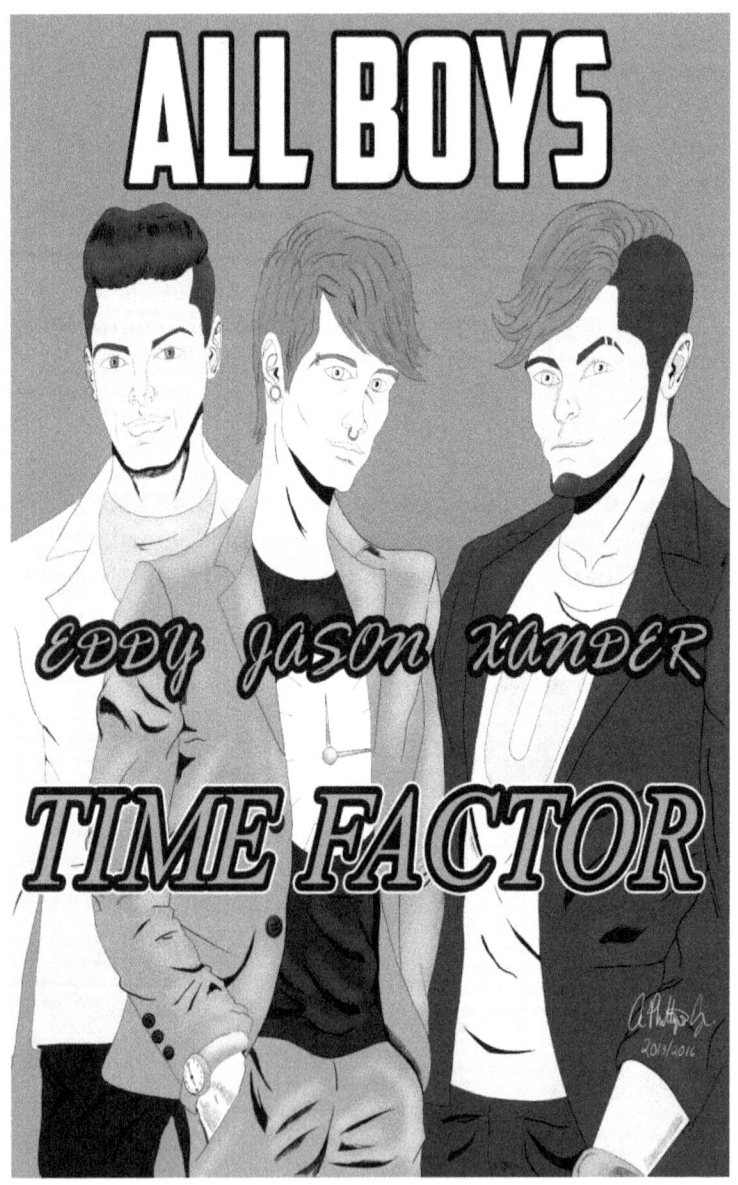

# All Boys

**I WOKE UP TO THE** sound of hard rain hitting the exterior of the ship. The shock of the change was still fresh. Alone at the desk in my room, I stared aimlessly outside as rain saturated the vast green landscape. Dark, brooding gray clouds filled the sky and prevented any light from shining through. Staring at the rain made me think about how bad things had gotten. I felt the lowest of the low. I was anxious and worried about everything. The fate of my parents, the impending war against the reptilians, it was all too much to accept. I stayed up with Jackson for most of the night, which wasn't a bad thing because he's not the person I expected him to be. He is pleasantly the opposite of the persona his physical appearance alluded to, that night really taught me something. The saying, 'Never judge a book by its cover,' truly applies to Jackson. He is quite profound. His shaggy, unkempt appearance does a great job of masking his true beauty. We talked about everything from our favorite video games, to end time prophecies. I found out that we have so much in common that it's crazy. I discovered that he actually likes some of All Boys' music, which was definitely a plus.

When we ran out of things to talk about, we entertained each other with our powers. I watched as he tried to turn into fifty different animals in under five minutes. He only managed to change into forty-two, though he disagreed and firmly believed it was forty-four. We settled on forty-three. After that, we played 'guess what I'm thinking' (which I won of course), and then he led me into a room filled with large heavy objects and dared me to see how much weight I could lift. I practically lifted every single item in the room without even straining the slightest muscle or breaking a sweat. Upon witnessing my seemingly limitless strength, he affectionately gave me the nickname "Mini Hulk", which I took as a strange compliment.

Eventually, Jackson tuckered out and decided to get some rest, and I for some reason chose to stay up. I stayed up thinking about everything that was going on. I thought about the surroundings that I viewed outside of my bedroom window. I wondered if we were still on Earth, or somewhere near it, or light years away from it. My mind ran wild with ideas of the type of life that inhabited it. Regardless of where we were, I was far from any and everything I knew. I drifted off briefly, but my slumber came to an abrupt end courtesy of the recurring 'dragon in the woods,' nightmare.

While sitting alone in my room, I remembered my cell phone. With so much going on, I had completely forgotten about it, which was amazing in itself considering that most teens are glued to them. I found it in the pants that I wore when I arrived. It had less than five percent of battery life left. It would soon be rendered useless thanks to me leaving the charger in my overnight bag. Tears formed in my eyes as I scrolled through the call log. My body trembled with grief as I quietly began to cry. My hushed whimpers went unnoticed as I sat alone on my bed. I was so engulfed in emotional pain, that even if someone had seen me, I wouldn't have even cared. It felt good to release everything that I had been holding inside. In the midst of my emotional breakdown, I accidentally dialed Liz's number. I thought about hanging up, but something inside urged me to wait and see what would happen. It took a while for it to connect, which only added to the anticipation. After a few moments, the call was connected and I could hear the rings through the phone's small speaker. Then, a low whisper brought an end to them.

"Hello," The small voice whispered as the phone rested in my lap. A mixture of shock and excitement flooded my senses as I slowly lifted it up to my ear.

*"Say something"* I thought as the hand holding the phone mildly trembled. "Liz," I whispered into the phone.

"Charisma, where are you?" She asked excitedly, abandoning her whispered tone.

"I'm not sure, but I know that I'm still somewhere on Earth," I replied.

"What happened to you?" She inquired. "Your house was on the news. Are you and your parents okay?" I hesitated to answer her. I didn't have time to explain everything, so I chose not to tell her anything.

"I can't really talk right now. I love you and I'll see you again soon bestie." I murmured before hanging up abruptly. I wanted to tell her everything, but my creepy encounter with Mr. Bemis came to mind. I didn't want to risk him finding out. After hanging up, my thoughts shifted onto another possible benefit that might be had by using my phone. Finding out that my phone worked really made me want to call my parents and see if they were alive.

The phone coverage was pretty much worldwide thanks to the fact that my father traveled extensively. I was just about to dial them when my phone began to vibrate. Liz was calling me back. I quickly swiped ignore and powered it off. Enki walked into my room with his same stone-faced expression. I still wasn't used to seeing a real life Grey Alien. He looked exactly like the depictions on film. I always wondered how someone came up with the idea to create such an odd physically unbalanced looking creature. His large head and frail malnourished underdeveloped body made it seem as if a gust of strong wind would cause him to tip over from the weight of his head. Maybe Enki had comparable thoughts about my race or about humans. Perhaps he thought humans and Enocians looked chimps with less hair.

"I deemed it advantageous to check on you," He said in his usual monotone voice.

"Thanks, I guess." I murmured as I inconspicuously slid my phone underneath my comforter.

"How are you and your suit, adjusting to the new partnership?" He asked.

"Great," I said with infused enthusiasm and a forced smile. My mind was preoccupied with my parents. I wanted to call them so bad. I wanted to know where they were, I yearned for the days when I could once again anticipate my father's return home from his latest business trip. More than anything else in the world, I wanted to hear my father tell quirky stories from his childhood, and see my mother leaving for work, or coming home from it in her plain Jane hospital scrubs. I needed them back more than I needed to breathe! I made up my mind right then and there, that I would get them back, regardless of the cost. "I'm ready to train again," I stated in a determined tone.

"You can train anytime you wish. The training facility is always open. Follow me and I will show you how to operate it appropriately," He responded.

I got up from the bed and did as instructed. We entered the Blue Room and Enki gave me a brief tutorial before letting me give it a go. I started it up exactly as he showed me and I was off into the simulation. The White House rose up out of the ground along with trees and a full, green lawn littered with crumbled parts of the iconic structure. A large menacing object hovered over the national landmark. The sky was dark and foreboding with a few stars scattered throughout it. Reptilians were wreaking havoc all around me. The President's secret service agents were held captive by fear. I was unfazed by all of it. I was ready to save the day. I sprung into action without giving it a second thought. I picked up a car, and tossed it, taking out two reptilians in the process. I then lifted off the ground, and flew directly into the ship, causing it to teeter off balance.

More reptilians emerged and began firing their weapons. I zipped and dodged through the air with more refinement than my previous sessions My confidence was high. I flew circles around their weak attempts. Then, the dragon appeared. It was ten times larger than a reptilian, with wings that were the size of the ones on a commercial airliner. It rose up from the ground with the speed of a jet fighter. It was headed straight at me! The irises of its eyes glowed ghastly green and were surrounded by blood colored sclera. They were as big as the tires on a Ford F-150. It looked exactly like the one from my recurring nightmare. I froze briefly at the sight of him, which gave another reptilian the clear shot he needed. Failing to react swiftly, I caught the brute sting of his laser fire in my shoulder. It sent me spiraling out of the air like a wounded bird. I caught myself seconds before hitting the ground.

I made a haphazard rebound and soared as if my life depended on it. The dragon stayed not far behind, snarling and roaring. I focused and flew as hard and fast as I could. I gained speed, but l still couldn't shake my determined foe. It increased its speed as well. I looked back and saw a huge claw flying toward me. It happened so fast that I was unable to react defensively. The hit made contact. It sent a stinging shock throughout my body and left me disoriented. I felt like a fly freshly whacked by a swatter. I spiraled helplessly, unable to regain control. I wondered if I would crash into one of the walls of the room or if it was much larger than I had believed it to be. Moments later, I crashed into a wooded area. I smashed through various branches before hitting the base of an oak tree. The impact sent me falling to the ground.

I hit the floor of the forest and almost lost consciousness. The simulation packed quite a punch. If it were the real thing, I probably would've died on impact or at least been rendered unconscious. My entire body ached as pain shot throughout it. I was disoriented and my vision was blurred. I struggled to my feet. Panic had set in. A dull throbbing sensation manifested on the right side of my body. My knees almost buckled under the intense urge to give up. It would take nothing for me to think myself out of the simulation. Knowing that it was simulated gave me a comfort level that I couldn't afford. If it was a real situation, I would have had to suck it up and fight through it all, the pain, the disorientation, and the burning desire to accept defeat. I felt the ground shake and saw a large shadow in the distance.

It was coming for me. The dragon was in hot pursuit. I heard the branches break as it forced its way through the trees. I hobbled along holding my side. It was moving fast. I contemplated launching a quick take off, but I was far too dizzy to do so. I started lightly jogging in an effort to put more distance between us. The dragon was moving at an unimaginably fast pace. My jogging did little to aid in my retreat. I realized that it was only a matter of time before I would have to fight for my life. In spite of the circumstances, I still held hope that I would come out on top.

*"C'mon Charisma you can do it,"* I thought as I continued pushing through the pain. I remembered my father and all of his comics. I thought about how the superheroes always managed to find the strength to triumph over their adversities. Those memories gave me exactly what I needed to face my fear, to confront my nightmare and defeat it. I made up my mind to take down the dragon. I stopped jogging and turned to face the direction from which it was approaching. I could hear its deep guttural snarls as it ran full speed, breaking trees and laying siege to everything in its path. The ground quaked exceedingly as it drew closer and closer. I prepared myself as it came into view. It was only yards away and I was ready, ready to conquer my fears and defeat my nightmare. I stood and watched as the agile behemoth burst through the last patch of trees that separated

us. I thought about my parents and felt a deep anger rise from within.

"ALRIGHT UGLY LET'S DANCE," I shouted with balled fists. Tears of anger ran down my face as I stared at the massive simulated threat. Our eyes locked in a brief hate-filled moment. The dragon let out a loud indescribable noise before charging directly at me. Its mouth was full of sharp, dangerous, teeth. They looked like large jagged off-white blades. As it neared me, I cocked back my arm and swung as if my life depended on it. The punch sunk into the creature's face and instantly stopped its charge. The force of the punch sent the scaly beast tumbling back along the path from which it came. My adrenaline kicked into high gear and forced back the pain. I ran after my foe with an absolute determination to finish it. I struck it again, it wailed in agony as the blow cracked one of the bones in its face. The second punch felt better than the first. I struck it a third time, and then a fourth time. Blood splattered and bones shattered as I pounded its face with full unrelenting hits. Its neck and head thrashed wildly in an effort to stop my assault. I was in the zone. Red was all around me. I wanted its death so bad I could taste it. I wanted it to hurt as much as I did. I wanted to translate the hurt held in my heart into an accurate violent physical equivalent.

The dragon's movements stopped, but I continued mercilessly punishing it. I couldn't stop. Causing it pain was therapeutic in a twisted sort of way. I continuously swung until my fists stung with numbness and my forearms burned from the extreme exertion placed upon them. I carried on in spite of it.

"Die!" I screamed at the top of my lungs as it convulsed violently. I couldn't stop myself even if I wanted to. I was far past that point and not wanting to stop only made it that much more deadly. The sensation that I felt while attacking the beast was intensely satisfying. I had so much repressed anger. Each deadly blow helped to dissipate the pent up rage. I held the power of death in my hands. I no longer felt like a victim. I felt far different from the clown fearing teenager that existed mere days ago. I felt closer to a God. The old Charisma was dead, and the new one wanted revenge! The new one wanted to show the Draakunaki that their days of tyranny were drawing to an end. She wanted to ensure their absolute extinction. I was so lost in my anger that I failed to notice Jackson as he entered the room.

"Charisma," he shouted, snapping me out of my murderous fit. Everything began to fade and crumble away. He must have stepped in and shut down my session.

"Huh," I responded, partially coherent, intoxicated by the power that dwelled within me. I turned to address him. The look on his face was full of concern. "I was kind of in the middle of something," I said abrasively. His interruption bothered me and I couldn't help but show it.

"Are you okay?" His question sounded like something one would ask a person who had just fallen off a bike or been a victim of some other ill-fated occurrence.

"I'm fine, just practicing." I uttered in a nonchalant manner.

"Don't you think you're overdoing it a little?" He asked. His tone of voice and body language evoked images of my father from our last disagreement over the sleepover at Liz's.

"No, I was doing it just enough," I replied unpleasantly. I instantly regretted the manner in which it came out. I didn't want him to think I had a problem with him because I didn't. The only problem I had was that I was making a drastic transition and there wasn't a 'For Dummies' book or an app for it. "I'm sorry, I didn't mean to sound snappy. I was just really engaged and you interrupted me."

"Charisma, killing virtual puppets isn't going to help you get through what you're dealing with." Jackson was being a sane voice of reason and it really struck a nerve.

"I just… I can't afford to lose when we encounter the real thing. There is far too much at stake and I don't want to be a weak link."

"Not knowing when too much is too much will make you that. You're overdoing it." He stated before leaning against the frame of the doorway.

"You don't know what you're talking about," I said as my irritation with his lecturing intrusion made itself known; I felt slightly offended by his preachy presence.

"I KNOW EXACTLY WHAT I'M TALKING ABOUT!" He said defensively. "You're losing it!" His remark was something a person might say to someone having a nervous breakdown or some other mental issue, not to someone that mere hours ago you were hanging out and having a good time with.

"HOW DARE YOU SAY THAT," I felt hurt. His words touched a nerve.

"Based on the performance I just witnessed, I'm stating the obvious."

"What are you saying?"

"I'm saying that you enjoyed killing that creature. Enjoying death isn't good. Once you get a taste for it, there's no coming back."

"So you mean to tell me that you don't feel that way? You looked like you were having a ball yesterday."

"That's where you're wrong. I had fun being in the battle, not killing my enemy, there's a difference." He retorted.

"So you mean to tell me that killing the creatures that killed your family doesn't bring you a sense of satisfaction?" I couldn't understand how Jackson could take such a stance considering the losses he had endured because of their kind.

"No, because no matter how many I kill one or a million, it won't bring my family back."

"But those creatures killed your parents and God knows what they did with your sister. If that were me, I would want to kill every last one of them!"

"Well, I guess it's a good thing that you're not me."

"What? YOU—" I felt myself getting flustered.

"Sorry, I shouldn't have said that, but all I'm saying is that just because some of them did it doesn't mean the whole race should be punished for it. I want to fight the good fight and have a clear conscience." Jackson's face turned somber and I knew that something else was bothering him. I tried to read his mind, but for some reason, I couldn't.

"What's really bothering you?" I asked as I walked over toward him.

"Remember when I told you about my half-brother Kenny?" I thought back to the almost three-hour conversation that we'd had the night before but I couldn't recall anything that stood out about his brother.

"I remember you mentioning him briefly," I replied honestly.

"Yeah, well… my brother fell into the wrong crowd, this anti-Muslim group and ended up almost killing a guy. Our family went through a lot because of it, and now our father is dead and—"

"I understand. So you both share the same father?" I interrupted.

"Yes, his mother died when he was a baby. Our father cared for him by himself until my mom came along. Hate, took my brother away from those he loved most." I felt ashamed of myself after Jackson finished. He was right, hating a whole race or species based on the actions of a group of misguided individuals makes the person with the hate the true villain.

"You're right, I guess I was so caught up in my anger that I failed to look at it that way," I responded while looking down at the floor. I didn't want to look at Jackson. I didn't feel like crying and the somber expression on his face would've surely triggered it. I wanted to leave out of the Blue Room and freshen up. Even though the mist did a better job than a good old fashion shower, I still longed for one. I longed to experience the simple things again. "How do you like the mist shower thing?" I asked as my mind entertained thoughts of warm hot steamy water running over my body. Sometimes, the simplest things in life are the ones we miss the most. The things we take for granted haunt us when they are no longer a given.

"Oh, the mist is the coolest thing here! It keeps you fresh all day without deodorant! It takes some getting used to, though. See, the trick to everything here is that it's all controlled by thought." I could tell Jackson was expressing his true feelings, it showed on his face. "I was never a big fan of getting ready in the morning. It was always too many things to do. Now, because of the cool technology here, I'm done with everything in a matter of minutes! The mouth tablets are kinda gross, but it beats brushing, flossing, and gargling."

"I don't know… that hair dome thingy does a rather basic job, what if I want my hair to look a certain way?" I didn't share Jackson's enthusiasm. As a growing woman, I needed options. I needed to have the freedom to change my appearance as I saw fit.

"Didn't you hear what I just said? Everything here is controlled by thought. If you want a Mohawk, simply think it and it's done. Hair streaks, no problem!" Jackson sounded more like a late night infomercial hawker and less like a super powered teen.

"And you can have all of this for the low, low price of never having a normal life again!" I joked in a voice similar to a cheesy product pusher.

"Ha ha, I see you have jokes huh." Jackson murmured.

"Hey, I'm just saying."

"I know, I know, but you can't fault me for trying to find the silver lining right?"

"I suppose Mr. Optimistic." I jabbed. I poked fun of Jackson's optimism, but I understood the reason for it. There was a huge burden on his shoulders. He had a burden that no one person should have to deal with.

"Gotta find reasons to keep smiling, and I think I just found another one." Jackson was obviously flirting with me but I wasn't comfortable reciprocating. I let out a slight giggle and briefly looked away. Even though we had great chemistry, I had eyes for Aiden. He reminded me of one of my favorite actors. Aiden was strong, masculine, and mysterious. I saw Jackson more like a goofy though profound brother, nothing more. I secretly wished that I had spent the night before staying up with Aiden instead. "Awkward moment," Jackson mumbled while looking away and scratching the back of his head. The redness starting to show in his cheeks was a sign of him blushing. I didn't mean to embarrass him, but I didn't want to lead him on.

"It's okay… I understand." I really didn't understand. I didn't understand why or how he could have a crush on me. The feelings I felt between us were those of a blossoming friendship and I guess he perceived it as something else. *"Did I send him any mixed signals?"* I wondered as I smiled at Jackson somewhat nervously.

"Maybe it's too soon…" He uttered, seeming as if he was directing it more so to himself than me.

"Yeah, perhaps…" I couldn't think of anything else to say. Thankfully, our awkward moment was interrupted by Alex.

"If you guys are done kissing, I would like to practice," Alex said, with an 'angry at the world' expression on her face. She was beginning to remind me of Paige Schuster.

"Actually, he was just telling me about the crush you have on him," I said deceitfully.

"Yeah, I was just telling her that you think we'd make a great couple." Jackson added, giving Alex the goo golly eye.

"WHAT? Really Jackson? Wow…" Alex paused, "Anyway, I'm about to practice so either participate or get out of my way." The way she responded was strange. She didn't corroborate the claim, but at the same time, she didn't deny it either. It made me suspicious. The weird moment ended when the room changed into a downtown metropolis. As Alex was lifting off into the air, I was walking out. I decided to do some more exploring. I didn't wait to see if Jackson would follow. I could've cared less. I was mentally writing him off when I heard footfalls behind me.

"Why didn't you stay to practice?" I questioned aloud while still walking, not turning around for a second.

"I was actually planning on practicing later, would you care to join me?" The voice stopped me dead in my tracks. I turned around and saw Aiden. He was dreamy as usual.

"S-sure," I mumbled taken aback by his boyish good looks. He looked as if he had just gotten out of the mist. "I… was just doing a little exploring to get familiarized with this place. Would you care to show me around?" I flashed a cutesy expression.

"Well, I'm not familiar with everything. I've only been here about a month. Maybe we can get familiarized together." He responded close to how I envisioned. I was so excited that I could barely contain it.

"Okay, lead the way," I said before stepping aside and letting him take the lead.

"Wait, first I have to do something." He stopped and suddenly changed into Jackson. "Do you still want to explore with me?" He said with a face that did little to mask his feelings. He was upset and it was quite evident as to why. I could sense jealousy in his tone and mannerism.

"What was that about?" I questioned as I played dumb. I had already figured it out. "I SEE, YOU CAN CHANGE INTO PEOPLE TOO HUH, REAL CUTE!" I fumed. I was bothered by his little trick and saw it as a betrayal of sorts. "If you want to know something, all you have to do is ask. That trick was so juvenile!" I barked. I was equally angry and embarrassed. If he were a reptilian, I would've decorated the walls with his insides!

"So I guess my assumption is right, and what about what you said? IT DIDN'T SEEM VERY MATURE TO ME!" Jackson's voice was now elevated and his golden colored eyes now had a red tint to them.

"OH SO NOW WE'RE DOING TIT FOR TAT HUH?" I was angry. I felt my face getting warm.

"NO, WE'RE NOT! IT WAS JUST A REACTION. I DIDN'T THINK ABOUT IT, I JUST ACTED. I'M MATURE ENOUGH TO ADMIT IT!"

"Maybe I shouldn't have said what I said, but I didn't mean for you to take it the wrong way. It was aimed toward Alex. It was really childish and stupid." We were arguing like a married couple. I say that because I remember the way my parents would argue. Jackson had a point, but I didn't want to admit it. "Look, this is silly. Can we just drop the whole thing? I think the stress that we're under is getting the best of us." I had grown tired of the conversation. It seemed so trivial for us to argue over something so petty, especially when you consider the fact that a race of giant reptilians was looking to wipe out our world.

"Yeah, you're right. We can drop it on one condition,"

"And what's that?"

"You admit that the reason you're not into me is because you have a crush on Aiden."

"Why would I admit to something like that? That's personal, and besides, that's not the reason at all." Part of it was in fact for that reason but what business of his was it?

"Okay, so what is it?"

"Well, for starters, we don't even know each other that well. I've literally only known you a couple of days! Plus—"

"It's not like I'm asking you to be my girlfriend or something, I just want the chance to get to know you without a crush hindering that, and maybe I am a little jealous. I know that besides Drave, Aiden is the guy that all the girls want, and I'm the one that they all end up liking, like a brother. I'm the guy that gets stuck in the friend zone." Jackson was right, and I felt guilty because that's exactly how I felt about him.

"Stop being so hard on yourself, you're great. You have a lot to offer."

"Really, like what?" I was hoping he wouldn't ask that question but he did.

"Well, you're funny, and you're quite profound for your age and you're cute." I really did think he was all of those things, which is why I couldn't figure out why I didn't have a crush on him.

"Cool," Jackson's face lit up which was definitely a good thing because his smile is priceless.

"Definitely cool," I murmured.

"Sorry about my behavior, I don't want to seem psycho, but I've been alone for so long, I guess I just latched onto the first meaningful situation that came my way."

"But you have the others here,"

"Yeah, but before you, Drave, and Sienna came there were only four of us and I was the uncool kid." I was confused by his statement. I wondered if he accidentally said the wrong number.

"You meant the three of you right," I asked anxiously anticipating the answer.

"No, there were four of us."

"Who—" I was curious as to why and how this mystery person left.

"His name was Jason. He wasn't the nicest person to know, he was somewhat of a bully. He's famous or at least he claimed to be, I didn't believe a word of it. He was also powerful and could probably take out a group of reptilians single-handedly."

"What powers did he have?" I was intrigued by the mystery person.

"He could warp time and space. I watched him single-handedly take out like eight simulated reptilians!"

"How did he do that?"

"Well, he used his time control capabilities to age some of them to the point where they literally turned to dust in front of us, and then he wiped out the rest by sending them through a time portal. When he returned them back to our time, there was nothing left but bits and pieces. It was brutal."

"Wow"

"Yeah, he was a real powerhouse. He left because he was sick of being away from the rest of the world. He said he would handle the reptilians by himself."

"How long has he been gone?"

"He left about a week ago." Drave entered the room in an excited manner.

"Hey guys, we might be going into action sooner than expected!" He blurted with an expression that looked as if he were about to burst.

"But, I— we're not ready, I mean... I've only been here a couple of days!" I exclaimed. I felt like a novice swimmer being thrown into the deep end of the pool. I wasn't ready to face flesh and blood Draakunaki, and I definitely didn't think that we were ready as a team.

"You'll be fine. You've got the rest of us with you and besides, I'm in the same boat as you." Drave said in a confident tone.

"What if I mess up? I'm not ready." I had a legitimate concern. I had just begun to control my powers. I felt that I still needed weeks, perhaps even months of training before engaging in real combat.

"Relax you're a natural, you were destined for it, we were destined for it. It's in our blood." Drave was passionate in his proclamation.

"He's right, sometimes opportunities present themselves when you least expect it. It's the unexpected that brings out the best in us." Jackson added. Further promoting the passionate rally started by Drave. Anaku appeared in a quick flash of light.

"We must go now. There is no time to waste." He communicated as his eyes blinked with every syllable. Sienna, Alex, and Aiden all entered into the hallway.

In an instant, we were in the heat of battle. People were running and panicking all around us as reptilians caused havoc.

"Alright people, let's send these overgrown lizards home," Drave yelled before charging into action. A reptilian fired its tornado box at Drave, he teleported just before impact. Aiden stopped it and hurled it back at the creature twice as fast. The creature fired more tornados, to deflect the first one, but that only gave it more power and fury. Aiden manipulated it like a spinning top. It crashed into the reptilian and sucked it up into its raging vortex. The creature howled in agony as the contents of the tornado ripped it apart. Its remains came crashing down on top of a sporty red car that still had a temporary license plate attached to it. Alex, now in the air, hurled monstrous fireballs down on the Draakunaki in rapid succession. Jackson was also engaged in action as a fierce lion. I watched as he dodged laser fire and sunk his large glaring fangs into the face of a huge reptilian. Sienna shot bolts of telekinetic energy as laser shots were deflected by her bubble.

I was so engaged in the things that were unfolding around me that I almost didn't notice a laser gun aimed in my direction. A shot was fired, and I reacted a split second too late. I spun around and the laser shot grazed my shoulder. I stumbled to keep my balance. It hurt far worse than the simulation. I instantly went into a state of panic. It was the real thing. I was definitely in the deep end of the pool. It was either learn how to swim, or die.

I broke out of the initial shock of my wound and ducked for cover behind a parked Toyota. I could hear the laser shots hitting the side of the vehicle as I cowered on the opposite side with fear. Thoughts of death and serious injury ran through my mind as I struggled to build up the courage to fight. I could hear screams and explosions all around me as I stayed behind the foreign made vehicle. My heart fluttered rapidly as I slowly worked myself into fight mode. I had to do something besides continue to hide; which I wouldn't be able to do too much longer considering the damage the lasers were inflicting.

"Okay, here goes nothing," I mumbled before getting a grip on the vehicle. I focused my strength and shoved it in the direction of my enemies. The vehicle flew fast and hard like a baseball pitched from the mound. It struck one of them while narrowly missing the other. I then ran full speed toward the remaining one. I attempted to tackle it, but it was tougher than I expected. The creature resisted with overwhelming brute strength. We wrestled back and forth for control. It wasn't going down easy.

"Enocian, you cannot defeat me." It barked in a harsh deep raspy tone. It eventually broke free of my hold and hit me directly in the face with the butt of its laser gun. The hit sent a sting through my whole body. I recoiled in pain and felt myself being forced to the ground. I landed on the hard concrete with a bone-shattering thud. Between the hit to the face and the hard fall, I was sure that I'd broken or dislocated something. The reptilian was on me and within seconds, I was pinned to the ground. I fought and struggled with all of my might, but it was unbelievably strong. We were deadlocked in our struggle. I was fighting for my life, and it was fighting to take it. "You're weak like the humans that you live among!" He taunted as he continued the fight.

"Get off of me!" I yelled as I forced my upper body muscles to work harder than they'd ever worked before. I slowly started to gain leverage. My arms quivered as I pushed against my foe. I wondered if the others were having as much difficulty as I was. "Ugh," I bellowed as I exerted all of my strength into one concentrated push. The force of my final push got the reptilian from off me. It flew a short distance before slamming into a bus shelter. Glass shattered as the creature's body plowed into the glass, metal, wood structure. I sprung up sore, but still functional and sprinted to finish it off.

Once inside the shelter, I ripped off the wooden bench and used it as a weapon to subdue the reptilian. I repeatedly swung the bench with as much force as I could muster. The wood cracked and splintered from the numerous impacts. The creature was left subdued and bloody though apparently still alive. I contemplated finishing it, but then I remembered the conversation with Jackson in the Blue Room. I was hesitant, but a part of me really had a curious burning desire to find out how much different it would be to take a real life versus a simulation.

*"It would do the same thing to you,"* I thought as I raised the remaining piece of the bench. "It's either you or me, and I'm not dying today!" I stated with absolute certainty before delivering the final deadly blow. It felt as if I was having an outer body experience. I watched as the mangled remnant of the bench came crashing down with lethal force upon the Draakunaki warrior's head. The final impact caused the bench to break completely in half and took the life right out of my foe. I stood momentarily in shock, staring down at the once menacing threat.

His cold, lifeless eyes remained open, with their final gaze fixed upon me. I was trying to process the fact that I had just taken a life. Regardless of the fact that it was a bloodthirsty alien that probably wouldn't have thought twice about taking mine, it was still a life. It was a justifiable kill, but I still felt remorseful for doing it. Taking the reptilian's life was a turning point. I knew that I would never be the same and could never return to the normal life of a teenager. I also came to the conclusion that I could never share my experiences with Liz.

Death would become a constant in my new destined life, something that I would have to accept and eventually grow accustomed to. I was so absorbed with my first kill that I didn't realize my body was healing. The only reason I took notice is because the pain that I had incurred from the battle was rapidly reducing. I could feel my broken bones and dislocated joints, set back into place. The parts of my body that were sore from the battle were itching like crazy.

Within minutes, my body was completely renewed. I felt stronger than I had ever felt. I felt more alive. I walked out of the shelter amazed, invigorated, and deathly frightened all at the same time. I looked at the rest of my team. I had fared better than the rest of them. We were losing. The reptilians were far stronger than the simulations led us to believe. Drave looked exhausted, and the new technology the reptilians had prevented Sienna from disintegrating them. Alex and Aiden were still fighting courageously, but Jackson could not be found.

In that moment, I realized how much I was truly starting to care for him. My eyes frantically scanned around the area searching for my golden eyed friend. I let out a gasp when I finally spotted him. He was unconscious on the ground. I felt my heart stop as the thought of him being dead, entered my head.

"Jackson!" I shouted before I began running toward him. I was mere yards away from him when, a different type of reptilian landed in front of me. It was oddly different from the rest. It was significantly smaller, a little less than six feet and had feminine characteristics. She was dressed in a glowing sleek metallic suit. Her eyes radiated with a pink light. Her hands smoldered in the same manner.

"YOU CAME HERE TO DIE! I will take you down in the same manner as your fallen comrade," She said. Her voice was coarse and otherworldly. She reeked of a scent that was comparable, to the smell emitted from an electronic device left running for an extended period of time.

"Not today!" I retorted before charging at her. I planned on hitting her with as much strength as I could physically muster. In hindsight, it was a very foolish thing to do, but at that moment, I was blinded by my concern for Jackson. She reacted faster than I could've imagined. Her entire body illuminated brightly, giving the appearance of it charging up. She blasted me with the glowing energy. The blast sent a numbing pain throughout my body. I felt myself helplessly fly through the air. I was paralyzed. Whatever the blast was that the reptilian hit me with, had zapped me into an immobile state. I struggled frantically to break the temporary paralysis, to no avail. I was as helpless as a fly stuck to flypaper.

Soaring backward through the air, not knowing what I would crash into or when, was the scariest experience that I had ever endured. I finally hit something; I crashed into the side of a brick building. The sound was a dull, heavy thud. Pieces of brick crumbled on top of me and around me as I came to a complete stop. The crash stung, but not as much as one would expect. I didn't know if I was partially numb from the blast, or the effects of another ability manifesting. Shortly after the crash, I slowly started to regain control of my body. My fingers were the first parts of my body that I regained control over. *"C'mon!"* I thought in frustration as I lay helplessly watching us lose the battle.

Alex went up against the powerful reptilian and was defeated in a matter of minutes. Aiden came to her aid and succumbed to a similar fate. She was extremely powerful. She turned the tide and ripped away any chance that we had of winning. She was a one-man wrecking crew.

As my team fought valiantly against the powerful reptilian, I continued to regain control. I struggled to get up as I watched Drave and Sienna double teamed her. Sienna's telekinetic blasts were deflected by the glowing energy that surrounded the powerful reptilian, and Drave's teleports and speed attacks were all rendered useless.

With our foe distracted, I decided to make one last strike. I saw a street sign pole jutting up from the ravaged concrete. I attempted to dislodge it as quickly and quietly as possible. It took a couple of tries, but I succeeded without diverting my foe's attention. I silently floated toward her. As I neared my target, I wound back the pole in the same manner that I had learned to do with a baseball bat. I had acquired the knowledge from my summers of playing softball. Once I was within reach, I swung for the fences. The pole smacked the reptilian and sent her shooting down the war-torn street. I watched in relief as she made a devastating crash into the windshield of a parked SUV.

We were far from out of the fire; more reptilians had landed and were closing in on us, and the sky was filled with more of their ships. There was no possible way of escape. Drave was weakened from battle and couldn't teleport all of us safely. Sienna was injured but still putting up a fight. Jackson, Alex, and Aiden were all down for the count. We were as good as dead. Just as I was abandoning all hope and preparing myself for one last fight, a blinding light appeared from out of the sky. The light grew, and engulfed everything around me. I couldn't see anything, not even my own hands as I raised them up to my face. I felt the weird, intense motion of my body being lifted, and then the light dissipated and revealed the interior of our ship. Robotic helpers lifted Jackson, Aiden, and Alex and carried them off.

"Where are the robots taking them? Are they going to get medical attention?" I expressed my concern.

"They are being taken to the sustenance chamber. The sustenance will fully restore them." Anaku replied. "You require some as well." I didn't want sustenance. I wanted a victory. It felt terrible knowing that we were brutally defeated. My dad always told me that I didn't handle losing well. I guess he was right. Losing my first battle was a stinging pain. I wanted to rescue my parents and almost getting killed was not how I would do it.

"Fine," I mumbled before reluctantly exiting the room. I was highly upset over the loss, but it still didn't deter my raging appetite. To say I was starving would be an understatement. It felt like I hadn't eaten or had any kind of nourishment in days.

As I slowly walked down the corridor toward the chamber, images of the loss replayed in my head. I tried to block them out. I wanted so desperately to find something to preoccupy my focus. My body was healed, but my mind was another matter entirely.

"Maybe I'll feel better afterward," I tried to convince myself as I reached the chamber. I went inside and saw the robotic aids setting Jackson inside one of the sustenance tubes. Alex and Aiden were already inside of their respective tubes. The sight of them unconscious and beaten helped usher out the tears that I had been keeping at bay. I lowered myself into the tube. The lid closed as I wiped my tear stained cheeks. The sustenance entered the tube and a peaceful rest soon followed.

I awoke fully rejuvenated and full but still a little worse for wear emotionally. The pain of loss still lingered in my heart. It tore at the very fabric of my soul. I recalled the battle and seeing Jackson injured on the ground. The tube opened. I jumped out of it and looked around the room wildly.

"Jackson," I called out as I looked for my newfound friend/comrade. The threat that we faced as a group was overwhelmingly brutal and more numerous than I had imagined. The simulations paled in comparison. The safety net that the Blue Room provided gave us a false sense of security. I relaxed a little after I noticed Jackson still receiving sustenance. Alex and Aiden's tubes were empty, and I wasn't sure if Drave and Sienna had gotten sustenance. I walked over to Jackson's tube, and looked inside. He looked so peaceful. I wanted so desperately for him to awaken. I needed to talk to him. I needed to let him know that I had gotten attached to him during our brief time together. I started to realize that maybe we needed each other for support, to stay sane and optimistic. "I'll see you in a few," I uttered as I placed my hand on the lid of the tube.

# Chapter 8

# So much for fresh air…

I STEPPED OUT OF THE ROOM with a head filled with troubled thoughts that I needed to clear. More importantly, I needed to know if my parents were still alive. As I began walking down the hall, a light went on in my head. Sienna's psychic abilities were pretty extraordinary. I wondered if it would be possible for her to find out if they were still alive.

"*Sienna,*" I communicated telepathically, to see if she would respond before I did the physical footwork.

"*Charisma, what can I help you with? You seem to be highly distressed.*" She communicated back.

"*I need to see you. I want to know if you can do something for me.*" I replied.

"*Sure, stop by the Rec Room.*" She said.

"*Where is—*"

"*Keep heading down, it's the fifth door on your right.*" She interjected before I could finish my question. I did as instructed and found Sienna meditating in front of a small pink glowing orb.

"Uh, hey," I uttered timidly as I entered the room.

"Hey Chariz," She responded. The pink orb faded and she stood up. "You want me to see if your parents are still alive right?"

"How did… oh, that's right." I murmured, remembering the reason why I paid her a visit.

"I was working on it when you came in. I got everything I needed while you were headed down here. I didn't pick up anything, but that doesn't necessarily mean that they're... you know... It could just mean that they're not being held on this planet." Sienna's explanation did little to overshadow the fact that my parents could possibly be deceased.

"Thanks for trying. I need to get out of here." I responded hastily before leaving out of the room. *"I need some fresh air. It would definitely help right now,"* I thought as I ran down the hall. I wanted to be alone. I had a lot of things to sort through and I preferred doing so in open spaces. I felt confined inside of the ship. Normally, when I needed to think alone, I would go to the park or the backyard to clear my head. Being cooped up inside of the Star Trek Enterprise wasn't cutting it. "How can I get out of here?" I questioned aloud while running down the hall. I remembered the first room I came in when I arrived. I hastily headed in that direction. I ran down the corridor and barely stopped to acknowledge Alex as I rushed by her. Her facial expression was disgruntled as usual. I didn't have time to engage in catty conversation. My brain was overloaded with pain, grief, and fear of the uncertain future that lay ahead. I ran through the ever-expansive Blue Room. After running for what seemed like forever, I finally reached the exit.

I went through the door and arrived at my destination. I saw a wooden door with what appeared to be some sort of futuristic security panel on the wall next to it. It didn't have numbers like a typical security panel, which made it even more foreign. I didn't know the access code and didn't recall Anaku using it when we arrived. I stood staring perplexed at the panel. I needed to get out and it was the only thing standing in the way of my freedom. I looked at the panel and took a guess. I pressed several of the lit areas on the touch panel and it blinked red. It was safe to assume that my guess was incorrect. "Ugh," I mumbled before trying again. I got the same result. "Third time's the charm," I uttered before giving it one last shot. The third time wasn't the charm. Instead of blinking red, the entire panel lit up.

In a fit of aggravation, I rammed my fist into the panel. Sparks flew out of it as a result of the impact. My hand sunk deep into it and left a gaping hole in its wake. The door sprung open and revealed the outside. I peered out across the lush green land that surrounded us. It was breathtakingly beautiful. As I gazed out at the picturesque scenery, I noticed what appeared to be a bluff in the distance. It seemed like the perfect place to sit alone and think. The ship was docked quite a distance from off the ground. I guesstimated it to be at least a fifty foot drop. At that height, flight was the only option of travel available.

I glanced back at the bluff. It was gorgeously inviting. I had always wanted to look out from one and I figured that it was definitely a good time to do so. I took a second to focus and then flew into the air. The air felt great as I soared. The fresh, crisp, high altitude oxygen filled my lungs. The intense sensation produced by the speed and the wind flowing through my hair brought back memories of riding with my dad on I-480 in his classic cherry red convertible. I miss those times. Having the ability to fly is priceless. The quick flight to the bluff temporarily helped to clear my head.

The landing wasn't the best, a little on the rough side to say the least. It produced a loud thud that echoed and sent a small quake throughout the structure. After taking a brief walk, I found the perfect spot to perch and think. It was a pocket right on the edge with a few small trees to offer seclusion. I took a seat and began mulling over everything that was weighing me down. I thought about my parents, the humiliating loss of our first battle, Liz, and last but not least, Jackson. Tears filled my eyes as I sat alone, staring off into the horizon.

Memories of past holidays and other special moments shared with my parents cycled through my head as I stared with blurry eyes over the vast landscape. I saw birds soaring through the clear blue sky. They looked as if they didn't have a trouble in the world. I envied them. The only cares that they had were where they would find food and build nests. They didn't have to worry about defending the world against a brutal race of aliens. They weren't burdened with having to adjust to major life changes. Their minds weren't overburdened with unsolved mysteries. While staring at the birds, one in particular, caught my notice. It flew slightly different from the others and while they were in flocks, it flew alone.

*"Maybe he's sick,"* I thought before writing it off and focusing back on my troubles. I continued sobbing uncontrollably. I cried so much that after some time, my eyes felt sore. I rubbed them for comfort, but that only seemed to make it worse. It added a nagging sting to the soreness. I was in the middle of trying to blink off the sting when a small noise somewhere behind me caught my ear. It was a slight rustling sound. It sounded as if a creature was scurrying through the grass. I turned and saw a fairly large brown rabbit approaching. As soon as it realized that I had noticed, it stopped dead in its tracks. We stared at one another silently. I deliberately made a small movement to see if it would run off. It did the exact opposite. It actually began to move forward toward me! This made me curious. *"What intentions, does this bunny have?"* I wondered. *"Is it starving and looking for food? Maybe it has rabies?"* I speculated as it continued uninterrupted. It settled once we were positioned side by side. It looked out over the vast green land.

"So… do you come here often?" A small voice murmured, taking me completely by surprise. What was even more shocking was the fact that it was coming from the rabbit!

"Wha…" I was at a loss for words. Then I realized who the rabbit really was. It brightened my day. I actually broke out in slight laughter. "Real cute Jackson," I uttered.

Jackson awake and back to his old tricks was definitely a sight for sore eyes.

"What's up Doc?" He said in his best Bugs Bunny impression. The small tone of his voice, made him sound more like a chipmunk than the actual character. It was so cheesy that it forced more laughter to escape from me.

"That was pretty lame." I eked out in between laughs.

"It doesn't matter. It did exactly what I wanted it to do." He remarked with what I assumed was a smile on his face. It was hard to tell given the fact that he was still in rabbit form.

"Mmm hmm, and what exactly did it achieve?" I asked with one brow raised. I kind of had an idea of what he was going to say, but I went along with it anyway.

"It brought a smile to your face and as a bonus, made you laugh." His response was similar to the response that I had envisioned beforehand.

"Thank you, I really needed that." I replied. Jackson turned back into his human form and sat next to me with his legs crossed Indian style.

"Try not to be too hard on yourself, everybody loses. It's a part of life." Jackson said.

"I know, but my parents and the world are depending on me, on us. We can't let them down. I don't want it to happen again." I said with determination in my voice and an overwhelming urge in my spirit.

"It won't trust me, we won't allow it," Jackson reassured.

"Bu—" The sight of a large fast approaching object in the sky stopped me from continuing. Jackson must've seen it too, because he stretched out his arm and pointed in the same direction that the object was in.

"Do you—" before he could ask the question, the ship disappeared. In the blink of an eye, it reappeared directly behind the pocket in which we were seated. It was as if it knew exactly where we were, like it was specifically looking for us. The shadow of the ship engulfed the area that we were nestled in. As we started to climb up from the pocket, an intense blast of energy shot out from the ship and completely decimated the edge of the bluff. Panic rose inside of me as I scrambled and tried to get a handle on what was transpiring. The ground beneath us crumbled before we had a chance to flee. We fell along with chunks of the bluff. Jackson and I looked at one another and instantly knew what the other was thinking. I caught myself mid-fall and Jackson quickly morphed into a bald eagle. I cut through the air like a rocket. Jackson flapped wildly and desperately tried to keep up. I looked back and saw a swarm of reptilians with special flight suits descending from out of the craft. Seconds later, bursts of laser fire danced in the air around us. Jackson and I did our best to avoid a direct hit. I twirled, spiraled, and zigzagged as if my life depended on it and Jackson tried his best to do the same. His large wings flapped with urgency.

It seemed like we had a fighting chance of making it back to the ship unscathed. Then things took a turn for the worse. A shot hit Jackson's left wing. The shot threw his flight off balance. Seconds later, another shot hit his opposite wing. I saw him go down hard and fast. A sense of urgency took hold of me and I quickly went into action. I dropped back and dived to save him. Terrified out of his mind, Jackson frantically flapped his damaged wings hoping to catch a good pocket of air.

"Hold on Jack, I got you," I yelled as I pursued my free falling comrade. Jackson looked up with fear-filled eyes and continued to flap vigorously in an effort to slow himself down. As much as he tried, his efforts were futile. His speed continued to increase rapidly. The reptilians were still hot on our tails. Laser fire zipped past me, barely missing by inches. I focused and forced myself to go as fast as my abilities would allow. Jackson was fast approaching the ground and there was still a lot of distance between us. The distance rapidly began to shrink as I reached my maximum speed. I was moving so fast that everything around me became a blur. I had tunnel vision. The only things that I could see clearly were Jackson and the ground not far below. More laser fire whizzed by and seconds later, I felt a stinging sensation on the side of my body. It was confirmation that I had just been shot. The initial pain was intense, but I fought valiantly to block it out. I didn't have the luxury of giving in to it. Our lives depended on my actions. I maintained my focus and the pain gradually started to subside. I got within inches of Jackson and yelled, "Morph and grab my hand!" Jackson obeyed and seconds later, I felt his panicked grip.

We were less than a minute away from being splattered Enocians. With Jackson in tow, I quickly turned my body in the opposite direction. I struggled to keep my focus during the transition. We continued to go down as I fought with all of my might to break free from the gravitational pull. Lasers continued to rain in our direction. I swayed to and fro in an effort to avoid them, all while keeping my focus on ascending. We gradually started to climb. The reptilians refused to let up the assault. They wanted us dead! "Hold on," I said before speed bursting. We flew directly through their laser assault and managed to get out with only minimal injuries.

Once I got us to a high enough distance, I was faced with another challenge. I couldn't take us directly back to the ship. I didn't want to risk leading the reptilians to it. I had to think of a temporary safe haven and I had to do it fast. The high-speed flying was taking its toll.

My muscles were beginning to ache. My eyes scanned over our vast surroundings. It was hard to make out a safe area to retreat. Everything around us was foreign. The only thing that I knew for certain was the direction of the ship. Having to make a split second decision, I decided to go the exact opposite of it.

I turned in the direction, and took off. Jackson, still hanging on, latched his remaining hand onto my arm and closed his eyes. I saw a wooded area in the distance and figured that it would probably be our best hope for survival.

"Jackson, I'm going to land in that wooded area up ahead. The coverage and density could be used to our advantage. It might be our best chance of losing them!" I yelled as the wind gushed past my face. "Hold on tight," I instructed before increasing my speed. As we were approaching our destination, I started to slow down. I looked back and noticed that the reptilians were far but not as far as I had hoped they would be. With little time spare, I made a shaky landing in the thick, dense wooded sanctuary.

As I looked around, I mentally put together a rough on the fly plan of escape. After giving a quick look over of the place, I set to work on my impromptu plan. I started by ripping off a couple of thick, sturdy branches from one of the trees. I handed one over to Jackson before proceeding with my work. He was hurt, but would still able to put up a fight. The branches weren't the best thing to use going against monsters with lasers, but they could prove to be deadly if used for sneak attacks, which was the last resort if my plan didn't work.

The second phase of my plan was to create a fake path that would give the appearance of a crash landing. It would throw them off our trail and buy us enough time to escape. Jackson tried to help, but his injuries and lack of super strength and enhanced speed hindered him from doing so effectively. I focused my strength before using it to knock over a medium sized tree. I didn't waste time watching it fall. I quickly started on another one. After that was done, I used the tip of my branch to create a series of imprints in the dirt. Finally, I ripped off twigs and leaves and scattered them along the path. I took a brief second to admire my handy work. It looked convincing enough.

"Let's find a good hiding spot." I uttered to Jackson. He nodded his head in agreement. We saw a thick group of bushes and ducked behind them. About a minute later, the first handful of reptilians arrived. They saw my faux crash landing and did exactly as I had hoped they would. More Draakunaki arrived and followed suit. I considered Jackson's condition and the number of reptilians. They outnumbered us ten to one. Escaping was the only logical choice, but if we didn't wait until they moved a far enough distance from where we were hidden, the plan would be futile. Jackson and I watched as they thoroughly searched through every inch of my work. As they were busy examining the path, a rustling sound in the distance caught their attention. One of them whispered something in their native tongue and then they all set off to find whatever had produced the sound. I was grateful for the distraction, it gave us the opening that we needed. Once they were far enough, I knew it was time.

"Jackson," I whispered as our enemies continued moving farther and farther away.

"Yes," He responded.

"We have to make our move now." I stated while my eyes stayed glued in the direction of the faux path. "Make sure that you get a solid grip on me," I instructed. He slowly wrapped his arms around my waist. "No funny business," I added.

"My arms are already sore, the last thing I need is for them to be broken or ripped off." He shot back. I turned and saw his usual handsome smile.

"I'm going to count to three and takeoff okay," I murmured.

"Gotcha," he replied.

I waited another moment to make sure they were far enough not to detect our movements. I felt beads of sweat form on my forehead and brow as I anxiously anticipated the moment. The sounds of the birds and other wildlife around us would help cover our big move but it was still unclear if more were waiting in the wings or if they had already found the ship. Regardless if they found the ship or not we couldn't stay hidden for long and it was our only viable option. Once they were far enough, I focused and began the countdown.

"1…" Jackson tightened his grip around me, "2…" I clenched my fists, "3!" Half of a second after 3 escaped from my lips, we burst out of the woods like a war missile.

*"Sienna,"* I sent out my mental beacon and waited for a response. *"What if they've already found the ship?"* was the terrifying thought that forced its way into my mind as I anxiously waited for her to respond. I shot a quick glance behind to make sure we weren't being followed. Other than a few scattered birds, the sky was clear. I assumed that the reptilians were still on a wild goose chase. I looked ahead in the direction that I remembered the ship being in. I was surprised not to see it.

"Where did the ship go?" I asked aloud while frantically looking about the landscape.

"Huh, what," Jackson responded.

"THE SHIP JACKSON, THE SHIP," I exclaimed as we drew ever nearer to where it was supposed to be stationed.

"I don't know." He replied. "It was just there before I left to look for you." He added.

"Do you think that they left us?" I questioned. I was past the point of being worried. I was completely distraught. It instantly evoked memories of the time I had gotten lost in a department store when I was five. I remembered sobbing uncontrollably as I frantically looked down isle after isle occupied by strangers. That same dreadful sensation had taken hold of me.

"I don't think so unless the reptilians got to them first." His response only added to my panic.

"Do you have any suggestions on what we should do?" I asked as I thought of an alternate place to land and take refuge.

*"We're still here."* Sienna telepathically communicated, giving me the pleasant surprise that I needed.

*"We don't see you,"* I responded, still unable to see any sign of the ship.

*"We're here trust me."* I didn't understand what she meant. There wasn't anything there. *"Look, with your mind's eye. I'll help you."* She said.

*"Okay,"* I replied. I took a deep breath and focused my mind. Like a mirage, the ship slowly started to come into view. It didn't fully materialize. It was semi-transparent, which was weird. It seemed to be cloaked. After a few seconds of examining the ship, I found the door that I had used earlier.

The cloaking technology didn't seem to affect the inside of the ship. The interior was completely visible. "I think you need to go rest in the sustenance chamber," I said to Jackson. He was looking worse for wear. The wounds that he incurred from our brief scrape with the reptilians looked pretty bad. The wound on my side was almost completely healed. My pain tolerance seemed to be increasing. The burns from the laser fire should have triggered more of a painful response. I barely felt anything.

We slowly moved out of the living room replica and into what appeared to be an active session in the Blue Room. We walked through crumbled structures and urban debris. I saw Drave engaged in battle. He was so preoccupied with battling the simulated reptilians, that he didn't even notice us as we quietly slipped past. We made sure to walk as fast as possible to get out of the simulation. After narrowly escaping with our lives, the last thing we needed was a simulated reminder. We made it to the other side of the vast room and exited into the hallway. I wondered where Sienna and the others were. It was clear that the reptilians didn't find them.

We journeyed along the corridor silently. Neither Jackson nor I were in a talkative mood. I wondered if being rescued by me bothered him.

"How do you feel about being rescued by me?" The question escaped before I had the chance to dress it up and make it not sound so straightforward.

"What do you mean, a save is a save right?" He replied. I wasn't sure if he absolutely meant it, or if he was trying to avoid giving me a straight answer.

"You know what I mean, by me being a girl and y—"

"Look, if I didn't say anything why are you thinking about it?" He uttered in a defensive tone. I guess I touched a nerve.

"Well, most guys—" He cut me off yet again.

"I'm not most guys." He shot back aggressively. I was definitely going somewhere that I needed not to go.

"I didn't mean it like that, I just meant… um, never mind." I decided to drop the matter entirely.

"That's fine by me," he retorted. "These wounds really aren't as comfortable as they advertised on the infomercial." Jackson changed his demeanor in a split second. He went from being seemingly irritated to his normal jokey self. He was quite the character.

"I see it doesn't take long for you to bounce back," I stated as I forced a slight smile.

"Sorry for being snappy," Jackson said, staring at me with his golden eyes. They were full of life as always.

"It's okay, I understand." I really didn't understand but it seemed like the best thing to say at that moment.

We went into the sustenance chamber. I decided to get a quick charge as well. I had taken a few shots so I figured that it might be needed. Jackson and I stepped inside of our respective tubes. He paused and turned toward me.

"Hey Chariz," Jackson murmured.

"Yes," I uttered.

"That was awesome!" He said in a sincere tone.

"Yeah, it was pretty epic," was my quick, simple response before putting the rest of my body inside of the tube. The tube closed and the sustenance gradually began to fill it. Some much needed rest soon followed.

I opened my eyes and realized that I was no longer in the tube. I was in my bed. I glossed around the room. Something on one of the walls made me do a double take. One of my All Boys posters was missing a member; my favorite member, Jason Niles. I got out of the bed and walked over toward the poster, not taking my eyes off it for a second.

"What..." I mumbled before slowly extending my arm and touching it with my hand. The poster was cold to the touch. While staring at the poster, I heard someone moving behind me. I turned around and saw Aiden and Alex in my room. It was unclear how they had gotten there or the purpose of their visit. I looked at them. They looked at me. None of us said a word. We stood silently staring at each other. At least that was what I assumed until I noticed that their eyes weren't directed at me, they appeared to be looking through me at the wall. I felt a cold draft on the back of my neck.

I turned and saw a weird glowing portal. I didn't recall it being there before. It was the size of a door, though not in the shape of one. It was oval shaped and pulsating with energy. I backed away from the mysterious portal and bumped into Alex in the process. I turned to address her. She didn't even acknowledge the fact that we had just bumped into each other. Normally she'd be ready to chew my head off with insults. She politely sidestepped and continued moving toward the portal. Aiden reached the portal first. I watched as he placed his foot inside. He turned and gave me a somber look before stepping completely inside. Then Alex began going into the portal. When she was about halfway in, she too turned and addressed me. The look in her eyes was one of the strangest, I'd ever seen. She opened her mouth and then...

I woke up back inside of the tube. The sustenance had almost completely dispersed. I looked over at the neighboring tube and saw Jackson inside. "Jackson," I called out as the tube began to open. Once it was completely open, I immediately exited. I wondered if Anaku knew about my brief venture outside. I found it weird that he didn't address us when we returned. I exited the chamber and went in search of him.

"Anaku where are you?" I questioned aloud while lightly jogging down the hall. "Anaku," I called out again. I was about to call out a third time, but then I saw someone step out of one of the rooms. I saw the one that Jackson had told me about, I saw Jason. Not just any Jason, the one, and only Jason from my favorite group, All Boys. I was star struck. For a moment, I thought that I was hallucinating. I didn't know if I should keep running toward him or turn back around. I halted my sprint. *"Am I really back on the ship? Am I even awake? Is this really happening?"* were the questions that skipped through my mind, as I began to turn and head in the opposite direction. I had made my first step to walk away when Jason called out to me.

"Hey," I stopped and slowly turned back to face him. As I turned, time itself seemed to stand still. Before I could blink, Jason was standing right in front of me looking exactly as he had on the posters plastered all over my bedroom walls. He was as dreamy as ever. At that moment, my crush for Aiden flew out the window. I was instantly smitten. Seeing as how Jackson was still in the sustenance chamber, I knew it wasn't him playing another trick on me.

"You, you're..." was all I could release from my lips.

"I know who I am now why don't you tell me who you are." He said smoothly in his hot British accent.

"I-I'm Charisma, Charisma Grey," was my shaky stammered response.

"Okay, well Charisma, it's nice to meet you and you guys really need my help." He said arrogantly. I felt insulted, but wanted to give him the benefit of the doubt.

"What do you mean?" I questioned. My mood instantly went from excited to slightly defensive.

"I mean that you guys need more training. I saw you get owned by the lizard boys." He bluntly stated.

"Well, that's a great thing to say when first meeting someone." I murmured sarcastically. "I would hope that you were raised with better manners," I said coldly. Superstar or not, I still didn't accept being insulted.

"Whoa, whoa, I didn't quite mean it like that, I meant that the simulations provided by the Blue Room are bloody inaccurate and can't possibly prepare you for what's really out there." He explained. I thought about the encounter from earlier and realized that there was some truth to his statement.

"I suppose, go on," I responded.

"Trust me, they are, that's why I left. I figured my chances were a lot better on my own. The experience I've gained while being in the real world is quite invaluable." He said before flashing the same signature smile I had seen on billboards and album covers. "Don't get me wrong, Anaku means well, but in my opinion, he's going about it all wrong." It all made sense. I remembered when there was a rumor spreading around about Jason leaving the group and not being seen for two whole weeks. There was also another rumor about attempts on his life.

"Hold on, if you're really Jason from All Boys, how are you here now? Aren't you supposed to be on tour?"

"The industry has ways of spinning something to make it sound quite common when really it's not."

"What do you mean?"

"They lie to the news sources and besides, I'm sure you've heard the rumors of me leaving the band and missing show dates correct?"

"Yeah well—"

"Don't you get it, that's how it always works; it's been going on for ages."

"So you never wanted to leave the group and all of the rumors of you starting a solo career are false?"

"Yes and so are the ones about me having an illness, it's all rubbish because the powers that be don't think the public is ready to know the truth." His words sounded sincere and the look in his eyes was that of a person with nothing to hide.

"And what exactly is the truth?"

"The truth is that reptilians have been eyeing to take over this world for quite some time, and the world's military forces have been diligently working to prevent it." The truth was frightening but considering the circumstances, it made all the sense in the world.

"So how are they able to cover it up so well? Wouldn't the truth have gotten out by now? The world is a big place and—"

"They hide it by putting it in our faces. They put the truth out in bits and pieces and mix it with wild far-fetched fairy tales. They put so much spin and bloody fluff on it that it all sounds like pure madness!"

"You mean—"

"I mean that most wars that you hear about between countries are really quite the contrary. Most of the time, it is the countries joining forces to prevent a reptilian invasion."

"I think I understand."

"Yeah, and for the record, I'm not sixteen. I'm really eighteen. It was just one of the many lies that they put together for my career."

"What are some of the others?" My mind was open and I was completely engaged in our conversation.

"Um, well," His voice changed from British to American, "I'm not from England, not even close. I'm from Toledo, Ohio."

"Wow, that's some truth." I uttered.

"Yep, and that's just the tip of the iceberg!"

"But it's really you guys singing right?"

"Yes, that's the one thing I can say is true."

"Great, well at least I can still be a fan of your music."

"You're a fan?" Jason sounded surprised.

"Of course I am what teenage girl isn't?"

"I can think of a few, my ex-girlfriend being one of them."

"So, Jackson told me that you time travel, how does that work exactly?" I asked while my mind ran wild with the possibilities.

"Yes, I can travel through time."

"Do you have to be careful when time traveling? Can you run into a future version of yourself or get stuck or—"

"That's not how it works." He said apparently frustrated by my lack of knowledge on the subject. "When you go forward in time, it alternates the linear path of the time continuum."

"Speak English, please!" I murmured.

"Basically, it changes how things would've gone if you never went ahead. So if someone expects to go into the future and see themselves, they are going to be very disappointed when they find out that the leap changed their course of history."

"Okay," I mumbled as I digested the information. Before we could continue our conversation, Anaku appeared.

"Hey Mr. A," Jason said in a cordial manner.

"Hello Jason, I am elated that you decided to return." Anaku replied.

"You guys need me." Jason stated arrogantly.

"I see your bumptious nature has returned as well." Anaku retorted. I wanted to say something, but I didn't know if it would be appropriate. I was self-conscious and didn't want my comments to seem out of place. "Charisma, I would like a word with you later." He added.

"No, let's talk now," I responded with a hint of anger. "Why did you let us go into battle? What was the purpose of sending us to almost get killed?" My words escaped my mouth before I had a chance to properly process them.

"We needed more data to update the simulations, and there was no other choice. You are Earth's last hope." Anaku responded.

"What if someone would have died? What would you have done then?" I asked the questions and expected sufficient answers.

"I have precautions in place to—" Anaku was explaining before Jason interjected.

"All of the so-called precautions and I never see you engaging in combat." Jason spewed angrily. "We're the ones risking our lives, so why do we need you?" Jason made a valid point. It was precisely what I was thinking. We were on the same page. There was a brief moment of silence. I wondered if Anaku had emotions like humans. I wondered if the things Jason said bothered him. Thoughts of going rogue and leaving with Jason pushed their way into my psyche. I briefly looked away from the two of them and realized I wasn't the only one listening to Jason give Anaku an earful. Sienna and Drave were in the hall as well.

"I've heard about you! I don't think it's a good idea for you to be here, stick to making music!" Drave barked flexing his alpha male nature. He was tense with anger. His fists were balled, his jaw was tightened, and his eyes were full of disdain. If looks could kill, I would've been a witness to a homicide.

"I guess you're another noob huh? How about you be a good little soldier and run along now." Jason shot back as a sneer formed on his face. "I'm sure Anaku will summon you when you're needed," He added. He was the exact opposite of the sweet British boy he portrayed in the limelight. I was seriously rethinking my crush.

"How about we go to the Blue Room and I show you just how good of a soldier I am." Drave challenged.

"You need to practice a little more before challenging me, I saw your battle," Jason said as a means of further provoking Drave.

"You can't be serious! I can definitely hold my own against you. You're too full of yourself and need to be DEFLATED!"

"Really, well who's gonna do it? OBVIOUSLY NOT YOU! I wouldn't want to embarrass you in front of your girlfriend," Jason said before winking at Sienna.

"THAT'S ENOUGH," Anaku interjected. "The reason why I cannot participate is because it goes against my beliefs. I am not permitted to engage in combat. Under the laws of the Religion of One and the Master Creator, devoted followers are only permitted to assist in nonviolent ways. That is the way it has been and the way it will always be.

"If Jason is right, how are we supposed to possibly defeat them? What's the point of hiding?" I now saw the clarity in Jason's stance. There wasn't a point in hiding until the next battle. Precautions in place or not, we needed to know our enemy. We needed to know their weaknesses, if any, in order to eliminate them as a threat. "I can't even leave the ship to get some fresh air without almost being killed!" I stated boldly. I wanted Anaku to say something in response. I needed him to acknowledge just how crazy things were.

"We're not hiding, don't listen to Jason we're preparing and Anaku is doing what he needs to do to assist us. It's up to us to decide Earth's fate." Sienna interjected obviously siding with Drave and Anaku's view. We both had biases, hers because of her obligation to Drave and mine because of my adulation for Jason.

"The reptilians have nonhuman detecting devices that are always searching for us. Outside of this ship, there are very few places that we can hide from the Draakunaki." Anaku's said.

"I highly doubt that. I've been doing just fine on my own." Jason retorted.

"Oh, so is that why we almost got killed today?" Jackson said as he entered the hall. "I find it really odd that on the day you happen to show up, they show up as well." He added insinuating that there was some sort of connection and not merely a coincidence.

"Well, well, I see little Jack has joined the party." Jason insulted.

"I see you're as full of yourself as ever," Jackson retorted.

"Anyway, I didn't come here to quarrel. I came with an offer, a chance to live a somewhat normal life." Jason said. "I have a proposition."

"What are you up to?" Drave asked, with one of his eyebrows raised.

"I'm not up to anything, hear me out." I tried to read Jason's thoughts but they were scrambled. I assumed he was mentally blocking us. "I came back to bring you guys with me. I came to offer you a full expense paid trip to freedom."

"How do you propose to do that?" Anaku asked. He seemed as curious as the rest of us as to what Jason's plan might be.

"I propose to do so by making them a part of my entourage. My band has a massive world tour coming up, so they would go along for the ride." Jason announced which sounded like my dream come true even if under stranger than fiction circumstances.

"That is not a very sound plan," Anaku replied.

"It's very sound. I have every aspect of it thought out. I will have around the clock security, plus our powers and you know how powerful I am." Jason was so full of himself that I doubted anything could've deflated him.

"What makes you think that will work? Do you honestly believe what you're saying? You're as crazy as the typical celebrity!" Drave shot back. It was obvious that he wasn't going anywhere.

"I have it covered, oh and thanks for the compliment," Jason replied. "I say that you let everyone decide what he or she would like to do. If they choose to stay so be it." I saw through Jason's arrogance. It was obvious that something had occurred, and it was the motivating factor for his return. He knew our enemy was too powerful for him to face alone. He needed us more than we needed him.

"Although I highly advise against it, it is ultimately up to them to decide." Anaku conceded. Jason presented the option, and it was up to us to choose. I had wished it was an easy choice, but like most tough decisions in life, it wasn't. There were advantages to both, but there were drawbacks as well. For those who did choose to stay, they would be at a disadvantage as far as real life experience, and being in the know. Whoever chose to leave would have to accept the fact that their lives would be in constant danger. There would be no safe zone. According to Jason, our enemies were far more of a threat than we could've possibly imagined. The enticement of his celebrity status and lifestyle was fading. The old me, wouldn't have thought twice about the decision and would've been on board before he even made the offer.

After the heated debate in the hall, cooler heads prevailed and it was decided that everyone would take a moment to process and then regroup in the main control room to get things finalized. I had just started walking toward my room when Anaku stopped me.

"Charisma, I would like to converse with you in private." He said in a slightly softer tone than usual.

"Um, okay," I responded.

"Follow me," He instructed. I nodded my head in agreement and did as he asked. I already knew what he wanted to address. It was exactly what I wanted to happen. I followed Anaku into an unfamiliar room. The room had the appearance of a futuristic study. I say it was futuristic because it didn't have the typical things that one might find in such a room. The books, shelving, and trappings of a typical study were replaced by numerous metallic racks. The racks housed a vast assortment of weird glowing tablets that were all about the size of an iPad.

"Okay, talk." I dryly uttered. My body language exuded the anger that I held. My arms were crossed, my brow was furrowed and my mouth was frowning.

"I wanted to discuss your actions from earlier. Why did you leave?"

"I... I needed to clear my head and I couldn't do it cooped up in this ship." was my answer.

"I understand that being confined inside of this vessel isn't something that you're accustomed to but it's the only way to keep you safe." He said as he did something that totally caught me off guard. He gently grabbed my hand. I assumed that it was his way of expressing his sincere concern for my welfare.

"Yeah, this transition is pretty rough on me. I'm still getting used to it." I confessed, with tears starting to form in my eyes.

"I promise you that one day soon our mutual enemy will be defeated and you will once again regain your freedom." He said. "And if you choose to go with Jason, please help him to see the fallacy in his thinking. I will summon you when it is time for us to meet." Anaku added before disappearing. I stayed in the room and glossed over the vast array of tablets, wishing that I had asked Anaku what they were for and why there was so many of them. They were as numerous as the books in a library. Being as curious as a cat, I grabbed one of them. It was cool to the touch. It had a whole bunch of weird symbols flashing on it. I didn't know what to make of it so I returned it to its proper place and left.

When the time came for the meeting, I was in my room, sitting on the bed in deep thought. A telepathic summoning from Anaku brought it to an end. I hesitantly slid out of my bed and walked slowly toward the door. Once outside the room, I saw Jackson further down the hall.

"Hey," I called out to him and quickened my pace. He turned and smiled instantly when he saw me.

"It's that time," He remarked as I neared him. He looked as if he were unsure of the whole matter. He wasn't the only one. I was on the fence as well.

"Yep," I murmured and smiled faintly. "Have you decided yet?"

"I don't know... I have nothing to go back to but on the other hand, I need better preparation so I won't end up getting owned again." What happened in the battle really bothered him. The simulations did nothing to help him prepare. In my opinion, it gave us all a false sense of security. Jackson was lost. He needed something more than what Anaku was providing. He needed a reason to believe in himself.

"Well, you're not the only one. I'm still a little unsure as well." I placed my hand on his shoulder. "How about we decide together?" I suggested.

"What, are we making a pact or something?" He quizzed, with one of his eyebrows raised.

"Yes, that's exactly what I was thinking," I said while keeping a sharp gaze upon him.

"Okay," He shot back quickly with a smile. "Besides, I'm used to being rescued by you." He let out a slight chuckle and flashed his signature humorous smile. "I don't know if I would be able to live with myself if Jason saved me. He'd never let me live it down."

"You got a point, maybe I should start rubbing in all the saves," I shot back jokingly before giving him a playful nudge. We walked together for the duration of the trip to the control room.

When we arrived at the meeting, Jason and the others were already gathered around Anaku and Enki, whom I hadn't seen in a while. Enki was very mysterious. I was still very intrigued by the fact of him being an actual Grey Alien. I had so many questions that I wanted to ask him. I really wanted to know if the rumors about his species were true. In hindsight, I know it was a bit naïve on my part to assume that he would have the answers, but if I had encountered his kind before, it wouldn't have crossed my mind.

"Okay everyone, you know why we're all gathered here, so what have you? Are you going to stay here and remain in isolation, or come with me and LIVE?" Jason asked as he looked around the room at all of us. I already knew that Drave and Sienna were staying. I wasn't so sure about Alex and Aiden, especially after our performance in the battle. I wrestled with the choice while I waited anxiously to see who else would stay.

"You already know where we stand," Drave spoke up for both he and Sienna. She nodded in agreement and placed her arm around his waist.

"It figures," Jason remarked, "Who else wishes to stay?" He asked looking directly at Aiden and Alex.

"We're definitely not staying here," Alex responded with a sense of displeasure in her tone. "I'm not a loser, so I don't want to be associated with any!" She said in a rude manner before cutting her eyes in my direction. She must have already had a feeling of how I would choose. I thought that things had gotten resolved between us, but the look that she gave me let me know otherwise.

"I'm staying," I announced with forced confidence to mask any hint of doubt. I didn't want to give Alex the satisfaction of letting her know that her remark bothered me.

"Me too," Jackson chimed in before giving me a slight nudge. "Oh, and just for the record, we're not losers, heck Charisma has only been here a couple of days so—"

"Anyway, are you sure you want to stay Charisma?" Jason asked in a softer tone, giving me a concerned look. It made me have doubts about my decision.

"Yes, she is sure. WE are sure!" Jackson said in a bold, authoritative manner. It was clear that he felt threatened by Jason's presence. I didn't think about it at the time, but with Aiden, and Jason out of the picture, it gave Jackson the opportunity he needed to win my affection.

"Okay cowboy, so be it. Alright, you guys ready?" He said before the area behind him warped and stretched. A small glowing orb emerged in the center of the area. Swirls of energy manifested around the orb. The area turned into a time portal. I watched as Jason stepped through the newly formed portal, then Alex, and finally Aiden. Aiden turned and gave one last look before he and the portal vanished.

"Well, I guess it's up to the four of us now," Drave commented with a sigh.

"Maybe it's better that way." Sienna said before smiling at Drave. Her devotion was undeniable. She would follow him anywhere, even through the flames of Hades if need be. I wondered how someone could have that strong of a bond. Up to that point, I had never even imagined myself being in her shoes. Sure, I had my crushes on celebrities and what not, but I couldn't fathom being that deeply in love with another person. Heck, I couldn't even fathom the concept of being in love! It was something that I didn't understand but wanted to experience when the time came. A brief thought of being that way with Jackson flashed in my head. I quickly dismissed it and focused on the uncertain road that lay ahead of us.

"I got dibs on being Johnny Storm!" Jackson quipped

"Fantastic fail Jackson," I murmured as I placed my hand on my face and shook my head in disapproval.

"Too soon, huh," Jackson uttered sheepishly with the proverbial egg on his face.

"Yeah," Drave uttered with a look of disappointment.

"Tough crowd… how about we go practice. Anaku, is the Blue Room updated?" Jackson said changing the subject swiftly. "We need to show Jason and Co. what we're made of!" Bad comedic timing aside, Jackson was driven. The disappointing battle and the harrowing escape had awoken something inside of him. I found myself oddly attracted to whatever it was.

"Yes, it is ready," Anaku replied. Knowing that the Blue Room was updated made me feel a lot better.

"Okay team lets hit it," Drave said. We all exited the control room. I looked back just as Anaku and Enki were vanishing. In a weird way, I felt a bond forming. It was starting to feel like home.

Once inside the Blue Room, we formulated a plan of attack based on what we knew about our enemies. Our plan was to use Drave's speed and teleportation powers to pull a sneak attack while Sienna used her powers to disorient the reptilians. Once the plan was set, we readied ourselves as the environment around us changed into a downtown metropolis. The reptilian mimics looked exactly like the ones from our previous encounter. I felt myself tense up at the sight of the female reptilian that had bested me.

"Is everyone ready?" Drave questioned loudly. I nodded in response as Jackson and Sienna vocalized their responses. "Alright honey, do your thing." Drave murmured affectionately to Sienna. She lit up with telekinetic energy before I teleported with Jackson and Drave. We appeared further down the street, about thirty yards from where the reptilians were. There was more than a handful to dispose of.

I grabbed the first car I saw and hurled it directly at the female reptilian doppelganger. The car flew with unrivaled speed and accuracy, hitting its target dead on. Several others turned in response and Jackson leaped into action. I watched as he morphed into a tiger while in midair. He landed with unbound fury onto the biggest of the reptilians. The creature tried to fire his weapon but was no match for Jackson's unbridled rage and speed. Drave ran circles around another one, distracting it long enough for me to knock it senseless with a well-placed punch. The force of the punch sent it flying through the air, and into the side of a building.

"Good one," Drave said as he gave me a thumb-up. The eruption of laser fire brought our congratulatory moment to an end. I ducked as Drave ran in a zigzagged blur directly at the culprits. He was so fast that their shots were far from near misses. Jackson finished off his foe and joined me as I used Drave's distraction to my advantage. I wrapped my arms around a mailbox and ripped it from out of the ground.

"Once I toss this, we take to the air and strike," I instructed before throwing the mailbox with all of my might. The mailbox sped through the air like a fast pitch fresh off the mound. Jackson turned into a large vulture and we ascended into the air. The mailbox struck one of the reptilians like a freight train and sent it flying down the street. I had a bird's eye view of the street. I pinpointed the area that I wanted to hit with a special attack that I told Drave about, it was something that I had yet to attempt. I had seen it performed in a video game. "Wish me luck," I murmured as I got myself into position.

"Ladies first, and good luck," Jackson squawked. It was strange seeing a vulture talk. I took a deep breath and aimed my body in a downward position. I focused and began my dive out of the sky. I picked up speed quickly. I was nervous about the impact. I promised myself that if I survived unscathed, I would definitely perfect it. Within seconds, I was directly above a group of reptilians. Then, like a scene out of an epic movie, I smashed into the concrete. The force of my attack sent shock waves through the ground, causing an explosion like effect, knocking over all of the reptilians like bowling pins. After regaining my bearings, I quickly glanced above and saw a large elephant descending. I sprinted out of the way, seconds before Jackson slammed to the ground, killing at least three reptilians in the process. It was a gory sight, to say the least. Only a couple of reptilians remained, and we now had them surrounded.

"Give up now or suffer the consequences!" Drave commanded. His voice was strong and his face held a fearless expression. One of the remaining reptilians spoke something in a weird foreign language before it began to morph. The other one followed suit. They grew rapidly. Large horns sprouted over various parts of their bodies. They grew to roughly 30 feet in height. I went off instinct and rushed the one nearest to me. I rammed one of its legs with all of my might. My attack forced the gigantic reptilian off balance. It stumbled and eventually tripped over a parked delivery truck, sending it falling backward into a neighboring building. Fragments of the building crumbled on top of and around it as it tried to brace itself. While the reptilian tried to get its bearings, a large chunk of the building fell on its head. The impact rendered it unconscious.

I turned and noticed Jackson had grown as well. His new size rivaled that of the remaining reptilian. What happened next was a battle of huge proportions literally. Jackson made the first move. He swung a quick jab, missing the creature's face. His mistimed punch made him stumble and left him open to a swift knee in the gut courtesy of the reptilian. The creature's counter strike looked as if it knocked the wind out of Jackson. His face creased up with pain as he staggered before falling to his knees. The impact caused the ground to quake. A sense of urgency instantly overtook me. I flew into the air right at the creature's face.

I had almost reached my mark when the palm of a huge hand swatted me out of the sky as if I were nothing but a mere bug. The hit stung all over my body. It was a shockingly unexpected sensation. It was as if I had just been dunked into a pool of ice water. I fell hard and fast. I was bracing myself for impact when something stopped me. It wasn't a gradual, somewhat natural stop, it was more like when a car is seconds from having an accident, and the driver slams on the brakes. The sudden stop sent my heart into overdrive. I hung, suspended in midair like a puppet on strings.

*"It's okay, I got you,"* I heard Sienna's voice and was relieved. She slowly lowered me to the ground.

*"Thanks,"* I communicated back before turning my attention to the battle. Drave was using his speed and teleportation as a diversion to give Jackson time to recuperate. He was teleporting; dropping bricks and other debris on top of the towering humanoid. The giant looked frustrated as it tried to strike Drave. While it was distracted, Jackson recovered and took another swing. This time the punch landed, hitting the creature directly in the chest. The hit stunned the reptilian and caused it to crash backward into a large skyscraper. The sound of the impact was extremely loud. It sounded as if a wrecking crew was doing a demolition job. Parts of the building rained out of the sky.

A woman had gotten her leg trapped under a piece of concrete and would've surely been killed by the falling debris if something wasn't done to prevent it. I leaped into action. The clock was ticking. I flew hastily to her aid. I reached the woman, and effortlessly snatched away the piece of concrete. Her leg looked bad. I was sure parts of it were broken. I grabbed the injured woman and flew like a jet out of the danger zone. The woman looked and felt so real, that for a moment, I had forgotten that she was merely part of the simulation. I wondered if she was derived from real life data, or simply just a random anomaly.

*"Where should I take her?"* I wondered as I surveyed the area. I was high enough to have a somewhat clear view of most of the city. I spotted a hospital a few blocks away and decided it would be the best place to take her. "Hold on tight," I instructed before increasing my speed. I had gotten the hang of flying. I carefully landed with the woman in my arms. Luckily, medical staff members were outside in front of

the entrance. I relinquished her into their care, and headed off back to the battle.

I returned just as the giant was defeated. Drave, Jackson, and Sienna all appeared to be in good shape.

"Where did you go?" Jackson asked as he returned to his normal size.

"I took an injured woman to the hospital. I'm glad it's just a simulation." I murmured shortly after landing.

"It's good to see you're taking this serious," Drave said in approval of my deed.

"There's more to being a hero than just beating the crap out of baddies!" I said with a small giggle.

"My point exactly," Drave walked over toward me as the room returned back to normal. "We may not have all of the experience in the world, but I think we're going to make a great team," Drave stated proudly as he placed his hand on my shoulder.

"Got that right, we'll show those other guys you just watch," Jackson interjected.

"How about we do a couple more simulations to get our chemistry together and smooth out the edges," Sienna suggested. "We should focus more on what you did Charisma. We need to be more aware of innocent bystanders." It felt good for someone such as Sienna to acknowledge me. Someone that I had looked up to and sometimes secretly envied. "By the way, good job," She added, further boosting my confidence.

"Thanks," I humbly uttered.

"Yeah, you looked just like a real life superhero." Jackson furthered with his golden eyes sparkling brightly. "Alright, it's my turn to load up a Sim. Just wait until you see it." He stated while keeping his enthusiastic gaze upon me. Within seconds, the room morphed into Paris, France, complete with the Eiffel Tower. "How do you like it?" He inquired like an eager child waiting for their parent's approval.

I had only seen the Eiffel Tower in World Studies class and on TV. Seeing a life-size replica of it was breathtaking, to say the least.

"Wow, it's pretty neat," I replied, wishing I had used a better descriptive. "I mean… it's pretty cool." I wanted to say something romantic, but given the circumstances, it was best that I didn't.

"What are you up to Jack?" Drave questioned suspiciously with his brow slightly raised.

"Something that you should be doing, I hope you didn't forget our special day is soon approaching," Sienna said, reminding Drave of their upcoming anniversary. The two had been going steady for longer than most Hollywood celebrities stayed married. My mom often scoffed at the stories she would read about the celebs and their microwave marriages. She would almost always make the comment that they didn't have what real couples had. She stressed that they lacked the patience, selflessness, and dedication to go the distance. She always told me I would understand when I got older. Being a hero is sort of like that, I suppose. It takes a lot of sacrifice and dedication to devote one's self to such a selfless life.

"You're making me look bad Jack," Drave joked and gave Jackson a playful jab. "Honey, I have something special planned, you just wait and see." He murmured to Sienna "Now let's get down to business."

The room changed from Paris, and morphed into another scenario. It transformed into a decimated version of Downtown Cleveland. I could tell by the familiar landscapes that surrounded us. Living most of my life near Cleveland, I was very familiar with it. Screaming citizens hastily ushered past us. They were fleeing from the chaos erupting at the opposite end of the street. The reptilians were laying waste to everything in their path. They had to be stopped. The need to defend kicked into high gear. I launched into the air. I wanted to be the first one in. Sienna wasn't far behind. I was determined to get it right, to master the art of saving the day.

I saw my targets. There were at least ten reptilians clustered in the middle of the chaos. They were armed with weaponry that varied greatly. Some had lasers and others had tornado boxes or energy blasters. A replica of the female Draakunaki powerhouse stood out from all of the rest. She looked exactly liked the real reptilian that bested us in our first battle. I watched as her metallic glowing suit charged up and glowed even brighter just before expelling a powerful burst of energy. The energy was powerful enough to knock everything out of her path, mailboxes, cars, trees, and even parts of the street itself. She was powerful.

The fallout from the blast instantly killed the souls unfortunate enough to be in its blast radius. Others were lucky if you want to call it that, to either be maimed, or trapped under the heavy debris. I could hear their urgent screams for help, as I got closer to the mayhem. This one voice, in particular, stood out from the rest. It was the voice of a child. His screams conveyed just how dire the situation had become. I had to make a choice whether to begin the assault or save him. I decided on the latter. *"Sienna, give me cover."* I communicated telepathically before diving in to begin my search. She began expelling telekinetic energy blasts as I descended to the rescue. The distraction from Sienna gave me the cover I needed. I made a somewhat discreet landing and wasted no time starting the search. Jackson landed seconds later and morphed into a bloodhound.

"Lead the way," I directed as I lifted and shifted a heavy concrete slab out of the way. The simulation was gravely real. I could feel the panic mixed with adrenaline as I searched for the boy. His screams echoed loudly through the caved in rubble. The sight of Jackson as a dog sniffing for a scent would've been quite humorous in a normal situation, but this was definitely an exception. Jackson stopped at a pile of crumbled brick and mortar. He stepped aside and I

182 Anthony D. Phillips Jr.

frantically hurled away chunks of the broken building. I was too absorbed in the search to pay attention to anything that was going on around me, which was a big mistake. A reptilian had gotten wind of our search efforts and was fast approaching. I cleared away enough of the rubble and uncovered an outstretched arm.

"Help, get me out of here please!" The boy said in a weak quivery voice.

"Hold on I gotcha," I replied as I continued removing rubble. I finished removing the wreckage and lifted the boy out of a small hole underneath it. The boy appeared to be in his preteens. He was covered in dirt and blood. I had almost completely removed him when a laser blast penetrated his chest cavity. The boy let out a sigh of pain and began to shake as his eyes rolled into the back of his head. He collapsed and I subsequently turned to see Jackson in the form of a black bear, attacking the reptilian responsible for firing the fatal shot. Anger shot up through my bones and I rushed into battle. As Jackson struggled with the treacherous reptilian, I saw my window of opportunity. I did a quick jet burst and struck the reptilian with a monstrous punch to the face. I felt its jawbone break as my fist sunk into its hard leathery skin. It lifted off the ground and moments later, hit the hard pavement. Jackson morphed back to his normal form with a disappointed look on his face.

"I had it, why did you go and do that?" He questioned in an exasperated tone.

"Obviously you didn't or the person I was rescuing wouldn't have been shot!" I fired back almost as a reflex, not really taking into consideration the effect it would have on the already tense situation. I had a right to feel how I felt. Simulation or not, we had just lost an innocent life.

"I responded as soon as I could." He reasoned.

"Well, I responded how I felt I had to," was my retort. Our tempers flared and we totally forgot that we were in the middle of a session. The Blue Room returned back to normal and put an end to our petty squabble.

"What's wrong with you guys?" Drave asked, frustrated by our lack of focus.

"I was saving someone and they ended up getting killed because Jackson didn't cover me" I fumed. At the time, I felt that I had every reason to be mad. If it had happened in real life, there would be blood on our hands.

"You guys would've lost more lives arguing like children in the middle of a battle! This isn't a game. If that were to happen in real life, we would be dead, along with the people we're trying to rescue!" Drave lectured like a disappointed parent. He had only been there a little longer than me and had already assumed the role of leader. He was a natural. He made me realize how foolish my actions had been.

"Sorry. I, I guess I just got too wrapped up in rescuing and losing that boy angered me," was my attempt at apologizing and at the same time rationalizing my behavior.

"Yeah, I guess we got a bit out of hand," Jackson added.

"You two need to get over whatever it is that you're hung up on. When we're in a real battle, we need to operate as one, no weak links," He paused before continuing. "The odds are stacked against us and they outnumber us one hundred to one. And Charisma," he shifted his focus to me, "It would probably have worked better if we cleared out the area before you tried to rescue someone." He took his focus off me and resumed. "We're done for the day. We will start again tomorrow. That should be enough time for you two to work out your issues." Drave exited the room with Sienna not far behind.

Jackson and I were now alone and staring at one another. I struggled for something to say, but it was of no use. I had already said a mouthful and I was sure Jackson felt the same. He looked just as awkward and remained silent as well. I slowly started to walk away. I reached the door and turned to give Jackson one last look.

"Sorry," I murmured before walking out. I hastily retreated to my bedroom and locked the door behind me. I plopped down on the bed and mentally went over the event.

The rest of the day was awkwardly strange. I stayed in my room for a few hours thinking and wishing that I would've left with the others. I had missed my one shining opportunity. I kept hoping that Aiden and Jason would return. It was really more of a wish. I knew they wouldn't be back for a long time, if at all. I was somewhat envious of them. I wanted the freedom of being home, but with my parents gone, it was more of a wish, a hoop dream, something that wouldn't be possible. *"How are they going to adjust to life on the road?"* I wondered as I thought about Aiden, and Alex. *"How long will they travel in Jason's All Boys' entourage? Will they eventually part ways with him? Can they survive a full-scale reptilian attack?"* Were some of the many unanswered questions that came to fruition in my head, even though Alex was a moody jerk, I still couldn't bear the thought of her getting killed by our common enemy.

A slight knock on the door interrupted my thoughts. I had a hunch that Jackson was the person on the other side of it and if that was the case, I wasn't ready to be bothered with him. I contemplated remaining silent until whoever it was got the hint.

*"I know you're up, I want to talk."* Sienna's voice echoed in my head.

*"Come in,"* was my mental response. The door opened, Sienna floated in, and the door closed back behind her. "I guess making a normal entrance would've been beneath you." I joked and gave her a smile.

"No, it's not that. I just like to work on my abilities. Practice makes perfect." She responded. "That's how I mastered my powers in such a short period of time."

"How long did it take you?" I questioned.

"About a month,"

"Really?" she had such mastery over her abilities that it seemed as if she came out of the womb using them.

"Yup, I got my psychic ability first at the end of my sophomore year. The other abilities started to manifest at the beginning of my junior year."

"So can you read all minds, both human and alien?" I asked.

"Yes and no. I tried to read Jason's but I couldn't seem to get a fix on it and I can't read Enki's to save the life of me."

"I can read human minds." I confessed. "Can you read Anaku's?"

"Most of the time I can but there are certain moments where it seems like he blocks me."

"Wow, I've only read his mind once and it was by accident, but anyway, have you discovered all of your abilities? Do we have a limit?" I felt like someone in need of prescription glasses. I definitely needed clarity.

"I'm not sure. I really wish I had an answer. Maybe there isn't a limit, maybe we continually grow in our abilities." The possibility of endless growth was both promising and disappointing. It was disappointing because it meant that there was a possibility of never reaching my full potential. I'm not an immortal, at least not that I know of.

"So there's a chance that we can become even more powerful than we already are?" I asked highly intrigued by the possibilities.

"Yes, it all depends on your alien DNA. At least that's what Enki told me."

"Speaking of Enki, why is he hardly ever around? I've only seen him a handful of times since I've been here."

"He's always busy creating and fixing things. That's his forte. According to Anaku, the suits were his creation.

Anyway, Jackson's outside of your door. Do you want me to let him in?"

"Um, yeah, I guess," I replied and watched as the doorknob twisted, followed by the door swinging open to reveal a bashful Jackson.

"Come in," I murmured with a smile. Jackson had a bashful grin on his face as he nervously strolled into the room.

"Hey Sienna, do you mind if we have a moment?" He asked politely.

"Go ahead, I was just leaving," she replied before leaving in the same manner in which she came.

"Look Charisma, I'm going to get straight to the point, I... I shouldn't have snapped at you earlier. I'm sorry." He stated in a low remorseful manner.

"It's okay, I was wrong too," I replied. Besides, I couldn't have him take all of the blame. I could've reacted differently, but the heat of battle triggered something in me. It triggered a side of me that I was quite unaware of, an edgy, aggressive side that if used properly could be quite an asset.

"I think we both need more practice. I should've handled that reptilian. If it were real life, I would have that boy's blood on my hands and—"

"We would've and he wasn't, so let's not allow it to happen in an actual battle." I interrupted, putting an end to his remorseful rant. "Now let's cut this pity party short and go practice."

"Alright," Jackson replied.

We practiced for at least an hour before deciding to call it quits.

As I was preparing to take a quick mist, Sienna contacted me. *Why did we let them leave? Why did Anaku allow them to leave?* She asked, more as rhetorical questions. Neither one of us had the answers.

*"I really don't know, maybe Anaku knows something we don't,"* I responded, hoping that there was perhaps a grand plan in motion and that's why he allowed them to go.

*"I hope you're right because we're taking a big risk by letting them go off on their own."* Sienna projected. I understood her concern. They were as good as dead if the Draakunaki decided to wage a full-scale attack on them. I wanted to go on a mission to get them back before the reptilians got a chance to get to them.

*"I know,"* I stopped and thought about what she said. *"Hey, are you thinking what I'm thinking?"* I asked, wondering if she had read my thoughts pertaining to finding the others.

*"Yep, but the problem is going to be convincing Drave."* Sienna knew as well as me how much of an issue it was going to be to get him on board.

*"Well, hopefully, we won't have to do it without him."* I remarked.

*"We won't. I'll get him on board."*

*"Okay and I'll talk to Jackson and Anaku,"* I stated.

*"Sounds good,"* She responded. We ended our conversation and I proceeded to take a quick mist.

# Chapter 9

# A win for the home team

"WE NEED TO GET TO THEM BEFORE THE REPTILIANS DO," I stated with my eyes locked on Drave. I was hoping that the talk with Sienna had softened him up. Boy was I wrong.

"You're kidding me right," Drave said with a look of disbelief.

"No, I'm serious. Working together may be our only hope of winning this thing." I stated, undeniably confident in my decision. "We shouldn't have let them go in the first place!"

"We don't need them! They chose to leave, and we're better off without them!" Drave was being stubborn and still holding a grunge despite the lengthy conversation Sienna had with him before the meeting. It was definitely not the type of attitude that we needed from someone who considered himself the leader. I really wanted to chew him out but I knew that it would only further complicate things.

"Look, I know you and Jason, don't see eye to eye, and you feel betrayed by Alex and Aiden's decision to leave, but we need to push all of that aside and focus on the common good," I said, sounding like a leader within my own right.

"That was very well put," Sienna said.

"Thanks," I replied humbly.

"She does have a point," Jackson added, which surprised me considering his competitive feelings toward Jason and Aiden concerning my affection.

"Thanks, Jackson." I murmured. I felt a smile form on my face. It was three to one. The odds were in my favor. Drave stood in silence obviously mulling over the situation.

*"I know she's right, but I don't think it will work."* Was one of his thoughts that I accidentally read.

"What do you have to lose?" I uttered in response to his doubt.

"The whole world if we're not careful. Jason is reckless and egotistical and Alex is a hot head with a less than favorable disposition."

"Okay, but what about Aiden? He seems to follow along well with the team concept." I said as a means of infusing a pro against Drave's cons.

"He was never my concern."

"We have no other option, and you know it."

"Fine, but since you want them back, you're going to have to handle them." Drave's words were a complete and somewhat pleasant surprise. It was the beginning of a transition that would eventually lead to a shift in leadership; something that I was completely unaware of at the time.

"So you're saying that if and when they return to the fold, that I will be responsible for managing them." I wondered if he actually thought that I was capable of such a feat or if he really just wanted to discourage us, mainly me from carrying out such a plan; or maybe, just maybe, he wanted me to learn firsthand how difficult it was to keep clashing personalities working toward the same common goal.

"Exactly," He responded with his trademark smile.

"Okay, I'm up for the challenge. Now we have to find them. Sienna, I need you to do a scan and see if you can pick up any of them. If you do, let them know that we need to talk." The clever smile on Drave's face quickly faded as a direct result of my response. He must have surely hoped that I would've gotten discouraged, but I was quite the opposite. I love a challenge. Life needs challenges to keep us from getting bored.

"I started on it five minutes ago," She murmured. Her eyes had a bright pink glow. "I think I found them. They must be pretty far, because their scans are faint." She said as her eyes glowed brighter. "I'm sending them a message now," I wondered how far was far. I also wondered if they were on the All Boys tour.

"Do you know roughly about how far they are?" I asked.

"They're in America." She responded as she continued scanning.

"Okay, well, we need to get to them. Drave, are you ready?"

"Yeah, I suppose, but shouldn't we tell Anaku about this?"

"There is no need to, I was already informed," Anaku said as he made his appearance in the room. Drave was about to say something, but Sienna interjected.

"She already told him about it before I told you," Sienna stated with a smile. "I found them, they're in Seattle," She was amazingly brilliant with her abilities. I wondered how she could pinpoint them so precisely.

"So I guess I'm the last to know," Drave asked with a hint of dismay.

"Yes, because you're as stubborn as they come, so we saved the most difficult for last," Sienna replied.

"Be aware that the Draakunaki will be able to track you anywhere outside of this ship," Anaku stated just as Enki walked into the room.

"Not if you have on one of these," He said as he held up a device that looked something like a wristwatch.

"What is that?" I asked while pointing at it.

"It's a portable DNA scan jamming device." Enki answered. "It will allow you to go unnoticed while out looking for the others. Anaku informed me of the incident from earlier." He said before walking over and placing the device on my wrist. "I have one for each of you, as well as for Alex, Aiden, and Jason." He added.

We arrived on the roof of a building in downtown Seattle just before sunset. It was vibrant with life. The smell of fresh rain still hung in the evening air. The lights of the city illuminated the thick dark cloud filled sky. It substituted for the barely there light from the setting sun. I looked out over the vast landscape and was overwhelmed by the sheer size of it. It looked so much smaller in pictures and movies. It was quite a surreal experience. I wondered if Jason was prepping for a concert. I also wondered what Aiden and Alex would be doing while Jason performed at the concert. It was foolish of Jason to carry on with his fake pop star lifestyle in spite of the impending doom that awaited all of us at the hands of the Draakunaki.

"Follow me," Sienna instructed. She went over to the rooftop exit and forced it open with a telekinetic blow. We all shuttered down the stairwell after her. She led us to the penthouse suite level. As we walked down the hall, I began receiving thoughts from occupants of the suites as we passed them. Most of them were things I cared to know nothing about. They made me really want to get what we came for and split sooner than later. One of the penthouse suites that we passed had loud music resonating through the walls with two big burly guards stationed on opposite sides of the suite's door. They shot us weird glances as we passed them. I guess four young people in weird outfits would garner that kind of reaction. I was sure that the guarded suite was the one. It threw me for a loop when Sienna didn't stop. She kept walking right past the guards and continued down the hall.

*"Huh,"* I thought as I followed her. We walked a little further and Sienna stopped in front of a suite that seemed to be the complete opposite.

"This one right here," Sienna uttered as she stopped in front of the door. The noise resonating through the walls sounded quite different from what I expected to hear. Sienna gently forced open the door, and casually entered. I wasn't far behind. The inside of the suite looked like something out of an E3 special as opposed to a hotel party. There were several gaming consoles set up in front of massive flat screen TVs. It was quite refreshing considering the things that were often rumored to go on in musician hotel rooms. I guess Jason was right. Everything wasn't what it seemed in the entertainment industry; or maybe, just maybe, he was smarter than I gave him credit for. I glanced at the screens displaying various matches currently in session. I didn't see any sign of Alex, Aiden, or Jason.

*"Where are they?"* I asked telepathically. It was shocking to see how much the video games captivated everyone in the room. They barely noticed us as we continued through the luxury suite. The glances were so brief that I don't even think the fact that we weren't suppose to be there registered in their brains.

"Cool, Cosplayers," One of the gamers mumbled before turning his attention back to his game. A slight chuckle escaped from my mouth in response to it. The lack of security and the odd theme of the party, I started to understand the reason for the massive pre-concert gaming session. It was the perfect cover for someone famous wishing to hide from life-threatening bloodthirsty aliens and crazed fans alike. We walked into one of the bedrooms and found Alex and Aiden playing cards. I wasted no time with formalities. I got straight to the point.

"Are you guys ready?" I asked bluntly.

"Ready for what," Alex asked. The freedom of life on the go did little to soften her hard disposition.

"You know why we're here Alex." Sienna stated.

"What's the rush? We're safe right where we are." Aiden added. I was surprised by his statement, but more so by the delivery. He seemed to have adopted the same nasty disposition as his sour sibling.

"What's with the tude'?" I asked as I positioned my hands on my hips.

"I don't know what you're talking about Chariz, it seems like you're the one that has one. Look at how you came in here, no hi how are you doing, just straight business."

"It's not like that it's—" I tried to interject, but was quickly cut off.

"Wait, let me finish. You didn't ask if we were okay or if we've been attacked. You seem to be more concerned with your own interest than with ours." Aiden's verbal chastising was something that I hadn't expected. Had I indeed been that rude or was it some type of guilt reversal trick? Whatever it was, made my thoughts stammer and forced me to mentally take a step back and analyze what had just occurred. He had a point, that I must admit, but he didn't understand the sense of urgency that was burning inside of me.

"Sorry for being rude, but things have really gotten out of hand. They're planning something big and we all need to be ready!" I stated with tears forming in my eyes. The image of the bloody handprint on my parents' door was permanently burned into my memory.

"It was inevitable," I turned to see Jason coming through one of his time warp portals. He had a serious look on his face.

"What do you mean?" Drave asked in a less than cordial tone. He instantly went into aggressive mode.

"Think about it, by there not being a real threat on Earth, it's up for the taking," Jason stated coldly. "Either you go along with the change or get destroyed for resisting." His words were brutal but held a cold harsh truth.

"Look, we know that you don't need us, but in order to win this war… we need you, all of you." I stated humbly. I laid it all out for them to sort. They were either going to really consider it or reject it and send us back out into the cold, dark world outside of their sheltered high life bubble. The room grew silent. My plea had touched on something that everyone understood regardless of his or her stance. Jason was the one that broke the silence.

"I'm pretty sure that I speak for Alex and Aiden as well as myself when I say that we would gladly rejoin you for one last hurrah of sorts, but I don't think your comrades feel the same," Jason stated before shooting an incriminating look at Drave and Sienna.

"If you're talking about us," Drave wrapped his arm around Sienna before continuing, "then why don't we just settle this once and for all. I'M DONE PLAYING NICE!" Drave proclaimed with his fangs bared and anger in his tone.

"Are you sure you want this, cause I'll gladly give you the trouble you're looking for." Jason threatened with clenched teeth and balled fists.

"THAT'S ENOUGH!" I yelled as my frustration reached its boiling point. I was sick of everything, sick of the arguing, the petty rivalry. I had had enough and I was willing to throw my weight around to ensure the safety of everyone. "If you guys can't put your petty rivalry aside for the sake of something more important, WE'RE ALL DONE FOR!" I yelled. My rage was out and there wasn't any containing it. Everyone became silent and all eyes and focus shifted onto me.

"You know what, maybe you're right Chariz." Drave mumbled humbly.

"Yeah, I guess we were being a bit childish." Jason added to my surprise.

"Good, now can we focus on getting ourselves together for the war?" I asked rhetorically.

"Alright, well the ball's in your court, so tell us the plan." Drave said.

"I will but first, Jason, are you going to help or stand by and watch everyone, including your adoring public be laid to waste?" I asked hoping that the mentioning of his fans would be enough to persuade him.

"I never said that... well, it's... not that simple. I don't have the luxury of ruffling any feathers." He said, fumbling through his words.

"Ruffling feathers?" I questioned as I tried to process his cowardly response.

"I can't because as soon as I do, I'm dead and that goes for Alex and Aiden too since they're with me. The cause you're fighting for is dead." Jason talked like a coward. There was a lot about the real Jason I had yet to learn. The teen heartthrob that I had kept in my head was gradually fading away and being replaced by the delusional, conformist one.

"You have to fight against them. You can't just be concerned about the three of you while the fate of the whole free world hangs in the balance. We can prevent this, but only if we work together, all of us." Drave interjected in a passionate rallying tone.

"Drave, you really are naïve. It can't be stopped, merely postponed. They are meant to come and take over this world. It has been prophesized for years. It's only a matter of time." Jason's view was very pessimistic. I wondered how he had gotten that way. I wished I had asked him more questions when we first met aboard the ship.

"I don't mean to interrupt your argument, but you guys really need to see this!" A person from Jason's entourage said urgently as he entered the room. Jason and Drave put their disagreement on hold and followed the rest of us as we headed out to see what was so urgent. I stepped into the front gaming room and noticed everyone's attention was focused on the large balcony window overlooking the city. I looked outside of the window and saw a large ship hovering above the city. The invasion was here. The Draakunaki were here.

"So what are you guys going to do?" I asked while my eyes remained glued on the ship. I felt a terrible sensation in the pit of my stomach as the image triggered flashbacks of our defeat. There was no way around it, we all needed to work together to ensure victory.

"What other choice do we have?" Alex asked. "We can't allow them to take over." She stated in a tone that was as dire as our circumstances.

"Right, we were born for this." Aiden added. I turned my attention away from the window and looked dead at Jason.

"Well, are you in or out?" I asked with my arms folded and my intense stare focused on him.

"I guess it's no point in me being the only one not in on the fun and games so I'm in," He uttered reluctantly. "I hope you guys know what you're doing. If not we're dead, right along with everyone else on this crazy ball of yarn." Before anyone could get a chance to respond, a strong quake rattled the building. Another one soon followed, along with a series of explosions. I ran out onto the balcony and saw Draakunaki soldiers pouring out of the ship's belly adorned in flight suits and heavy duty battle armor.

"Whelp, there goes the neighborhood." Jackson joked. No one released a single giggle.

"I don't think now is the most opportune time for jokes Jack," I stated in response.

"You're supposed to laugh in the face of danger, it makes it less dangerous." He replied, which was weird but somehow logically sane.

"How do you want to do this, rooftop or ground level?" Drave asked.

"Both, it might give us the element of surprise." I answered.

"Alright, Charisma you, Sienna, and Alex attack from the roof. Jackson, Jason, Aiden, and I will take to the streets." He instructed. "That way, me and good ole' Jason here can get properly acquainted." He joked as he shot a quick smile at Jason.

"Yeah, I'm really looking forward to it," Jason responded sarcastically.

We arrived on the rooftop and I got a clear view of the mayhem that was ensuing. Some of the reptilians had grown into mighty giants and were knocking off large portions of neighboring buildings with single swipes. Others were rapidly firing their tornado boxes. While yet still others were hovering and raining down laser fire and energy blasts from above. They were within a ten-block radius of the hotel. I felt a lump form in my throat, and the muscles in my stomach tightened as the butterflies began to flutter wildly. The mere sight of the destruction around me was enough to trigger them.

"GIVE US THE ENOCIANS OR DIE!" A voice boomed and echoed. It was clear that they were here because of Aiden, Alex, and Jason. Unlike us, they hadn't had on the scan jamming devices and even if we would have given them theirs when we arrived, I doubt it would've prevented the attack. The Draakunaki had more than likely already picked up their scans prior to our arrival.

"Better late than never, you guys might need these in the future." I said before giving the DNA scan jammers to Jason, Alex, and Aiden.

"You got the late part right." Alex said with a giggle. Her response actually made me smile.

"Alright, let's do this." I said before leaping off the roof. I put all nervousness and doubt on the back burner as I flew right into the danger zone. One of the giants was the first enemy that I encountered. He was preoccupied with demolishing a building when I seized the opportunity. I charged up and flew right at the creature. The impact was fast and brutal. I plunged into the creature's gigantic jaw and burst through the opposite side in an explosion of blood, teeth, and spit. Calling the experience gross would be an understatement. I hovered in the air as the behemoth collapsed, clutching its injured face. I saw Drave and the others below engaged in combat.

"That's one way to do it." I turned and saw Alex staring with bewildered eyes.

"I don't have time to play. I've got an entire world to keep safe." I responded.

"That was pretty gruesome." Sienna added. I looked around and saw her inside of her telekinetic bubble firing energy blasts at our foes. Alex broke out of her awestruck trance and began hurling fireballs wildly at the Draakunaki. They retaliated with laser fire and energy bursts. Sienna's bubble deflected the shots intended for her, while Alex maneuvered frantically to avoid them. I received a direct hit from an energy burst. It didn't hurt, which was absolutely not, what I was expecting. I didn't feel a thing. I was changing. The reptilian shot another blast at me. It was met with the same result.

Another reptilian took notice of his comrade's failed efforts and fired a tornado in my direction. I attempted to move, but the gravitational pull of the furious engineered typhoon sucked me up into its vortex. I swirled around in the hellish cyclone. I closed my eyes tightly and covered my face, as various pieces of loose debris scraped me as they whirled by. In spite of being scraped more times, than I could count on both hands, I still didn't feel any noticeable pain. The scrapes were the equivalent of a fingernail scratching an itch. It was as if I had been injected with a numbing agent.

*"I wonder if I can break free of this?"* was the thought that popped in my head as I tumbled around like a sock in a dryer. It was dizzying. It instantly brought back memories of the first time I went on a roller coaster ride and came down with

an extreme case of motion sickness. If I had had actual food contents in my stomach, it would've escaped my body before I could escape the tornado. I was getting dizzier by the second. *"C'mon, you can do this."* I thought before I began to focus my attention inward. I tried my best to block out everything. The uncontrolled motion, the sound of the howling wind in my ears, the one-hundred-something mile per hour debris scraping and slamming into my body, was something that a mere mortal would have never been able to withstand.

Focusing while enduring those conditions was close to impossible. *"C'mon girl, do it!"* I urged silently as I wrestled with the outside interferences. Then, in an act of pure raw strength, I regained control over my body. I was no longer being swirled around helplessly. With my face still partially covered, I attempted something that I remembered my father telling me about from one of his numerous comic books. I concentrated, and then hovered out of the tornado as smooth as a hot knife slicing through butter. I looked down at the Draakunaki soldier. He seemed befuddled, to say the least. He fired another Tornado. This time, I met it head on and sliced right through it on a straight path toward my aggressor. He continued firing, but couldn't stop my descent. His manufactured typhoons had no effect on me The panicked reptilian let out a shriek and attempted to flee as I closed in for the kill. The sight of it brought a smile to my face. I effortlessly flew and within mere seconds, landed a power punch that sent him flying through a building close by.

After disposing of him, I turned my attention to the other Draakunaki firing their ineffective lasers and energy bursts. I was hit with a barrage of shots and blasts as I headed toward them. They all begin yelling to one another in their native dialect as I continued full speed in their direction. I reached them and began my assault. The first one received a bone breaking punch to the ribs. My small but powerful fist went right through his armor. He stumbled backward, clutching his wounded area before falling over and releasing a freakishly intense howl. I silenced him with a swift kick to the face. *"If only Dad could see me now,"* I thought as I looked down at my now unconscious foe. I was determined to get back my quirky but loving dad, no matter the cost.

There were now three Draakunaki troopers left, and they all ran like the dickens. I laughed as I pursued them and took them down one by one like a choreographed fight scene. I took down the first one by drop kicking him into a large parked SUV. He was meters away, but a quick sprint closed the distance. I stopped the next one dead in his tracks, with an insanely powerful well-placed uppercut. The force of the blow sent him flying into the air like a popped champagne cork at a New Year's celebration. The last was the easiest. I had grown tired of chasing by the time I got to the final reptilian and decided to outsource the task to a parked car. I hoisted the vehicle in the air and hurled it. The vehicle flew through the air and crashed with a force comparable to a head on collision. The result was an incapacitated reptilian smashed against the side of a building.

With my foes disposed of, I glanced around for the others. I saw Drave running laps around a reptilian, while Jason was literally taking the life out of another by using his rapid aging power. Jackson was going toe to toe with a giant. Aiden was forcing back tornados at the Draakunaki, and Alex and Sienna were working together rescuing injured innocent bystanders. Alex provided cover with furious fireballs while Sienna searched for victims. We were winning, and we were doing it as a team. Seeing the others work hard toward a common goal was a refreshing experience that kept my spirits high.

While my team kept the ground forces at bay, I took it upon myself to destroy the ship. I charged my power and flew into the air like a rocket. The ship had stopped deploying enemy troops and was hovering idly above the city. It was vulnerable, or so I thought. I reached the ship and as soon as my hands touched its otherworldly metal exterior, it discharged a huge surge of energy, knocking me clear across the sky. The currents of the discharge surged throughout my body as I flew through the air. I was finally able to feel some viable pain. It felt as if I had been electrocuted. I felt my body tremor as I continued soaring in my immobilized state. The weird powerful energy produced an unsavory taste in my mouth. It was a taste that can best be described as a cross between rusty iron and dish detergent. Finally, after getting knocked halfway across the attack zone, I crashed onto the rooftop of a small dilapidated building.

The painful crash only added to the aftereffects of the shock from the ship. My head spun dizzily and throbbed uncontrollably as I lay on the roof. After a moment or two, I regained movement. I slowly rose to my feet and cleared the cobwebs out of my head. The energy packed even more of a punch than the female reptilian from the first battle. The energy expelled from the ship was unlike any I'd ever encountered. It made me wonder why they hadn't used it against us. An asset such as that would definitely give them a clear advantage in the war. I stammered to the edge of the roof. I was out of it. It was as if I had just gone toe to toe with a tank.

My conscious swirled around as I looked across the city. My vision was blurred, but it didn't take clear sight to notice that the Draakunaki warship was gone, and all that remained was the damage left in its wake. My ears rang mildly. In spite of the mild ringing, I could clearly distinguish the sounds of police and rescue sirens in the distance. I wasn't sure if there were many human casualties or if the rest of my team was in good condition. I couldn't seem to snap out of the disoriented state that was induced by the mysterious energy.

*"I gotta focus."* I thought as my vision began to clear and the ringing dissipated. I closed my eyes and tried to focus my abilities. I took a few minutes to clear my head. Then, I

attempted to fly. I took a leap of faith… off the roof. As opposed to taking off into the sky as I was supposed to, I fell. It was a shock. I descended rapidly. I tried to focus and catch myself, but it didn't work. I continued falling helplessly through the sky. I wanted to scream out of both fear and frustration. *"I'm the hero. This isn't supposed to happen to the hero!"* I reasoned mentally. I didn't want to end up splattered across the ground or have every bone in my body broken. *"It can't end like this, not like this!"* I objected as the possibility of a non-heroic death took center stage in my mind. It was non-heroic in the sense that it didn't have that signature, villain added element. It seemed like it was more of a fluke, an accidental death, which sucked because it meant that I would be responsible for my own demise.

The wind rushed past my face as I got closer and closer to the end of the ride. I wondered if my parents would ever be found. Furthermore, I wondered how they would feel upon hearing the news of my accidental death. I also wondered a thought that was particularly odd. I wondered what Jackson would do without me. "C'mon girl, you gotta get out of this!" I commanded. The ground was fast approaching and that feeling that one gets right when things are about to take a turn for the worst had taken complete control over me. I closed my eyes and tried to focus yet again. It didn't work. I slammed into the ground.

The cold hard concrete cracked and buckled from the force of the impact. I would be lying if I said it wasn't painful. It was, more so than any other pain that I had experienced. I should've been dead, yet I wasn't. The energy had somehow weakened me, but hadn't taken away all of my powers. I rose and saw a pair of dim glassy eyes looking at me.

"Hey Miss, are you okay?" A man with a scruffy beard, tattered clothes, and a shopping cart full of cans asked with a look of astonishment plastered across his face. He was covered in dirt and grime. The wind carried a whiff of his scent, which was a nauseating mixture of unwashed funk,

Anthony D. Phillips Jr.

stale cigarettes, and booze. As far as the astonishment factor goes, we were on the same page. If the shoe were on the other foot, I would've definitely not understood. I went from being a normal teenage girl to a super powered titan in less than a week's time.

"Yeah… I'm fine," I mumbled in between staggered steps. I looked back at where I had landed and saw a crater. It was surreal. I was fortunate to be able to hobble away with minor bruises.

"That was like something right out of a comic book!" He exclaimed. I stopped briefly and gave him a weak smile.

"I just have to walk it off." I uttered before continuing my slow, painful trek to where the others were. It was a pretty awkward moment. There wasn't anything else that I could've said. It's not every day that a teenager falls from a building and breaks the ground when she lands.

As I shuffled through the city block by block, a great heaviness began to manifest in my heart. I looked at all of the carnage left in the wake of our battle. I saw children crying, I watched as Paramedic EMTs rushed to help the injured. I felt a deep sadness for all of the victims. Their lives would never be the same. It reminded me of the senseless tragedies I would often hear about on the news. Except this was different, there wasn't a lone gunman with mental issues looking to go down in infamy or a terrorist cell with radical religious beliefs sending a message to the western world. This was something more malevolent, something that the people of Earth would never truly understand. The threat was ten times worse than a suicide bomber or a wacko with an arsenal. This was a threat to the entire world and no one was left out. The normal citizens, crazies, egomaniacs, black, white, gay, straight, would all be extinguished or enslaved alike.

By the time I made it back to the others, my strength was mostly restored. The pain from the fall had decreased greatly and I was able to walk without looking like a zombie or an injured athlete. Aiden was the first one I met.

"Hey, where did you go?" He asked as our eyes met.

"I took a little trip courtesy of the energy field on the warship." I replied with a somewhat weak attempt at humor.

"What?" He responded, obviously not picking up on the joke.

"Never mind, so are all of the Draakunaki disposed of?" I asked as I further examined the mangled city that surrounded us.

"They're done. I think we can chalk this up as a victory." Aiden stated. Jackson and Drave appeared suddenly courtesy of Drave's teleportation ability.

"Yeah, we kicked their tails all the way back to their home planet." Alex added as she descended to the ground along with Sienna.

"You mean we kicked a—" I interrupted Jackson before he could finish.

"Yes, but we probably shouldn't celebrate just yet. Their warships are probably everywhere."

"Charisma's right," Drave paused before continuing. "This seemed more like an assessment, a side mission. Like they were testing us, gauging our strengths and weaknesses,"

"Like they're getting to know their enemy," I added and finished his statement.

"Exactly, either that or distracting us while they put their master plan into place,"

"Where's Jason?" I asked as I looked around and noticed that he was suspiciously absent.

"I don't know… he's a real wild card. That's why—" At that moment, a time warp appeared near us and interrupted Drave.

"Well, it's good to know that my mates think of me so fondly." Jason said as he stepped out of the portal.

"I'm just saying. You don't strike me as very dependable." Drave said.

"Yeah, okay, whatever," Jason replied before dismissing the subject.

As we continued our conversation, a crowd had begun to gather. First, it was just three kids gawking at us in our weird suits. Then, more and more people started to join them. Within a matter of minutes, there were three times, the number of people gathered around us. The onlookers chattered amongst themselves as they watched our every move. The street lights cascaded a strange glow over the weary disenfranchised lot. A police officer assessing the damage around us caught my attention. I found it odd that instead of being preoccupied with helping the citizens, he seemed to be more concerned with the condition of the area.

"Are you responsible for this?" He asked as he boldly stepped forward interrupting our conversation. We all turned and looked at him. *What is this, some type of new gang?"* was an idiotic thought taking up space in the cop's mind.

"If you're referring to this, as saving the city from a brutal race of aliens, then yes we are responsible." I stated confidently. "And no we're not a gang. We're Earth's last hope!" I added letting him know that I knew what he was thinking

"Okay, well do you know how many crimes you guys have committed?" He asked in a slightly shaky voice.

"Are you serious?" Alex asked in her usual 'annoyed with life' tone.

"Y-yes, the city budget—" A bright light appeared where we were standing and silenced the police officer's nonsense. I looked above and saw our ship. Seconds later Anaku appeared. The look on the officer's face was priceless. He stood flushed with his mouth gaped open in shock. The rest of the bystanders were equally shocked. They all stood stunned, with frozen expressions on their faces. One little girl began to cry.

"We need to go to your nation's capital now!" Anaku stated in the same booming voice as when he had first rescued me.

"Y—you're not going anywhere, Fr—freeze!" The cop shouted with his gun aimed in our direction. It was a very foolish thing to do considering that we had just taken on a barrage of brutal alien warriors. His gun was a toy compared to that.

"Have you lost your mind? We're the good guys and—" Before I could finish my statement, we were inside of the control room, back aboard the ship.

# Chapter 10

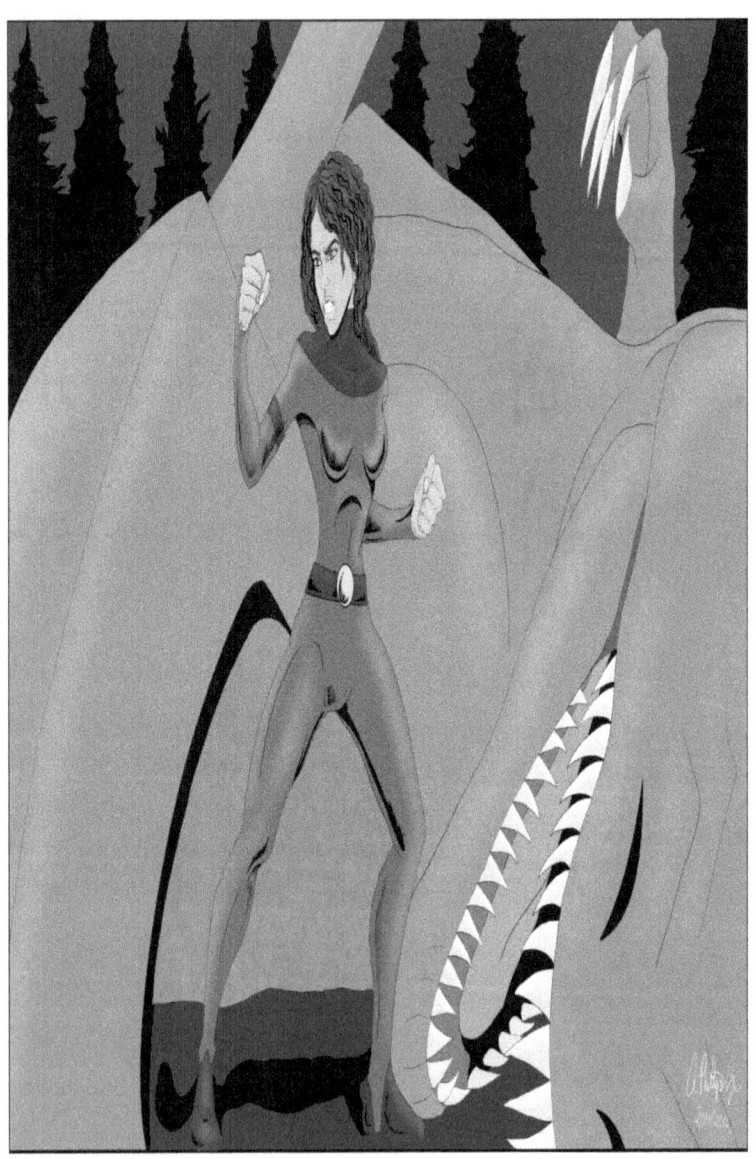

# Fright Night or Fight Night?

**IT HAD BEEN LESS THAN AN HOUR SINCE** we defeated the first wave of Draakunaki in Seattle. As we approached our next destination, the monitors inside of the ship displayed the chaos that was unfolding in the nation's capital. Reptilians rained down from an armada of Draakunaki warships that hovered over the White House. The night sky was illuminated with explosions and energy blasts. Secret service agents and U.S. military personnel were valiantly engaged in battle against the brutal Draakunaki menace. They fought hard in spite of the fact that they were clearly outgunned. Even their most advanced weaponry failed to compare to the highly advanced reptilian arsenal. Their tornado boxes dispensed ravishing typhoons that ripped apart tanks and other military vehicles. I watched in horror as a Draakunaki energy burst downed a fighter jet and reduced it to fiery rubble on the White House lawn. The pilot ejected in the nick of time, narrowly avoiding an excruciatingly horrible death.

"How are we going to enter into the battle without the military mistaking us for enemies?" Alex asked as we continued looking at the carnage unfolding before us.

"We will have to directly address them," I stated as I thought about the possible reactions that could occur from doing so.

"But what if they attack us? That's not—" I stopped Alex midsentence.

"I understand what you're saying, they may want to attack us, but I think that we would stand a better chance with the direct approach," I stated.

"Oh, so we're just supposed to stroll up to them offering help and expect not to get our heads blown off?" Alex exclaimed.

"Yeah, that's exactly what we're going to do," I responded. "We'll teleport from off this ship, to somewhere inconspicuous and then walk right up to them. We all look completely human, it's not like we're freakish looking."

We arrived inside of the subway station a few blocks from where the carnage was ensuing. Aside from a few homeless people, it was empty.

"Alright, here's the plan," Drave said. "We change our suits and try to look as normal as possible. We don't want to raise any red flags. Us offering them assistance is already weird enough,"

"What if they refuse?" Alex asked. It was a valid question that definitely needed to be considered before engaging in such a risky move.

"Then we will show them why they should accept," I interjected boldly. "And we will do that by showing them what we can do," I added.

"I guess you guys have it all figured out, huh?" Jackson commented.

"I hope so," I mumbled as I thought about the worst-case scenario of what we were about to do. We were taking a huge risk.

As we walked through the desolate subway tunnels thoughts of my parents occupied my mind. I thought about how I would successfully go about rescuing them. I had no clue where the Draakunaki were keeping them, whether they had them on Earth, on their home planet, or on some mother ship orbiting out in space. The ground beneath us vibrated, as we got closer to the battleground. I felt like an athlete prepping to step out on the field before a big game.

"Is everyone ready?" Drave asked as we walked down the sparsely lit tunnel.

"We don't have a choice, the world can't wait," I responded. I was trying to convince myself as well as the others. I saw the exit up ahead and braced myself for battle. When we reached the exit, Drave was the first to go up, followed by Sienna and Alex.

"Good luck, break a leg or two, just not your own," Aiden joked before heading up after the others. Jason stopped and turned toward me. The look on his face was a mixture of fear, doubt, and false confidence.

"This is it. I hope you know what you're doing Chariz." He said with a forced smile.

"We're going to be just fine," I replied and smiled back. Jackson and I were now alone. It was awkward, especially knowing that death was a real possibility. We exchanged glances as we stood in silence, unsure of what to say. I tried not to think about the possibility of him dying. "Okay, let's go." I murmured before turning toward the exit. As I started to walk, Jackson grabbed my hand.

"Wait," he said with a slight tug. I turned and caught a direct line with his golden eyes. "I just want to say I… I care about you." His words were soft and sincere. I didn't expect for something so simple to sound so sweet, so meaningful. I paused and thought about how to respond. I didn't want to say too much, but on the other hand, I didn't want to say too little either.

"I, I care about you too, so don't die," I said. At the time, I felt it was the right response. It wasn't too sappy and it was borderline edgy.

"I'm not worried about dying. It's your job to save me right?" He shot back with a grin.

"I suppose so silly." I murmured before giving him a hug. It was a friendly hug, nothing romantic about it what so ever.

"What was that for?" He asked with a shocked expression.

"I don't need a reason to hug you. Now let's go win this battle." I stated with a smile before walking through the exit

We reached the surface and saw the damage from the ensuing battle firsthand. The sounds of rapid gunfire and the booms of tank cannons echoed in the air. Explosions rocked everything around us and the bright bursts of light produced by them appeared throughout the dark night sky. The presence of war was undeniably tangible. The thick smoke from the numerous fires burning hung in the air and the scent accompanying it forced its way into my nostrils.

I looked ahead in the distance and saw soldiers running and firing frantically around the White house. Their weapons were doing damage, but nowhere near the amount needed to defeat the unrelenting war hardened foes that seemed oblivious to fear. They fired their lasers, energy bursts, and tornado boxes with little regard for their own welfare. When one fell, another quickly took its place. There seemed to be an almost endless stream of Draakunaki troops. More and more of them descended from their ships.

A single, partially burned flag hung frayed and limp atop of the broken crown of the nation. The pillars that held up the front of the structure were broken and had chunks displaced from them. One of them was completely gone. They looked like damaged teeth, barely clinging to the structure that they had been a part of for ages. We continued walking along the outskirts of the desecrated area. In the short distance, I could make out what appeared to be a general. There were numerous others gathered around him listening to the orders that he barked. He definitely seemed like the one that we needed to approach.

"That's the guy we need to talk to," I stated before boldly walking toward the general. Once we were within yards of him, the men around him directed their rifles toward us.

"STOP, DON'T TAKE ANOTHER STEP!" One of them yelled. He had the look in his eyes of a fierce war hardened man. It was clear to see that he was willing to die to protect his commanding officer and his country.

"We need to talk to him." Drave uttered as he pointed to the general. "You're not going to shoot a bunch of unarmed kids now are you?" He questioned. The look on the man's face softened and he lowered his gun. The other soldiers witnessed this and lowered their weapons as well.

"You know you guys shouldn't even be here. This is a war zone!" The soldier stated. He seemed genuinely concerned for our safety.

"We're here to help," I stated.

*"Here to help? Is she for real?"* The soldier's face matched his thoughts, it instantly changed from a serious war-torn mug to a belittling smirk. "Are you serious?" He asked while struggling to contain himself. Before I could answer, Alex stepped forward.

"Of course we're serious." She stated as she revealed a hand covered in flames. The soldier's eyes widened and the others backed away.

"Show-off," I mumbled as I shot her a quick friendly look.

"I know," She uttered, and responded with a smile.

"We really need to speak to him," I added as I put on the face that I had used on my father countless times when I wanted to have my way. The officer stood briefly thinking in silence. After a moment of consideration, he spoke.

"Alright, but make it quick," was his reply to our request. We walked toward the general that was stationed behind a big hulking armored vehicle. He appeared to be communicating with someone via a com link.

"Sir," I addressed the general. His back was turned to us. He was so engrossed in his conversation that I failed to get his attention with my first attempt. "Sir," I said again in a louder, more assertive tone. The second time did the trick. He turned to face us. His appearance, for all intents and purposes, was stereotypical of how one would envision the general of a platoon of elite soldiers. The clean shaven, oily, moist with sweat, dark brown skin on his face glistened from reflected moonlight. His eyes were piercing as they gazed upon me. He stood well over six feet. His frame was a mix of husky and muscular. I looked up to him, literally. His sheer size dwarfed my small petite body.

"Why did you let them pass?" He yelled to the soldiers that surrounded us.

"Sir, they needed to talk to you. They said that they can help sir," The soldier that gave us access responded.

"Okay private and just how are a bunch of kids supposed to help us?" He asked as he looked us up and down.

"Well, uh, sir..." I walked over to the back end of the hulking multiple-ton weighing vehicle, and focused. I effortlessly lifted it in the air and lowered it back to the ground with the same amount of ease. The general and his soldiers were all shocked. Some stood with their jaws slack and gaped open, while the others simply had wide-eyed expressions on their faces.

"What the..." The general finished his statement with an unintelligible word.

"So are you going to let us help you or what?" I asked in a bossy tone.

"What are you waiting for, go and win this battle." The general said while motioning toward the battlefield. With the general's permission granted, we revealed our suits and sprung into action.

"The pot calling the kettle black," Alex said as she flew past me. The Draakunaki noticed us and immediately shifted their attention. Alex showered a group of them with fire, while Aiden dehydrated them with his manipulation over water. Drave and Sienna tag teamed a squad of foes, while Jackson morphed into a Rhino and stomped his way through another.

Before Jason could begin in the battle, a Draakunaki warrior sideswiped him and sent him slamming into the ground. I saw it and immediately went into action to save him. While the creature was preoccupied with finishing Jason off, I was headed straight toward it. The creature removed a weapon that resembled a sword from a sheath on its waist. It powered up the hi-tech blade and was just about to kill a dazed discombobulated Jason when I crashed full force into it.

The force of the hit knocked the blade out of its hand and sent both the reptilian and the blade into the air. The blade plunged handle first into the ground, and the reptilian met a horrible demise via impalement. The hot energy blade sliced into its chest with zero resistance. The Draakunaki let out painful shrills, as it struggled to turn off the weapon. Its frantic movements became less and less frequent, and it became less and less audible. The reptilian's shrills were replaced by garbled moans of agony and the frantic movements were reduced to weak pathetic attempts. After fighting with its destiny for a brief few agonizing moments, it finally gave in to the appointment death had set for it. It stopped moving and released one last garbled sigh.

"Thanks," Jason said as I helped him up from the ground.

"You're welcome" I responded. "C'mon, let's send these creeps back where they came from." The next few moments were a blur. I effortlessly punched and ripped my way through numerous Draakunaki foot soldiers. Their shrieks of pain, echoed in my ears as I decimated their numbers. I was determined to win and get my parents back. It seemed as if the obstacle was well on its way to being overcome until my nightmare nemesis arrived. I was in the middle of dismissing the last of my opponents when a giant winged dragon descended from the sky. It was enormous and looked just as fierce and dangerous as the recurring nightmare dragon. Its big green eyes glowed malevolently as it traveled down to Earth.

"A dragon, you gotta be (expletive) kidding me!" Alex exclaimed. It was the size of a Draakunaki warship and smelled like sulfur. It landed and caused the ground to tremble terribly. It released a mighty roar before going into action.

"How are we supposed to defeat that?" Jason questioned as the enormous monstrosity lumbered toward us from across the battlefield.

"It can't be that hard." I reasoned.

"Well, everybody isn't like you, we're not almost invincible!" Jason shot back. I almost laughed at Jason's somewhat flattering statement.

"Hopefully, I'm more than just almost." I joked as more reptilians went on the assault. We were already outnumbered by the Draakunaki, and a big dragon in the mix was overkill. "You guys handle the rest of the reptilians, I'll handle big and ugly," I said before flying toward the hellish dinosaur-sized foe. Lasers grazed me as I flew toward my massive adversary. I met it in the middle of the field with a supercharged punch. My fist slammed against the creature's hard leathery skin. The punch caused it to skid back several yards. It let out a loud enraged growl and swiped one of its enormous claws at me. I put up my arms and braced myself for the hit. The strike sent a powerful shock through my body and knocked me back a short distance. I hovered to keep from falling to the ground. "Is that the best you can do?" I taunted fiercely. The hit stung, but I refused to let the monster see any signs of weakness.

The creature growled fiercely and charged. It was faster than I anticipated. Before I could blink, the creature was upon me, launching another attack. I blocked the second hit and countered with my own attack. I did a short sprint and followed up with a sloppy but powerful right hook. My form was a little off, a tad on the wild side but it landed effectively. The unorthodox swing caused the creature's face and neck to whiplash. Spittle flew out of its mouth. The punch temporarily dazed it. It staggered back a few steps and shook its large head. I wasted no time launching another attack. I was in mid-swing when the creature unexpectedly expelled an energy blast from its mouth.

The blast hit me right in the chest and sent me flying off into the distance. It felt similar to the discharge from the ship. My body was immobilized from the shock. I had once again met my Kryptonite, my Achilles' heel. The pain was intense. It felt like my whole body was on fire. I wanted to scream in pain, but I was unable to do anything. I just flew helplessly through the night sky. I flew much farther than the first time. If I were a baseball, I would definitely have been out of the park, a grand slam. I blacked out and came back to several times during the uncontrolled flight. The final time I came to, I was fast approaching the heavily wooded Theodore Roosevelt Island.

Seconds later, I crashed right into the thick of it. The impact of the crash shook the entire island. My whole body throbbed painfully and my head felt like a spinning top. I was disoriented and sore. My heart raced as I became more and more coherent and aware of my surroundings. I was in a dark dense forest section of the island. It looked exactly like the one from the nightmare. Panic began to rear its ugly head, as I lay helpless and alone on the dark cold forest floor. My heartbeat was intense as I struggled to move even the slightest part of my body, a fingertip, a toe, anything would've sufficed and given me hope, but nothing would work. I was frozen in a paraplegic state. I felt sweat trickle down the side of my face as I fought to regain control over my body. I was a sitting duck.

"*Move Charisma, please,*" I silently begged. I could hear crickets chirping and rustling sounds in the thick dark foreboding woods. I wondered if any of my teammates noticed my absence. "*Sienna,*" The idea to contact her flashed in my head. "*Even if she could hear me, what good would it do? What if she comes to my aid and gets killed, I can't risk it.*" I wrestled back and forth mentally with possible solutions to my conundrum as I desperately tried to move. The sound of branches breaking, and the accompanying sensation of a thunderous rumble let me know that my nemesis had arrived. The sound that I heard next really brought on the panic. I heard the menacing dragon's snarls. It was coming for me. It was coming to finish the job. Thankfully, it was around that time that I regained control over my hands.

As the dragon's boisterous footsteps got closer and more frequent, the rest of my body slowly started to recover from the paralysis. I gradually started to get up from the ground. It was an intense struggle. I pushed with every fiber of my being to rise from the dank, chilled ground.

"Get up," I mumbled in a somewhat slurred manner. My motor functions were off, and the chances of me using my powers were slim. "You can do it." I urged while still fighting to stand. My legs felt like limp noodles and my arms weren't much better. I knew the dragon was near. The slight tremors were constant reminders of the impending danger. Time wasn't on my side. Nor was luck, good fortune, or anything else. Flashbacks of my nightmare began cycling in my mind like scenes from a movie, a movie where the ending is exactly the opposite of happy. The type of movie where you've read the book and know that your most beloved character is going to bite the dust, buy the farm, kick the bucket, you know, die. I made it to my feet. It was a wobbly attempt. I took a step forward and almost fell flat on my face. My legs buckled under the force of gravity. My knees hit the ground hard. The impact sent a slight sting through my legs. I was still far too weak to fight, but I didn't have a choice in the matter.

I could hear my enemy fast approaching. I crawled along the ground with a determination unrivaled by any previous experience. I was crawling for my life, literally! My predator would soon be upon me and my powers were still seemingly absent. My chances of a full out escape were slim and hiding seemed like the option that was the most viable. My eyes scoured my surroundings anxiously trying to locate a hole or some other type of crevasse capable of rendering me invisible to the monstrous foe that was drawing closer with each wasted second that passed.

"Ugh," I exasperated as I searched for a place to hide. I found a spot that appeared to be suitable. I didn't consider the possibility of it being already inhabited. I threw caution to the wind and quickly dove in. The hole was pitch black and reeked of decaying leaves and forestation. I ignored the smell and focused on the safety that it provided. A short while later, I felt the ground quake, my enemy had arrived. I nervously peered out from my shadowy haven. The creature's large clawed feet made loud menacing crushing sounds as it moved through the forest. I sat motionless, silently studying my dark surroundings. I could hear the creature, but couldn't figure out from which direction it was approaching. It's loud stomps vibrated the ground. I smelled the sulfur scent that permeated from it. I continued scanning the dark vague forest. Once my eyes finally began to adjust to the darkness, I saw the enormous predator lurking in the distance. It was far, but not far enough for comfort.

"*Please don't let it find me!*" I prayed silently as I fought to keep from turning into a complete panicky mess. "*Keep it together girl, keep it together,*" I commanded as the distance between us shrank. Its large strides ate it up rather quickly. Within mere minutes, the creature was a few yards' distance from the hole. I could distinctly make out the outline of its massive body. It's terrifying green eyes glowed in the dreadfully dark surroundings. They moved around like two synchronized balls of illumination as the creature searched for me. The menacing glowing orbs stopped in my direction and hovered silently. My heart felt as if it was going to burst through my chest at any given moment. I heard a sound that was similar to when a dog sniffs to pinpoint a scent. I hoped that the sulfur smell emanating from its own body would be enough to block mine. My hoping was short lived. The beast let out a snarl indicating that its prey had been located. It's partially exposed teeth glimmered faintly as the almost nonexistent moonlight reflected off them. I slowly crept further into the hole, as far as it would allow, and waited for the inevitable. *"God, please,"* I pleaded silently. I bit my bottom lip as I gazed up at the horrific beast. I held my breath and remained as silent as a mouse in a house full of cats.

What happened next was unexpectedly fast, and completely unpreventable. In the blink of an eye, the creature opened its mouth and fired a powerful burst of energy into the hole. I managed to duck completely to the bottom of the hole a split second before and barely missed being hit head on by the blast. The blast tore open the partially covered hole and left me exposed. *"This is really bad,"* I thought as I looked up at the gargantuan dragon. Just as it was about to release another blast, I sprinted upward and delivered a quick precise uppercut. The punch knocked the creature back just enough for me to attempt an escape. I did another quick sprint in the opposite direction. I thought I was in the clear until an exposed tree root caught my foot. I fell forward. If not for me putting my hands out as a knee jerk reaction, I would have surely eaten mud-pie.

The root snapped and I landed on all fours. Pain shot up through my body from my snagged extremity. It was an indication that my powers were not yet fully restored. I crawled away through the pain. I turned to look at my foe. It had shaken off the sting of my blow and was now back in pursuit of its prey, me! I forced myself up from the ground. Once on my feet, I felt an intense pain in my ankle, indicating a possible sprain. I limped as fast as my injured body would allow. I had to get some type of leverage against the dragon. Its size and energy bursts gave it clear advantages and my condition only added to that.

I hobbled as fast as I could, but the creature stayed on my tail. It could've easily stumped me with one of its massive feet, but it appeared to enjoy the chase. It seemed as if it was toying with me and delaying the inevitable. At least that was what I assumed before its massive claw crashed into me and sent me flying through trees and brush. I hit the ground with a painful thud. I was too dazed and confused to register what had just occurred. I felt a warm trickle of liquid come from out of my nose. I brought my hand up to my face and wiped at it. It was too dark to make out what the liquid in question was. Was it snot, sweat, blood? My money was on the latter. My ears buzzed and the side of my body burned as I sat trying to gather myself.

"Get up!" I commanded as more liquid began to flow from my nose. I was hurt, but I wasn't sure how bad. I slowly began to rise. As I was attempting to stand, the creature blasted me with another burst of energy. The force of the hit sent me crashing through several more trees and ended with me lying on my back staring up at the starless night sky. It was weird surviving such a devastating blow. By all accounts, I should've died. Contrary to popular belief, epic comic book style battles are not cool, fun, or in any way enjoyable, they hurt, a lot! They hurt so much so that the word hurt should be considered an understatement when describing the pain incurred from one of them. I shook off the shock of the hit and wearily rose. My legs were shaky, my back was on fire, and my head was absolutely killing me. It was throbbing and pounding like nobody's business. It felt like it was on the verge of exploding. Oh, and my nose was still leaking. I was in bad shape. I cupped my head and reduced my oxygen intake. Normal breathing made the pain in my injured nose and back even worse. The pain was so intense. I was on the verge of tears.

Everything around me was spinning. I felt dizzy. I took a small step forward and collapsed to the ground. I hit the ground and momentarily lost consciousness. I regained consciousness. I opened my eyes, and my enemy was right in front of me. The odds were stacked against me, but I refused to give in, I refused to die. Its eyes glowed brightly as it anticipated the victory at hand. It opened its massive mouth and the sulfur smell intensified exponentially. The smell was nauseatingly unbearable. I felt my stomach churning. I definitely didn't want to end up inside of it.

"I'm not ending up as a late night snack," I mumbled in a strained weak tone thanks to the intense pain ravishing my body and the overwhelming urge to upchuck. In a last ditch effort, I put the pain and nausea on the back burner and rose to my feet. "I'm not dying tonight!" I proclaimed as I stared into its eyes. It snarled in response. I was hurting something awful, but refused to give up. I stared down my foe fiercely as we squared off. It reopened its mouth and I saw another burst of energy building up. It fired the burst. I put up my arms to deflect it.

The blast hit my forearms. It knocked me back, but didn't knock me out. It actually worked. My arms actually deflected the forceful blast. "IS THAT ALL YOU GOT UGLY?" I yelled tauntingly at it. It snarled and its eyes glowed brighter. It followed up the failed blast with a hard forceful swipe. Again, I quickly put up my block, and deflected the powerful hit. Pain shot through my forearms. It hurt, but it was a lot better than getting knocked through trees and like half a forest. "My turn," I retaliated with a swift punch to its face. It made the creature's head whip to the side and the rest of it staggered back. I wasted no time landing another punch. It knocked its head to the other side.

I continued connecting fierce forceful punches. I felt my power building with each strike. I finished up the string of hits with a debilitating uppercut. It lifted the creature off the ground and sent it crashing back down. The earth shook from the heavy body slamming into it. The creature was down but not out. It was disoriented and struggling to get up from the brutal combo it had just received. Before the creature could get its bearing, I sprinted and gave it a swift kick. The kick sent it crashing into several trees before finally resting against a large rock structure. It let out a long sigh. I rushed over to finish it. I was going to make an example out of it for the others. I was going to end the war and ensure Earth's safety.

I stood over my fallen foe. I couldn't allow it to live. It had to die. I lifted the massive creature and hurled it into the air. I zipped up after it and met it with a hard, devastating double foot dropkick. The kick sent the beast flying like an oversized beach ball. It shot back to the ground like a shooting star and crashed with the momentous impact of an asteroid. I landed next to the creature and instantly looked for any signs of life. The creature was alive, though barely. It's breaths were short and labored. I took a moment to collect my thoughts and then I did the unthinkable. I plunged my fist into the creature's chest cavity, through the bone and muscle tissue, and felt around for my intended target. Once I reached my assumed target, I jabbed my fist with great force. I felt the massive muscle burst from the impact. The creature expelled its last breaths as it surrendered to death. I felt the pain dissipating as my body healed and my strength returned. Partially restored, I grabbed the creature's tail and lifted into the air. The creature dangled below me as I soared through the clear night sky. I looked ahead toward the White House and saw Draakunaki warships still hovering over it. The battle against the Draakunaki was still raging. It was unclear how the rest of the team was fairing.

As I neared the battle, I thought of ways to put an end to it. I had just defeated one of their most formidable weapons, which should have been enough, but I really wanted to send a message to our foes, a message that would show them that I meant business. I also wanted to take down one of the ships and in the process, get information that would lead me to my parents. I decided to use their weapon on them. I got within a stone's throw of one of the ships and swung the massive dead carcass at it. The ship teeter-tottered from the blow, and its deadly energy shield activated. I swung again with as much strength as I could muster. The hit sent the ship crashing to the ground. My attacks garnered the attention of the other ships and they began firing their weapons at me.

I used the dead dragon as a shield as I made my way to the downed ship. Alex saw my efforts and began hurling fireballs to divert their attention. With cover provided courtesy of Alex, I tossed my fallen foe and approached the ship. The reptilians had just started escaping from it. They looked different from the ones engaged in battle. They didn't appear to be soldiers. They looked like they were of more importance. My gut told me that I should definitely capture one of them. I went for the weakest, most vulnerable one. He was a straggler. The others had fled, but he was still trying to get out of the escape hatch. I swooped down and wasted no time getting to the point. I punched the creature in its face. The punch wasn't one of my hardest, it was just enough to knock some sense into him and persuade him into telling me what I needed to know.

"I need my parents back and you're going to tell me what I need to know in order to do that!" I said with my hands wrapped around its neck.

"I-I know nothing Enocian" The reptilian stated. I knew he was holding out, so I tightened the grip around his neck.

"Let's try this again. You guys took my parents, and I need to know where they are!" I said in a forceful tone.

"I don't know. I didn't take them." He proclaimed in a slightly irritated tone.

"Okay, maybe I'm going about this all wrong," I said before yanking him out of the hatch and lifting off. Once we were a safe distance, I resumed my interrogation. "Look, I'm going to ask you one last time, where are my parents?" I wasn't letting him off easy. I began picking up his thoughts which was amazing considering he was a reptilian and I hadn't had that much experience with reading their thoughts.

*"I'll, n… tell y… anything… parents… closer than you think… very close."* His thoughts weren't as clear as I would've liked them to be. They were like picking up an AM station with a broken antenna.

"I know they're close, now unless you want to end up as a stain on the concrete, you'll tell me where they are!" I threatened. I had every intention to fulfill the threat if I didn't get what I wanted. His life was nothing to me. He was just another baddie. His mere existence posed a threat to the world that I loved regardless of its imperfections. I loosened my grip. "TALK LIZARD," I demanded as I increased speed and ascended. The creature looked rattled. He was on the verge of spilling the beans, all I had to do was give him a little more of a scare and he'd spill everything like someone knocking over a glass of milk. I flew higher and faster with little regard for anything else. I was going to get the information that I needed and I was going to get it from him. The reptilian started speaking rapidly in Draakunaki gibberish. He was a harder case to crack than I had anticipated. I decided to let him go. I released my grip and he fell screaming in Draakunaki. I waited a few seconds before diving to get him. I grabbed the reptilian and he was ready to pop.

"I'LL TALK, I'LL TALK, I'LL TALK," He blurted in a raspy voice with eyes as wide as light bulbs.

"Tell me what you know!" I demanded as I lifted him up to look him face to face.

"The humans that you speak of are aboard our space station." He said. I read his thoughts and they lined up with what he was saying. He was telling the truth.

"Okay, good. You're going to take me there." I stated. I needed to get back to the battle, but first; I had to find a way to keep my prisoner safe and under wraps. I descended onto a neighboring city street, ripped a stop sign from out of the ground, and wrapped the pole around my weak captive's upper body. I then grabbed another pole parallel from the first and used it to bind his legs. There were bystanders witnessing the whole thing. Half stood in shock with frozen expressions on their faces, while the rest had their cell phones out recording. "Alright, show's over," I stated before taking off with my captive.

I arrived back at the battle. The enemy forces were depleted and all of my teammates appeared to be doing well. The abandoned warship was still where I had left it. A plan was starting to come together in my head. We needed to end the battle and get aboard their main base of operations. But first, I needed somewhere safe to stash my captive before I entered back into the battle. Then, like a lightning strike of inspiration, I remembered the armored war vehicle stationed by the general. I needed to get to it, but I didn't want to risk the military trying to take my captured reptilian for research. I needed him for my own purposes and I didn't want to hurt any of them to keep him. I decided that I would stash my victim, confiscate the vehicle, and use it to confine him at Theodore Roosevelt Island for safe keeping. "Wait here," I said before stashing the reptilian in a dense, bushy area a short distance away from the battleground.

I returned and went right to the general. He was still in the same area where we initially met. "General" I called as

I landed before his armed soldiers. "I need to have a word with you."

"You have the floor, Ms...."

"Grey, Ms. Grey," I finished his statement. "I have to borrow your vehicle," I said as I pointed to the vehicle that looked like the byproduct of breeding a tank and a gas guzzling SUV.

"Well, Ms. Grey I'm not sure that I'm authorized to do that. It's government property, and besides, do you even have a license?" I had to try my best to keep from laughing. I have the power to fly so driving it was the last thing on my mind.

"Sir, with all due respect, do you seriously think I want to drive? I can fly for Christ sakes." I said with a smile. "I just need it to hold something. I will bring it right back in the same condition as I found it I promise."

"Give me a second to think about it." The general said before going into silent mode. *"What in the world could she need my vehicle for?"* He questioned mentally while scratching his head.

"I need it to end this battle," I added as a means of persuasion.

"I wouldn't do this under normal circumstances, but these are definitely not normal circumstances, so do what you need to do. Just be quick about it." He turned to one of his men. "Give her the keys private." He instructed as he gestured his hand toward me.

"Sir, yes sir," His subordinate responded before tossing me the keys.

*"Where can I put them?"* I thought as I realized that I didn't have any pockets. "Wait, that's right..." I mumbled before making a pocket appear on the shoulder area of the suit. I had forgotten that the suit and I were mentally linked and that I could alter it at any given time. "Thank you." I murmured before lifting up the truck and taking off.

I returned back to my captive. He was just as I had left him. "Alright, up you go," I said before grabbing him from off the ground. I carried him with one hand and used the other to retrieve the keys from my pocket and open the trunk of the massive commandeered vehicle. I threw my captive inside.

"Sit tight, I'll be right back. Oh, and if you have to pee hold it because this isn't mine and I plan on returning it in pristine condition." I said before closing the trunk. I lifted the truck and took off into the night. I reached the forest in no time. I parked the truck behind a series of large trees. Once the vehicle was securely stashed, I took off.

I arrived back at the battle and I couldn't help but notice every single news station, both local and national was surrounding the perimeter of the battle. CNN, Fox News, you name it, they were there. *"News reporters really have a death wish."* I thought as I looked for a decent place to land and avoid them. The military did its best to keep the press and public at bay, while still trying to assist in the war efforts. They were being stretched thinner and thinner between the ever-growing crowd straying too close to the action and the relentless Draakunaki army. Something had to be done. I didn't want any more civilian casualties, so I took it upon myself to keep the threat's interest away from the naïve curious public. I began by using everything around me as objects to hurl at the enemy troops and ships and divert them as far from the growing population of spectators as possible. I hurled stones, broken pieces of the white house, and anything else that I could get my hands on in an effort to shift their attention onto me. My teammates caught on to what I was doing and began assisting.

"Focus on crowd control, we can take it from here," Drave instructed to the soldiers diligently fighting alongside us. They did as he instructed and we continued to draw the remaining reptilians back. In the midst of diverting, three brooding reptilians confronted Drave. I quickly came to his aid. The first reptilian swung and it barely missed Drave's eye. He ducked the punch and countered with a rapid combo of jabs. "So where did you go? We haven't seen you for like half of the battle." Drave said as he finished off a reptilian.

"After defeating the dragon," I sidestepped and avoided a hit. "I was working on a plan to put an end to them once and for all." I eked out in between delivering a swift kick to one of the reptilian's knees. Its kneecap cracked and it screamed in agony.

"So what's the plan?" He asked as he started fighting with another one of them. The reptilian with the busted knee tried his best to keep his balance. Just as I was about to finish him off, another reptilian joined the fight and attempted a sneak attack. I deflected it, shifted my attention, and swung a bone-shattering blow.

"I'll tell you once we're done with these overgrown house pets," I said as my fist rammed through the reptilian's chest armor.

"Fair enough," Drave responded as we continued to fight. "Are you sure you're a girl?" He asked as I delivered a solid hook to the reptilian with the busted knee's jaw, completely dislocating it.

"As girlie as they come," I replied with a smile as I cracked my knuckles.

"Remind me never to get on your bad side." He uttered as he kicked a reptilian in the groin and followed up with a fast hard hook. The creature howled in agony before collapsing to the ground. He finished it with a barrage of rapid-fire punches. Although he wasn't as powerful as I was, he was still a formidable threat to an unarmed reptilian. His lightning fast combos reminded me of this martial arts guy named IP man whom my cousin Preston idolized. IP man's punches were supernaturally fast for a normal human. I remember this one time I visited Preston and he forced me to watch two movies starring the masterful fighter. Since he was babysitting me, I really didn't have a choice in the matter.

"It's bound to happen, but we're like family so I won't rough you up too much," I stated. We continued fighting side by side. His super speed and my slightly enhanced speed and brute strength were an overwhelming combination against our remaining weary foes. We were fighting with everything we had and racing against time. In the midst of battle, I looked up and noticed that the ships were retreating. "I think it's over," I said as I pointed to the sky. The Draakunaki forces on the ground had been all but eliminated, and the ones operating the warships didn't seem to care about the stragglers left behind. There was only a handful left, and once we surrounded them, they didn't hesitate to surrender. *"Maybe I didn't need to hide the other one?"* I thought as I looked at the captured group of reptilians.

The general and a group of soldiers had also gathered around them. "Alright general, you can take all but one of these scumbags. We need one to lead us to their home base." I stated as I looked over the lot. I was trying to figure out which one might be able to help operate the ship if it needed more than one of them. I picked the smallest one. He was drastically smaller than his counterparts were but his cranial mass was larger in comparison to them. He looked like one of the ones that retreated from the ship earlier. "Oh, and we're taking the ship too," I added. We had the superpowers and were also responsible for turning the tide of the battle, so it was only right for us to call the shots.

"Under normal circumstances, that wouldn't be possible, but as I stated before, this is far from normal and if you guys can put an end to those walking handbags, then be my guest." The general responded. "Oh, and make sure you bring my vehicle back, and the gas needle better be where I left it." The general added jokingly and cracked a smile. It was weird seeing him smile.

"You got it, sir," I responded with a generic military salute. "I'll be right back." I zipped into the air and went to retrieve my captive. I arrived at my hiding spot a short time later. Without a moment to spare, I grabbed the truck and was back in the air in a matter of minutes. While flying, I thought about the impact that our battles would have on the world. We were the world's first legitimate flesh and blood proof of extraterrestrial life. Aside from thoughts of making history, I also wondered if Jason would be able to return to his thriving music career. I thought about the unwanted fame that our exploits would bring to us. Jason was used to it and at times seemed to crave the attention. I for one had never wanted to be famous because most of the people that get famous at a young age crash and burn well before they reach thirty.

I returned to the war-torn landmark and saw that the media circus and general public surrounding it had increased. I wondered how the government would manage to cover up such an exposed event. The floodgates had opened. Aliens and beings with extraordinary abilities were now confirmed pieces of reality. A reality that prior to the revelations had been carefully filtered and managed, in order to give the public the world that the governing powers wanted them to know. The change would force everyone to think outside the box. Knowing a part of the truth would make the public's appetite for more of the truth insatiable. Our existence would give hope to believers of Bigfoot and the Loch Ness Monster. It would make Vampires and Werewolves seem plausible.

I lowered myself to the ground with the vehicle in tow. The crowd seemed stunned by the sight of such a small being handling a gargantuan vehicle. I tried to block out the onlookers as I set down the vehicle with the greatest of ease. I tried to ignore them as I opened the trunk and removed my captive, but their oohs and aahs, and chatter only made things worse. They wanted to be acknowledged so I did the only thing that I could think of doing in response, I waved. The way that I waved was not in the manner that one would wave when greeting another. I waved in the manner of someone of importance. I felt myself blushing as I fought to keep a straight face. The moment was quite surreal. Facing the multitude of unfamiliar faces that we were responsible for protecting was a turning point. I realized that just as much as I wanted to rescue my parents, protecting the masses of strangers was equally as important.

"Okay, end of the line," I murmured as I dragged the reptilian out. I closed the door and tossed the keys to the general. "She's all yours, sir," I said before carrying my prisoner away as if he were a duffle bag. "Alright guys, let's end this," I said as I rejoined my group.

# Chapter 11

# Final Showdown, who are you?

**THE INSIDE OF THE DRAAKUNAKI WARSHIP WAS VERY DIFFERENT** from what I had grown accustomed to. It was smaller than Anaku's and not as sleek in its interior design. The control room was crude and somewhat archaic. Even though it appeared to be much more advanced than anything I had seen on Earth, it still evoked images of an ancient race. Both of the reptilian captives were stationed at ship control panels, and we were right behind them watching their every move.

"Just a word of advice," I paused and walked in front of them. "If either one of you tries anything funny, I will make sure that you die an agonizingly long death. Do I make myself clear?" I stated boldly as I placed my hands on my hips and donned a serious facial expression. They looked at one another, then looked at me and nodded in agreement.

"We want no further quarrel with you Enocian. Our brethren have left us to die so now they are our enemies." One of the reptilians said. It was a shock, but I completely understood.

"Fair enough, I guess that makes us allies," Drave said as the ship began to lift off. We were weary and in need of rest, but the mission had to be completed. We'd won the battle, but we didn't have the luxury of resting on our laurels. We were headed to fight another battle and hopefully the last.

I stared out of one of the ship's windows as we rose rapidly above Earth. I watched it shrink and slowly fade as we ascended higher into the atmosphere. The view was scary, yet picturesque. As we ventured into the unknown, I wondered what awaited us outside of Earth. My emotions were mixed. I was excited to be one step closer in my quest to reunite with my parents, while at the same time afraid of the tangible danger that lay ahead. We were going to the opposing team's home court and I didn't trust our captives.

*"They could be taking us right into a trap."* I thought as I studied them. I watched as they pressed various buttons on the control panels and whispered in Draakunaki to each other. I focused on trying to decipher their thoughts, but they were fuzzy like bad reception. The only thing that I could decipher was that the lack of trust was mutual.

*"They might be setting us up."* Sienna communicated telepathically.

*"I know, and that's what I'm afraid of,"* I replied. *"Can you read their thoughts?"* I asked, figuring that she would fare far better than I had.

*"Not really, it almost seems as if they have something blocking us."* She responded. *"All I'm getting is bits and pieces, something about Nexus, Daaminus Traccus, and a Dragon King."* I had no idea what any of it meant, but none of it sounded good. *"It doesn't matter what they're talking about, we have to get your parents back!"* It felt good to know that Sienna cared. It was something that I needed to take the edge off everything. As the ship reached space, an enormous metallic structure appeared. It was a thousand times the size of the warship we were on and about a third the size of Earth. A chill swept over me as I gazed at the foreboding structure.

"We have arrived." One of the reptilians announced as he pressed one of the many buttons on the panel stationed before him. The button activated some sort of beam that shot out from the station and engulfed the ship. In the blink of an eye, the mysterious beam had sucked us inside of the station.

The ship idly hovered in the center of what appeared to be a ship hanger. Unoccupied ships were lined up on both sides. It was a massive fleet. The fleet dispatched to the White House was only but a fraction of it. For a brief moment, I started to have doubts. Fear was slyly trying to persuade its way in. *"There is no way we're going to win. This may have been a bad idea. What are the chances of my parents still being alive?"* were the doubtful thoughts that invaded my mind. I was in deep thought when I felt someone place a hand on my shoulder. I turned and saw Sienna.

*"It's going to work out."* She communicated with a smile on her face.

*"I hope so,"* I responded. I still had reservations about the reptilians on the ship. I pictured myself in their shoes. They were probably not too pleased with being left for dead, but at the same time, they had the leverage. They had the power. I realized that the roles had been reversed. We were their captives. As I processed this obvious disadvantage, an idea started to form.

*"I've got a plan,"* I communicated to Sienna. I looked out of the ship's windows and saw reptilians entering the hanger. They weren't dressed in warrior garb. They were dressed in gray unarmored suits. They appeared to be utility workers. *"I need you to communicate it to the others."* I communicated my plan to Sienna and wasted no time putting it in motion. "Hey, uh Draakunaki… I don't know your name—"

"Drexen," The reptilian to the left of me interjected. "I'm Drexen and he is Zarconus." He added as he pointed to the other reptilian.

"Okay Drexen and Zarconus, I want you to capture me," I stated. The reptilian turned and gave me his full, undivided attention.

"What are you up to Enocian?" He questioned with a hairless scaly brow raised.

"The only way I'm getting in is if you bring me in. So for all intents and purposes, I'm your prisoner." I said as I extended my wrists in a manner of someone ready to be handcuffed.

I exited the ship bound in Draakunaki restrictive energy shackles. The reptilians from the ship were my escorts. Sienna, Jason, Drave, Alex, Aiden, and Jackson stayed behind inside the ship. Having only me as a captive seemed more believable than all seven of us, and since they were holding my parents as prisoners, it was only fair that I shoulder the majority of the risk. Once I found my parents, I would contact Sienna and let her know when it was time to move to the next phase of the plan. As we walked through the hanger area, all reptilian eyes were on me. They whispered amongst themselves as we walked past. Their cold hard stares were chilling. The weird manner, in which they blinked, made my skin crawl. Nervousness began to set in as we continued the trek.

I wondered how my parents were doing and for a split second, I thought about us being trapped on the space station. We were thousands upon thousands of miles above Earth. I tried to keep focused on the positive and not even consider any negative outcome. I had made too much of a sacrifice to have any doubts or negativity. My parents and my team were counting on me. I switched gears and thought about the risk that my ruse posed for the reptilians escorting me.

*"Would they be put to death if things didn't go accordingly, or would they sell us out to save their own necks?"* I wondered as we came upon a seemingly solid metallic wall. *"Why are we stopping here?"* I questioned silently as I gazed at the wall. Then, as if I had asked the question aloud, the wall faded away and revealed a large gunmetal colored passageway. We continued toward our destination.

While journeying through the passageway, we encountered another type of Draakunaki. The others we encountered were twice the size of my escorts and had what appeared to be wings. Their footfalls made the floor of the corridor quake. I didn't want to look into their eyes. They were more frightening than the dragon I had defeated in the woods. I felt an undeniable malevolence permeating from them as they passed us. If not for the fact of being a super powered extraterrestrial myself, I would have probably died with fear upon looking at them. They were unlike any of the others that we'd faced in the battles. They were easily over twelve feet and ripped with muscles on top of muscles. I knew that I would probably end up going against one before we made our escape.

Judging by the deviations between the Draakunaki that I had already encountered, it was clear that reptilians varied in appearance almost as much as humans did. I was walking with two of the smallest that I'd encountered. They were dwarfed by the lumbering giant menaces with wings. I wondered how far up the social ladder they were. I wondered if they were peons or something of some significance in the Draakunaki society. I seriously doubted the latter, but I didn't exclude it as a possibility.

As we were on the verge of passing through another phased opening, a reptilian in a silver suit stopped us and said something to my escorts in their Draakunaki language. Drexen responded. The silver-suited reptilian said something else and then pointed at me. I assumed that he was asking them where I was being taken. Drexen again responded. The silver-suited one seemed apprehensive in regards to the response. I felt a nervous rumble in the pit of my stomach.

*"Please don't let him figure us out."* I thought while trying my best to stay in character. They continued back and forth with their conversation. Something Drexen said must have satisfied his apprehension because he ceased with his questioning and allowed us to continue our journey. We

passed through several more phased-away walls before reaching the prison section of the station. It wasn't like the prisons on Earth. The prisoners all appeared to be asleep, and their bodies hovered off the ground. There were easily over fifty prisoners neatly arranged and housed in one large room about the size of a gymnasium.

The color scheme of the large room was far different from the other parts of the station that I had seen. The walls, ceiling, and floor were pitch black and looked like liquid. As they ushered me inside, I expected to sink into the floor, but it was solid to the touch. The prisoners housed within the room ranged in size, shape, and overall appearance. A handful of them were the size of small children, most were around the average size of a human adult, and others maxed out at around nine feet or so. Some looked similar to humans and Enocians, others were drastically different. One prisoner, in particular, caught my eye. His body was bright red, and his hair was as white as fresh snowfall. I scanned over all of the faces hoping to see my parents. I found my mother first. She was close to the entrance. I found my father over on the far opposite end of the room. I felt tears start to form as I stared at my parents in their helpless comatose state.

*"I've got to find some way to wake them up."* I thought as we walked further inside of the room. Another idea hit me. *"What if I find a way to wake up all of the prisoners?"* was the idea that illuminated my mind. It was a brilliant idea in the sense that it would offer a great distraction to aid in the fruition of my plan. *"Sienna I have an idea, I will let you know when it's time to strike, oh and watch out for the other reptilians. I saw some new ones on my way in."* I communicated to Sienna as I analyzed the room. "How are the prisoners kept asleep?" I whispered to my escorts.

"It's this room. All of the prisoners have an implant in them that reacts to the energy that is emitted from the room itself. As long as the energy is circulated in the room, they will remain in their current state." Zarconus answered.

"So how can we shut the energy off?" I asked as I looked around the room for some type of switch or button.

"We have to gain access to the control room." was the answer I received.

"Okay, let's go do it," I responded. Both reptilians turned toward me. The expressions on their faces were sinister. Something didn't feel right. I was getting a bad vibe from them.

"We can't allow you to do that. As a matter of fact, we can't allow you to leave this room!" Drexen said in a menacing tone.

"What do you mean?" I asked in an astonished manner. The seeds of a double cross were blooming.

"You didn't actually think we were going to assist you now did you?" Zarconus asked mischievously with a wicked look of glee.

"Thanks to you, we'll be hailed as heroes." Drexen chimed in excitedly.

"You're making a big mistake!" I warned. "Either you take me to the control room, or I paint the walls of this room with your blood!" I threatened.

"Foolish Enocian, your threats mean nothing. You are outnumbered, and have already lost; you're just too unintelligent to realize it!" Zarconus's words were cold and harsh. They made my blood boil. I wanted to rip him into pieces right then and there.

"WE'LL SEE ABOUT THAT!" I said aggressively. In a fit of rage, I attempted to break free of my restraints. Breaking free was harder than I imagined. For the first time since I discovered my powers, I felt completely helpless!

"You cannot break those restraints; they are specifically designed to reduce Enocian abilities," Zarconus responded before maniacally laughing. I pulled and twisted as hard as I could, but the restraints didn't give in the least.

*"Oh boy, I've done it now!"* I thought as I continued to work on getting free. The distraction of the restraints gave

Drexen the opening that he needed. I looked up and saw the sole of his boot, coming toward my chest. The kick was dead on. It sent me flying backward, bumping into a few of the sleeping prisoners on my way to the floor. I fell with a hard thud. *"Sienna where are you?"* I communicated desperately. I had fallen right into their trap. They had turned the tables on me. *"Sienna,"* I tried again, still nothing. Drexen was now walking toward me. *"Sienna,"* I mentally yelled, desperately hoping to get some type of response. *"What am I going to do?"* I pondered as my foe drew closer. I was on the verge of having a panic attack when Sienna responded.

*"Sorry for the late response. We're up to our eyeballs in reptilians."* Her reply pulled me back from the brink. As Drexen came upon me, I remembered a defensive move I had learned while watching a show on self-defense. I had never tried it before, but I figured that I didn't have anything to lose. Drexen took another step forward, and I burst into action. I did a scissor leg sweep. The move made him stumble into one of the sleeping prisoners. The momentum and loss of balance brought him down upon the sleeping hapless victim.

"Sorry about that," I murmured to the sleeping prisoner before bringing myself up off the floor. Once I was back on my feet, I sprinted and kicked my foe with as much power as I could summon. It worked; the kick sent him flying out of the entrance. Zarconus looked on with astonished wide glossy green eyes. "If you know what's good for you, you'd take these things off me now!" I said fiercely. He complied and within seconds, I was free. "Now show me how to wake them," I commanded.

"O-okay, follow me." He uttered nervously. He led me back out of the room. Drexen was unconscious against the wall on the opposite side of the passageway. Zarconus ushered me into a neighboring room. There were three reptilian guards waiting for us. They witnessed the debacle in the prison room and refused to succumb to the same fate.

"Cease!" One of them said in a deep raspy tone. He had his laser weapon aimed directly at my head. I felt my strength returning, which was bad news for them.

"I don't think you want to do that," I warned as a smile formed on my face. The reptilian fired his weapon. I dodged the laser shot with above average speed. I then rammed my fist into the side of his face. His face spun around with such force that the momentum broke his neck. He collapsed. The remaining guards were frightened out of their wits and began firing wildly. The death of Zarconus was the result of the panicked attacks.

A laser headshot was how he met his demise. The remaining reptilians kept firing. Their weapons had little effect on me. I quickly dismissed another with a swift, brutal punch to the chest. I heard his bones breaking as my fist made contact. He staggered back and dropped his weapon. His eyes rolled back and he collapsed. The remaining guard kept his weapon aimed at me as he cautiously stepped back further into the room. His hands shook nervously as he strained to maintain proper aim.

"St-stay back," he said in a trembled voice. I looked at the foreign controls on the console behind him. There were so many buttons, switches, and touch points, that it would've taken me forever to figure out how to awaken the prisoners. I needed him alive.

"Look, you know your weapon is pretty much useless against me, so how about we do things differently." I took a step forward. He shakily fired his weapon. The shot went just past my shoulder. "Okay, perhaps I didn't make myself clear. You," I pointed at him, "are going to put your weapon down and wake up the prisoners. You got that?" I finished. He looked dumbfounded.

"Are you serious? You want me to release all of the prisoners?" He asked in an astonished tone.

"Yes dead serious," I replied.

"As you wish," He said before slowly walking over to the console. I wondered why he was so hesitant to release the captives. Then I realized why. All of the different species being held together inside were a recipe for disaster. I wasn't familiar with most of them, and I didn't know how they would react to humans, more importantly, what they would do to my parents. The guard pushed a series of buttons, and his actions triggered an alarm.

"Why did you do that? You really want to die, huh?" I said, trying to keep my anger in line.

"I did as you asked." He replied nervously. "Releasing the prisoners automatically triggered it."

"Okay, so how do we shut it off?" I asked. I looked into the room housing the prisoners and noticed that they were starting to stir. In a fit of frustration, I slammed my fist into the console.

"You just broke it!" The guard exclaimed.

"I know, I'll be back," I responded before running out of the room. I entered the prisoner holding area and saw my mother sitting on the floor. She looked confused and frightened.

"Mom," I called as I ran to her.

"Charisma, where are we? And why are you dressed like that?" She murmured as she gave me a look over.

"I'll explain it later, right now we have to get dad and get out of here," I responded as I helped her up. I hoisted up my mother with one hand and sprinted over to my father. He looked just as disoriented as the rest of the freshly awoken prisoners.

"Charis—" I grabbed up my dad before he could finish.

"I'll explain everything later," I said as I hustled past the other roused beings with a parent in each arm. Chaos erupted before we could make it out of the room. Some of the prisoners began attacking the others. I focused and sprinted out of the entrance. As we exited the room, I noticed that reptilians were coming from both ends of the passageway. I did the only thing that I could think of, I sat my parents down and rammed into the wall parallel from the prison room. "C'mon," I yelled as the reptilians closed in. I ushered my parents through the hole.

The hole led to another passageway. It was vacant and smaller than the one we had just exited. The new passageway did not have phasing walls, which made an uninterrupted sprint possible. I could see clear down to the other end of it. My parents were moving far too slow. I realized that at the rate they were running, the reptilians would catch us in no time. I decided to take advantage of the situation. I lifted my parents onto my shoulders and took off with an incredible burst of speed. We were halfway down the passageway in a matter of seconds.

*"Sienna, where are you guys?"* I asked as I continued traveling at high speeds.

*"We're still by the ship."* She responded.

*"Okay, I'll be there shortly."* I communicated.

I began to slow down once I got close enough to where I figured that I should make another hole. *"This has got to be it."* I thought as I placed my parents down and prepared to ram through the wall. I focused and ran full speed into the wall. As I expected, the wall put up little resistance. I burst through the other side in a manner that could instantly evoke comparisons to the Kool-Aid man from those beloved wacky commercials that often interrupted my favorite cartoons when I was a child. What I didn't expect was that I would slam right into one of the giant reptilians that I had passed earlier. The impact knocked him across the hanger. His large muscular frame barely missed colliding into Jackson.

"Whoa," Jackson exclaimed as he turned to face my direction. The massive creature couldn't catch himself; he stumbled and fell to the hard metallic floor. The impact shook the entire hanger. I looked and noticed Anaku's ship had arrived.

"How—" Before I could get out my question, Drave interjected.

"Get your parent's in the ship!" He yelled as he delivered swift punches to the face of an unfortunate reptilian.

"C'mon guys," I said to my parents as I helped them through the makeshift opening. Draakunaki forces were rapidly converging on the ship hanger area. I rushed my parent's to Anaku's ship. The hatch opened, the ramp lowered, and Anaku greeted us.

"Charisma, I see that you have recovered your parental figures." He said, his blue eyes glowing brightly.

"Yeah, I did," I replied as I hurried my parents aboard.

"Wait but—" I interrupted my mother.

"That's Anaku, he's on our side," I said, gesturing toward Anaku.

"But—"

"Mom, I'll explain everything later, just get on the ship," I said, cutting off my mother again. I had gotten my mother aboard the ship and was helping my father aboard when he forcefully grabbed my arm.

"Da—" Before I could finish my sentence, I was thrown from the ship's ramp. I crashed into a Draakunaki warship docked several yards away. I watched as my father transformed into a female reptilian. Her appearance was unlike any of the others. She appeared to be some sort of hybrid. With a mighty leap, the reptilian left the ship's ramp and landed in front of me. Jackson took notice and reacted. He turned into a fierce panther and lunged at my foe. She caught him with one hand and rejected his attack. She tossed him away as if he was a stuffed animal.

"You were naïve to think that you could come here and rescue your parents." She said in a cold bitter voice. "I've been waiting to settle the score."

"Settle the score?" I had no idea what she was talking about. I didn't even know who she was! "I don't know you or what you're talking about," I said as I got up from the ground.

"I am Nexus and I require your death as vengeance for the Dragon King!" She responded, stopping within a few feet of me.

"Okay, I get that you're on your cryptic villainous rant, but I—" Before I could finish, she sprinted and grabbed me by my throat. Her insanely strong grip interrupted my words.

"Silence Enocian, your ignorance won't save you. YOU MUST DIE!" Nexus stated as she tightened her grip. "My Kinship shall be avenged!" I focused my strength and delivered a swift knee to the reptilian's gut. She released her grip and flew back toward Anaku's ship.

"I still don't know what you're talking about, but you picked the wrong girl to start a fight with." I weakly responded as I rubbed my throat and caught my breath. I sprinted and hit my foe with a hard left hook. The punch sent her crashing into a neighboring wall. She recovered and wiped the reptilian blood from her mouth. "Where is my father?" I asked as I prepared for another attack.

"Oh, the male human, he died while attempting to be a hero. He was such a fool. I had fun killing him." She flashed a sinister smile exposing her vampire like fanged teeth before continuing. "I brought back the female human alive because I knew that you would come for her." The news sent a bitter chill through my body. Images of my father flashed through my mind. I felt a part of myself die as the news started to sink in. "You cannot win. Surrender and succumb to your fate." She said venomously.

"You're going to die! I'm going to kill you and feed your body to the first pack of wild animals I find!" I threatened as the warm salty tears began their journey down my face. In hindsight, it was foolish to continue fighting. The reptilian army outnumbered my team. I was so consumed with anger and grief that I couldn't focus on anything else but my enemy's death. I made another attack. I punched the reptilian with all of my might. Her head whipped away in reaction to it. I followed up with another punch and followed up that one with yet another. Nexus was far more superior as compared to the other Draakunaki I had faced. A punch that would have normally knocked out a reptilian only stunned her. Even the dragon I defeated didn't compare. "What are you?" I asked as I studied her features. She was reptilian and something else, possibly human or Enocian.

"I'm your worst nightmare Enocian." She responded as her wounds rapidly began to heal. "I am a part of you, you are a part of me; we are a part of each other." Her words were confusing and quite frankly, irritating.

"You know what, I'm tired of talking." With that said, I grabbed my foe and hurled her into a docked ship. She crashed into the ship. The impact rendered her unconscious. She fell to the ground headfirst. I heard her neck snap. I waited a few seconds to see if she would get back up, but she remained motionless. *"Wow, that was so lame,"* I thought as I stared at her lifeless body.

"I guess that was a dud firecracker." Jackson joked as he walked over.

"Yeah, super fail," I added. I looked at a wall just as it was fading, and noticed that the reptilians had another problem on their hands. A large group of their prisoners had made their way to the hanger and had joined the battle. "C'mon, I think they have it under control," I said before turning in the direction of Anaku's ship

"I think you're right." Sienna responded.

"Alright team, let's go," Drave said as he took notice of what was happening. We all ran to the ship and wasted no time getting aboard. I was the last to board. I looked back and saw that Nexus had managed to recover from her injury and was fighting the red, white-haired prisoner.

"I guess you were a little too late," I mumbled before completely stepping inside of the ship.

"It is good to see you all in one piece," Anaku said as the ship's hatch closed.

The atmosphere of the ship was mixed. It was a confusing time. Our enemy hadn't truly been defeated, which meant that they would remain a threat to Earth and everything on it. I still had a million unanswered questions about Nexus. I wondered who she was and why she had such a deep hate for me in particular. I sat huddled in a mess of mental anguish with my mother in my arms.

I was torn internally. I was glad to have her back alive and well, but at the same time, my heart was breaking into pieces as thoughts of my father haunted my mind. I had held hope that I would find them both alive. Fate had played a cruel joke on me. It left the signs. I just failed to see them or maybe I subconsciously shielded myself from accepting the clues for what they were. The blood on the door and in my parents' room, the manner in which the reptilians brutally disposed of the other people that they encountered; I was actually lucky to have one of my parents alive.

"So what was the deal with that one reptilian you were fighting?" Alex asked, snapping me out of my world of thoughts. It came as a surprise. We had never really had any sort of rapport, so her asking me a question was weird, to say the least.

"I'm not sure. She calls herself Nexus. She said that she wants vengeance for the Dragon King." I responded.

"Dragon what," Alex was just as perplexed as me. I shrugged in response.

"Should we consider this a victory?" Jason asked aloud. His tone seemed a bit sarcastic. I wasn't sure if he was serious or if he was being a jerk as usual.

"I don't know Jason you tell me," Sienna said in a somewhat harsh manner.

"I'd consider it one. We successfully thwarted an invasion and we got Charisma's mum back." He said as he shot me a look. "Right Chariz,"

"Well, if you look it at that way, I guess so," I replied and looked at my mother. It was a victory, though not the one that I expected to achieve.

"It is indeed a victory Jason," Drave said. "Unfortunately, it may not have turned out the way we wanted it to," He paused and looked in my direction," I'm sorry for your loss," he said before turning to address the rest of the team. "It's a victory because we worked together and now the Draakunaki know for a fact that Earth is protected." Drave walked over to Jason and extended his hand. "We earned this victory as a team and that's definitely something to be proud of." Jason grabbed it and they shook.

"I guess you got a point. I don't hate you as much as I used to." Jason admitted and smiled.

"All of you worked together in perfect harmony. The world will remain safe because of your combined efforts." Anaku stated, with his eyes glowing brightly. Looking around at the others, I started to feel better. I had lost my father, which is a loss that I will never truly recover from, but I had gained a whole new family. We may not see eye to eye on everything but that's the way families are and I couldn't picture my life without them. THE END

# ABOUT THE AUTHOR

**Author, writer, illustrator, comic book creator, and all around free thinker,** Anthony D. Phillips Jr. creates stories and art using both traditional and digital mediums. He has an unrelenting passion for all things creative. His beliefs are somewhat unorthodox, but that's what makes him unique. See more of his creations at www.adpbooks.com. **THINK AND LIVE OUTSIDE THE BOX**

www.ingramcontent.com/pod-product-compliance
Lightning Source LLC
Chambersburg PA
CBHW060734180626
46819CB00001B/27